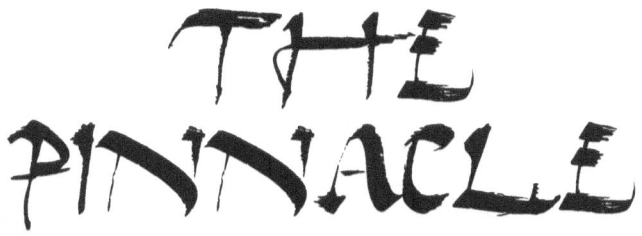

THE PINNACLE

Sequence:

Judas Gene
The Pinnacle
Almost Human

Gary Moreau

The Pinnacle
Gary Moreau
First Edition Copyright © Gary Moreau, 2017

Published by Yard Dog Press at Create Space

Print Version ISBN 978-1-945941-09-2
The Pinnacle
First Edition Copyright © Gary Moreau, 2017

Yard Dog Press
710 W. Redbud Lane
Alma, AR 72921-7247

http://www.yarddogpress.com

Edited by Selina Rosen
Copy Editor & Technical Editor Lynn Rosen
Cover art and Design by Mitchell Bentley

First Print Edition September 15, 2017
Printed in the United States of America
0 9 8 7 6 5 4 3 2 1

DEDICATION

For my mother, Vel Moreau

CHAPTER 1

Casey Conklin was empty. He sat at the console and leaned forward with his head cradled in his hands. His mind drifted, an empty boat on a vast sea. Rituals and habit ruled his skeletal existence.

Occasionally, one of the screens in a bank of screens would blink to life, bright with symbols indicating well-being. "All is as it should be," they would say. The same message had been repeated for fifty years. The content of the screens no longer held meaning. It was like the rest of his minuscule world, changeless in its small, repetitive changes.

There had been a time when he had been special, chosen to serve on this, the seed ship of humanity. It was survival of the species as expressed by the remnants of Earth's civilization. It was humanity's insurance policy against extinction.

It wouldn't be long now. Soon he would join his charges in cryogenic sleep to await journey's end. Midpoint was only five days away.

A chime sounded. As if clicked on, he pushed himself to his feet. He shuffled across the deck toward the curved passageway, which was lined with cryogenic capsules. The long row of vertical tubes glowed with the ghostly light of stasis. He began his daily inspection of the capsules; each contained one well-preserved youth, deep in winter's sleep. During the first years of the journey, he had intervened to save the lives of many of the sleepers, but that was long ago. The capsules had stabilized.

He paused before the first capsule. He focused on the faint reflection from the convexity of the clear, ceramic surface. The face that stared back at him was balding with wispy, white hair. There were shadows under the cheekbones and sagging skin beneath the eyes. He didn't recognize this old man.

He looked beyond his own reflection. The sleeper's face, with its sharp nose and square jaw, proclaimed confidence and strength. Even though wearing the death mask of cryo-sleep, the face was fresh with youth. The narrow, almost lipless mouth perversely reminded Casey of a gluteal cleft. Butt-face had a future; he had a real face, preserved for real life.

He continued down the passageway. Except for an odd few, he knew all their personal information, everything about them that was stored in the ship's computer. He was keeper of the living dead. Halfway down the passage, he stopped in front of his favorite, Lisa Bouviet. Lisa was her given name but he wasn't fooled. He knew her real name was Virgin of the Woods. As always, she remained unchanged, but he took time to study her round face and the curves of her body. His gaze glided over the jeweled communication collar around her neck and settled on her pink nipples, which were contracted and erect as if sexually aroused. Her scant pubic hair was as blond as the hair on her head, but she was forever beyond reach. He had grown old, but she had escaped the inexorable passage of time. She reminded him of a woman he'd left behind. It might have only been the shape of her face, but it was enough. What he imagined and what he remembered were mixed together like the marbling of a cake.

Through the years, many of the sleepers had come to life in his mind and had revealed their real names. The small woman with the straight black hair, delicate epicanthic folds, and unblemished olive skin, the one with the child-like breasts, had become the Child Princess. The giant man, who could have been a sumo wrestler, became the Unsmiling Buddha. There was Prissy and Shrew, Mister Attention and Little Pecker, Teddy Bear and Gingersnap, and all the rest. They were his collection, his ice people, neatly lined up along the passageway for his daily inspection. If he'd been capable of rational thought, he would've admitted that he didn't like them all but, whether good or bad, they had all become his children, even Butt-Face.

Raucous laughter echoed down the passageway; it sent a shiver of fear down his back and he hurried back to the command center. He had been hearing it for some time but, regardless of how quickly he turned, he could never discover the source. There were times when his scalp prickled with warning and he would pivot, but he could never catch the prankster. At first he had thought it was Vlada Bezdicek, the guardian of Deck Two, the one who had left a message that he could take it no longer and had cycled into space. He could imagine Vlada's boiled and bloated body hurtling through the void alongside the starship, a grotesque moon. But now, he was almost positive it was Julio Mendoza, the guardian assigned to Deck Three. He had found Mendoza's decomposing body years ago and had dumped it into ship recycling. He suspected Mendoza had merged with the ship and had oozed into the bulkheads.

There were times that he would hear a voice. It sounded like his own. It would say, "Fail-safe, fail-safe, fail-safe failed."

He thought that was a good joke and it brought a rare smile to his face. He began to think it was all a grand joke, an April Fools forever, and had decided to play a joke of his own; he had constructed his own cryo-capsule and it was well hidden. He wasn't going to be the only one not to get pricked by the magic spindle. They had told him at Midpoint his replacement would awaken and then he would join the others in frozen sleep, but he wasn't that gullible. A joke is a joke, but he wasn't going to shrivel up like Mendoza; that wasn't funny.

Wild laughter careened around the room.

"Where are you, Mendoza?" he yelled, and then stomped his foot on the deck. "Did that hurt?"

There was no answer. There never was. Meanwhile, the chronometer marked off another microscopic passage of time. Midpoint was coming ever closer.

He touched each capsule with the tip of his index finger as he shambled back to the bridge and then crouched behind the control chair to study the hall of sleep. It was dimly lit by the soft light of the crystalline capsules but he could only see a short distance into the passage because it curved to follow the contour of the ship. He switched his gaze to the opposite corridor. It was a mirror image of the hall of sleep, but there were no cryo-capsules; its inner wall was lined with doors that opened into rooms filled with instruments.

When he was certain no one was watching, he stood and crept toward the down-tube. His eyes jerked from place to place, first the passageway, then the bulkhead, then the overhead, and then back to the passageway. He had to be especially careful now; the time for his own joke approached. He slid as smoothly as a wet noodle into the mouth of the down-tube, but kept his hand on the lip. He raised his head so that he could peer with one eye into the bridge. There was no one, but he wasn't fooled. They were cunning, so he had to be even more cunning, but that was fair. It was one of the rules of the game; everything was fair.

He released his grip and floated downward, past Deck Two, past Deck Three. He was going all the way down to Storage. When he neared the short side-tube that opened into Storage, he touched the wall of the cylinder with his fingertips. His descent slowed until, with well-practiced precision, he flipped feet first into the side-tube and slid out to stand on the landing platform. The light-lines in the overhead came to life, revealing the cavernous hold.

A voice spoke, "Never fail, never fail. What a good ship am I, am I, am I...."

The words reverberated in his mind. He stood perfectly still and then screamed. "Ship, I'm warning you! If you tell Mendoza, or any of the others, I'll kill you!"

There was no answer.

After a few moments, his self-satisfaction reasserted itself. The ship understood. He was certain of it because it was fair.

He walked down the steps of the landing platform and over to the ladder that stretched upward to the control cabin of the land-shaper. It was a mammoth piece of machinery, the biggest, single artifact they had brought with them, other than the ship itself. He climbed the rungs and paused at the top, as high as the roof of a three-story building. He gazed out across the clutter of vehicles and machinery. It was quiet and still. When he was satisfied Mendoza hadn't seen him, he tugged on the handle of the massive hatch. It opened on its automatic hydraulics at its own rate; it could not be rushed. He climbed into the dark hole and activated the closing mechanism. The hatch closed with a muffled "clang" and a soft "hiss". His rigidly straight back relaxed. He was home again.

For years he had studied the information on cryo-capsules stored in the ship's computer and had become the proverbial, self-taught expert. He had connected power cables that were fed directly from the starship engine. He had successfully bypassed the ship's computer. His isolation was complete.

He reached with confidence to touch the control panel and activated the lighting and environmental systems. Then he turned to let his eyes feast on his creation: his very own cryo-capsule, built piece by piece, separate from the rest, and hidden in the bowels of this great, mechanical beast. It was his pea pod and he was to be the pea.

Suddenly he was furious! He kicked viciously at the capsule and pummeled it with his fists. Someone had beaten him to it. Tears leaked from his eyes and he cried loudly, a broken-hearted baby. Someone had cheated. Someone was sleeping in his bed. He leaned forward, flattening his nose against the glass-like surface, and began to giggle wildly, just as he had cried without restraint only a moment before. He was already inside the capsule; no, it was his dummy inside the capsule.

He smiled and rubbed his chest. *Is there anyone more clever than I?* Not likely, he admitted.

"It is a good trick," he declared out loud. "It's a trick, a treat, a teat to suckle."

He settled onto the deck of the cabin and curled up to suck contentedly on his thumb, to sleep in safety.

He awakened with a start. He slowly withdrew his thumb from his mouth. *What was that?* Little needles dashed up and down his legs and lightly across his arms. It felt like the cradle of his womb had slipped sideways. There was a sinking in his gut; all joy leaked out. Had he missed his time?

With trembling fingers he opened the hatch and gazed into blackness. He listened until he could hear his heart, but nothing more. Something had happened. He stuck his head out of the hatch and sensors reactivated the light-lines. He quickly glanced around; all appeared as it should be.

He climbed down the ladder of the land-shaper, all the while whispering, "Cheater, cheater, cheater...."

When he arrived at the up-tube, he stopped whispering and peered cautiously into it. The shaft was empty and quiet. He slipped soundlessly into the up-tube and exited on Deck One, where he immediately slithered onto his stomach and carefully worked his way over to the control console. Harsh laughter shattered the silence. He stopped, as still as any prey sensing a nearby predator.

"Shhhh," he whispered, "a joke is a joke, but fair is fair."

He listened; the control room had become ghostly silent. He continued his squirm across the deck until he could see down the hall of sleep; there was nothing but the quiet of glowing capsules. He took a chance and scrambled to his knees to look at the chronometer. His forehead wrinkled in puzzled concern; Midpoint was still five days away. He leaned forward and slammed the deck with both fists. His faced flushed. Someone was changing the game. Was it that tricky Mendoza?

He slipped back to the floor and worked his way over to the control chair. He pulled himself into the chair and kneeled to cautiously peer over the back. The blue of his irises was completely encircled by white. Eyes right, eyes left, back and forth.

"I'm looking now," he said in a soft voice, "so you can't move. It's the rule."

Almost at once the coarse rattle of the warning signal grated on his ears. The red, danger-light flashed insistently, demanding attention. He collapsed and curled deeply into the chair. His heart fluttered. The warning had sounded and flashed only once before, years ago, when Vlada had cycled into space to take his solitary walk. Vlada, the name struck horror in his mind, disfigured, exploded, monstrous. The airlock on Deck Two was opening to space. Vlada was coming to get him!

The light on the console changed to green; cycling was complete. His breath was coming in chest-heaving gasps. He could imagine Vlada gliding down the passageway of Deck Two. Soon, Vlada would enter the up-tube and burst onto Deck One, an overripe ghoul, dripping with putrefaction. He imagined the greasy remains smothering him, swallowing him whole.

He bolted for the down-tube, slipped and fell, and scrambled back to his feet. He jumped feet first into the mouth of the tube, barking his shin on the edge, but the pain was nothing compared to his fear. Vlada was coming! There was no doubt, but Casey could fall only as fast as the tube would allow. He floated gently downward in contrast to the hammer beating of his heart, feeling as if it were about to burst. He slid past Deck Two, past Deck Three, and then swung into the exit tube of the Storage Deck. Vlada was right behind him; he could feel it.

Before the light-lines had reached their final brilliance, his foot was on the bottom rung of the ladder that led to his secret hiding place in the land-shaper. He climbed the ladder with the speed of panic and slid through the hatch before it had fully opened. He slapped the close-switch and collapsed onto the cabin floor, shaking uncontrollably in absolute darkness. The air filled with the pungent odor of sweat. He crawled across the deck on quivering arms and legs and pulled open the cryo-capsule. He reached in and jerked the dummy out with such force that the dummy's head flew off and rolled to a stop at the base of the control panel.

He stripped, as if he would have the benefit of the watchful eyes of a guardian, and stepped into the capsule. When he activated the closing switch, power surged into the unit, lighting the darkness of the control cabin with an eerie glow. Time stopped. He didn't trust the master computer. He had timed his awakening to the chronometer in the land-shaper.

There was no sensation. His life was held in suspension by the wintry grip of cryo-sleep. Years weren't even a moment. When he awakened his heart was in mid-beat, but picked up its furious pace as if it had been uninterrupted. He stood still until his heart slowed and his breathing quieted. He had won! He was certain he had beaten them all.

The land-shaper cabin was invisible in the darkness, but he had no difficulty in activating the lighting and then the hatch. While he waited for the hatch to open, he stared absently at the dummy he had tossed onto the floor years before. The glass eyes stared back at him.

He climbed out and his movement activated the Storage Deck lights. The brightness was almost painful until his eyes adjusted. He looked for signs that the others had awakened, but could see no evidence that the sleepers had been down to Storage.

He chuckled. "Won't they be shocked when they find out I'm the winner? But, fair is fair." He spoke out loud, though there was no one to hear him. It had become his way.

He slid into the up-tube with confidence and flipped out of the tube onto the deck of the upper most level, jauntily landing on his feet, expecting to see the area buzzing with activity, but stopped without taking a step. It was quiet. He was annoyed. He looked at the bank of control screens. No messages declaring well-being scrolled across them. They were like black windows. The rounded shadow of a head protruded over the top edge of the console chair, but he saw no movement. He was impressed; the person was obviously deep in thought. He decided it wasn't proper to disturb such profound contemplation. After all, he was not irresponsible.

He looked toward the hall of sleep and was pleased to see the familiar glow of the transparent capsules. He was tempted to take a quick stroll down the passage so he could make one last inspection before the Awakening, but suppressed the impulse. He was early; they were late. And then he understood; it was just another trick. Every moment he was awake he was getting older, but they were staying young. He nodded. It was unscrupulous, but he had to admire their duplicity. He must never underestimate them.

Harsh laughter echoed around the bridge. It made the hairs on his arms stand erect. Mendoza. Mendoza was helping them. He stole a nervous glance toward the control chair; the head had not moved, but now he knew it was part of the game.

He backed toward the down-tube, feeling for the edge with his foot. When he felt it, he took a step backward and was silently swallowed by the shaft. He smiled a tight little smile. They evidently thought they were playing with an amateur.

He exited on the storage level and quickly climbed back into the land-shaper. He could hardly contain his glee. This time he set his cryo-capsule to open when the land-shaper's sensors detected light in the Storage Deck for an uninterrupted hour. This time he wouldn't be the first to awaken; he'd be the last. He was extremely pleased. He reentered his capsule and it took him once again into the timeless embrace of stasis.

CHAPTER 2

Casey awakened. His plan was fresh in his mind because, for him, no time had passed. He pushed against the smoothly curved, inner surface of the capsule and it opened soundlessly. He knew that his awakening meant that lights were on in the Storage Deck; the colonists had come back to life.

He stepped onto the cabin floor of the land-shaper, naked except for his jeweled com-collar. Debris coated the deck, feathery soft against his feet as he walked over to the control console. He didn't need the cabin lights to find the control plate and placed his palm flat against it. The hydraulics responded and the heavy hatch began to open, visible as a crescent-shaped crack of bright light in the darkness. His eyes were fixed on the growing opening. He was so excited he could hardly wait. He raced up the small ladder that led to the hatch, and then paused.

He scolded himself. "Control yourself, Casey. Don't underestimate them."

He waited until the hatch was fully open and then peeked over the rim, as crafty as an earthworm in sunlight. The Storage Deck was brightly lit and, not more than thirty meters away, he saw two men dressed in the pumpkin-orange of mechanical technicians. Both were bent at the waist while they inspected a drill press, but he wasn't fooled. He knew they were pretending. They were trying to sneak up on him but they were too late. He had won! It started as a soft cackle, but quickly grew into belly-shaking, breath-taking laughter. He had won!

The two men had started to walk away from the drill press, but the wild laughter immobilized them. They turned as if one to search out the source of the ghastly sound.

Casey recognized them. The tall, slim man, the one with the pointed nose, thick lips and prominent cheekbones was Barracuda. The other was massive, the biggest man on the ship, other than the Unsmiling Buddha. He was Meat-Man. Barracuda and Meat-Man made brief eye contact with one another and then walked cautiously toward the land-shaper.

Casey stopped laughing. They should have shouted their congratulations, but they hadn't. Clearly, they were cheaters. A tear rolled down his cheek. He was so sad his chest ached. They were bad children, evil. They would never admit they had lost. They were going kill him.

"It isn't fair," he whispered. He withdrew into the cabin and activated the lights. The light glinted off silvery tools he had used to construct his cryo-capsule. Among the tools he spotted a pick-like instrument. He grabbed it and concealed it in the palm of his hand.

"Fair is fair," he said and nodded in agreement with himself.

He climbed the small ladder and his head and torso popped out of the hatch, like a jack-in-the-box. He smiled a decent smile. The two men paused in mid-stride.

That confirms it, Casey thought as his head bobbed forward and back, they are assassins. He cleared his throat and maintained his smile. "Hello, Barracuda," he said, and then nodded toward the body builder, "Meat-Man." He kept his voice soft and smooth. "I've been waiting a long time for you."

Barracuda whispered to Meat-Man and then reached up to activate his com-collar. Casey couldn't hear what Barracuda was saying, but he was talking rapidly and waving his arms.

From his vantage point, Casey felt secure, but he wasn't comfortable with the secrets the two men passed back and forth. However, he knew how to play the game. He had his own secret. His smile was a taut slash of revealed teeth while he clutched the pick tightly.

"Secrets cancel out secrets," he whispered.

Meat-Man looked up, directly at him. "Who are you?" His voice was weak and high pitched.

"Wrong voice," Casey said to himself, "and wrong words. They know exactly who I am."

Meat-Man took two steps closer. "Who are you?" he repeated.

"You know who I am," Casey replied and snorted in disgust. "I'm the one you left behind. Give up. You can't fool me."

Barracuda's eyes narrowed to slits.

Casey could see double-edged thoughts behind those eyes, sharp and dangerous thoughts. He sensed that laughter would bubble up. "Not now!" he commanded, but the laughter burst forth anyway; it had a life of its own.

The men stood rock still and stared up at him. When the laughter subsided, the Storage Deck was again silent.

Casey expected them to come closer, but they stayed where they were. He tried to entice them into approaching. "Don't worry," he said in his most reassuring voice. "It was only Mendoza." He blew them a kiss. A happy thought came to mind. Perhaps a timeout would be enough to set them straight.

Barracuda spoke, his nasal voice escaping from every orifice on his face. "We are friends. Come down and join us."

"Friends." Casey shook his head with disappointment. "How sad. Is that anyway to speak to your father?"

Meat-Man shifted his eyes toward Barracuda.

It was a secret message. Casey was certain of it, but he needed to get closer. It couldn't be helped. He climbed the rest of the way out of the hatch and descended the ladder. The steel rungs were cold against the bare skin of his chest and thighs. He climbed down slowly, his head twisted so he could see them at all times. His confidence increased as he neared the bottom of the ladder. He could control them with his eyes; they hadn't moved since he'd begun his descent. He stepped onto the deck and walked toward them. They were only a few strides away, but they still hadn't moved, pinned in place by his power. His smile widened and filled in with teeth.

"Now!" Meat-Man shouted. He lunged forward and wrapped his exaggerated arms around Casey.

Casey couldn't breathe. He was suffocating! He arched his back with the strength of sheer terror and gained a sliver of space. It was enough. Up came his hand with the concealed pick. He placed it with the precision of a surgeon. The needle-sharp point pierced Meat-Man's larynx and passed upward and back, into his brain stem. Casey sliced the tip of the pick back and forth.

Meat-Man remained standing for only a moment. His last breath was expelled by the mechanical elasticity of his thorax and gurgled out of his mouth as he collapsed.

Casey was knocked to the deck, pinned beneath the lifeless hulk of Meat-Man. He struggled fiercely to escape, an animal caught in a trap. He had almost managed to free his hand, still gripping the pick, when his vision flashed brightly, followed by blackness.

When Casey regained consciousness, he was secured to an examination table with straps around his wrists and ankles, and a belt across his chest. To him, it was a spider's web. He pulled against the restraints and squirmed, but could not escape. A scream erupted from his mouth.

"Silence that maniac," the sharp-nosed man with the thin lips and blocky jaw snapped.

Casey heard the spider and struggled with renewed strength, trying to break his bonds.

"Help me! Please, help me!" Casey yelled.

"I told you to silence him," Slater demanded.

A young man with soft brown eyes and shaggy brown hair approached Casey. He spoke in a gentle voice. "Casey, it's me. You're on the Starship Pinnacle. You're safe."

Casey tilted his head quizzically. "Teddy Bear?"

Jon reached tentatively toward Casey's naked shoulder and touched him with his fingertips.

Casey jerked as if stung. He stared in horror as the teddy bear split along its seams and a black, glistening spider emerged, with a bulbous body and long, black legs. He saw the spider's mandibles, double sickles, clicking back and forth, and dripping with sticky, yellow venom. Terror broke through his skin as a soaking sweat that ran in rivulets onto the exam table. He was terrorized beyond speech, beyond sound.

"Give it up, Jon," Slater said. "He's obviously suffered a complete psychotic break. I have duties that require my attention. Just make sure he doesn't escape. He's already killed one man."

The naked man strapped to the table became still and repeated in a small voice, "He's already killed one man."

Slater continued, as if the restrained man didn't exist. "Because of our unexpected difficulties, we can't afford to lose another man, a healthy one that is."

"A healthy one," Casey repeated.

Jon looked down at the deck. He took a deep breath and released it as an audible sigh.

"As I recall, he was your friend," Slater said.

Jon looked up and nodded. "We were roommates at Copper Mountain. He was the most considerate and kind person I ever met."

Casey began screeching, pausing only long enough to take another breath.

"Come on. Let's go into the passageway so we can hear ourselves think," Slater said and put his hand on Jon's back to guide him through the door.

CHAPTER 3

As soon as the portal swished shut, Jon turned to face it. In his mind, he could still see the man strapped to the examination table. That man was old, dirty and wrinkled. His skin was thin and shiny. And his eyes, they darted about and his tongue, it flicked in and out.

"He was always so clean. I'm...I'm not certain it really is Casey." Jon said and looked to Slater.

"It's him all right. He's old and crazy, but it's Conklin."

Jon shivered. "How can we help him?"

Slater took hold of the smaller man and turned him, holding him firmly by the shoulders. "Jon," he began, "we're in a crisis situation that was never planned for, not in our wildest scenarios. We need to reach deeply and find the strength to do what must be done. There will be no help from Earth. We're on our own."

Jon looked up, into the taller man's eyes, eyes that were such a light blue they were almost colorless.

"Casey was my friend," Jon said. Tears glistened along his lower lids.

Slater's lips squeezed together and his grip tightened on Jon's shoulders.

Jon yelped. "You're hurting me!" He tried to twist out of Slater's grip, his eyes wide.

Slater eased his hold and finally released it, patting Jon on the shoulder. "I'm sorry, Jon. This is a difficult time for all of us, but we must rise to the occasion. Your secondary training was as a paramedic, wasn't it?"

"I was trained to be our librarian."

"That's not what I asked. You don't honestly think I called you here because of your training as a librarian, do you?"

"But...why me? I'm not a physician. It takes years to become a physician. Casey was older than the rest of us, twenty-eight...." He looked toward the door that hid the old man who was tied to the exam table. "And he had the benefit of computer assist."

Jon waited, but Slater merely stared at him.

"I heard we've had a computer crash and all our stored data was lost." Jon held his breath.

"That is correct."

"Oh, my God! Our culture, all the literature, music, videos...all our knowledge. I'm ruined. We are—"

"Shut up, Jon."

Jon's mouth hung open with unspoken words.

"You will become chief medical officer."

"Me?" Jon shook his head. "That's impossible. I'm not a doctor. What about Doctor Gupta and Doctor Ishak?"

"Their capsules failed."

"But, there were other doctors, the other guardians."

"Dead. All of them dead, except one."

"Geoffrey," Jon was nearly shouting. "We need Casey! I can't take his place." He wiped new tears from his eyes.

"First of all, don't call me Geoffrey. We are not friends. I am the Commander of this expedition and you will show me the respect I'm due. From now on you will address me as Commander Slater. Is that understood?"

"But, Geoff...I mean Commander Slater, we need him."

"Listen to me and listen good. I knew Casey back on Earth. We all knew Casey. He was stubborn, disrespectful of authority. He never knew when to stop pushing or when to shut up. He was a sarcastic son of a bitch."

"But—"

"But what? Mitchell Mason hated him. That should tell you a lot. If it hadn't been for that asshole Nichols, he never would've been included in the crew, much less have been appointed chief medical officer. And now we see the proof of Mason's judgment. When we really need Casey, where is he?"

"He's ill."

"I'll give you this, he certainly looks crazy...but I wonder. Is he really? The more I think about it, the more I think he's playacting. Hiding. Wallowing in there, feeling sorry for himself. It's sickening to see such weakness in a man. Sickening."

"You can't possibly believe this is an act. Anyone can see he's in terrible shape."

"Grow up, Jon. If you were a better judge of people, you'd know the extent they're willing to go to in order to avoid blame. I know what motivates people."

"But, he was the only physician to survive at all."

Under Slater's glare, Jon stepped back until he was against

the bulkhead. He raised his arms protectively, as if he expected to be struck.

Slater's response was unexpectedly mild. "Exactly...makes a person wonder doesn't it? It wouldn't surprise me if we find that Casey caused all the death and the computer crash too, for that matter, either out of cowardice or some kind of warped suicidal desire. It wasn't enough to kill himself. He wanted to kill everyone. It wouldn't surprise me at all." His voice trailed off in thought and then his eyes refocused on Jon. "You have one week to turn him around. No longer. If you're unable to talk some sense into him, I'll jettison his worthless carcass into space. Furthermore—"

Jon opened his mouth but, before he could voice his objection, Slater reached out and grabbed a handful of Jon's uniform, pulling Jon's face close to his own.

"Furthermore," Slater continued, "you'll take on the responsibilities of chief medical officer and, as such, you'll be held accountable for any failure. There will be a meeting of all guild chiefs on the bridge at sixteen hundred. Be there." He loosened his grip. "And, there's one more thing, as I think of it. I want that monstrosity sitting in the control chair removed." He released his grip on Jon's tunic and eased away. He smiled and smoothed out the front of Jon's uniform. "I'm sure you'll do just fine. Just remember what I've told you and," he paused, "remember, Jon, I'm counting on you. We're all counting on you. I'll be watching." He smiled coldly for a moment and then abruptly squared his shoulders, turned, and marched off.

Jon stared at Slater's retreating back until he disappeared around the curve of the passageway. He leaned weak-legged against the bulkhead while he considered the impossible task that had been assigned to him. He punched in the code for all-call on his com-collar.

"This is Jon Brent. I need the immediate assistance of anyone with a secondary training as paramedic. This is a priority request. Contact me at once."

He unconsciously held his breath as he waited. The seconds ticked by without a response and he was forced to exhale. The lengthy silence told him that death had taken many of those he'd spent time with during training. A cold emptiness filled his chest and he began to lose all hope when his com-collar switched on.

"Jon, this is Li Quon. Can I be of assistance?"

"Li, thank God! Please come at once. I'm in the passageway outside the medical suite on Deck Two. I need your help right now!"

Li's voice was cool in contrast. "What's the emergency?"

"Just come!"

"All right, Jon, I'll be there in a few minutes, but remember, my primary is history."

"Please hurry!"

"Sure, I'll be there in a minute." She broke off the connection.

Jon felt unbearably alone again and began tapping his foot on the deck while he waited. It seemed like a particularly long minute before he saw her walking along the curve of the passage. She walked toward him with graceful self-assurance, not hurrying, not hesitant. Her shoulder length coal-black hair shimmered and her dark brown eyes glittered with reflected light. He fidgeted while he waited for her to walk the last few steps. When she was within reach, he lost all reserve and hugged her. She tolerated this for a moment and then gently, but firmly, pulled his arms from around her.

"Why did you call me here?" she asked.

"Haven't you heard?"

"If you're talking about the capsule failures, I know of it first hand. I've been walking the decks. There are lines of pasty-white capsules, one after another, as if filled with milk." Her eyebrows pulled together and she closed her eyes. "So much death." She opened her eyes to meet his. "How could so many capsules have failed? How could any of them have failed? How the hell could this have happened?"

"No one knows," Jon said. "And that's only part of it." Seeing her self-control helped him and when he continued his voice was steady. "There's been a computer crash. Obviously, they've retained their functions, but the data storage has been wiped clean."

Li nodded. She had already heard rumors to that effect. "I've been thinking about that. I'm going to have to start recording what I know from memory. But, I don't see how I can be of any assistance to you. You'll have to do your own."

"That's not what I need your help with. You and I are the only ones left with any medical training," his voice began to quaver, "except for Casey."

"Casey Conklin's alive? Thank God. I'd heard all the doctors were dead. Why do you need me?"

"I'm sure you heard Mitch Klaus and Arnald Schmid's description of their confrontation with a wild man down in the Storage Deck."

"Yes, I heard it. So?"

Jon stared at her.

"You mean...." Li said with open disbelief.

"That's right. That was Casey."

"I can't believe he'd kill someone."

"Neither could I, but I guess we're all witnesses to Mitch's murder. He and Arnald Schmid were broadcasting on all-call throughout the entire ordeal. When Schmid said he'd 'smashed the bastard's head in', it was an exaggeration."

They stood quietly for a moment, each with their own thoughts, then Li spoke, "But...Mitch is really dead?"

"He's dead. I guess if a physician wanted to kill someone...."

"How do I fit into all this?"

"Geoffrey Slater has already been down here. He told me I had to heal Casey, or he's going to eject him into space."

"Absurd. He doesn't have the authority to do anything like that. I don't believe it."

"You obviously haven't had any contact with Slater since the Awakening." He lowered his eyes and added in a soft voice, "He always was so aggressive, but now...I'm afraid of him." He paused as he bit his lower lip. "I need your help. Please." His shoulders drooped. "Please," he begged.

She put her hand under his chin and raised his face. "We'll do what we can, but we can't be expected to do more than that. Right?"

He nodded. "Thank you, Li."

"I gather, when you say we need to heal Casey, he's suffering from some kind of mental illness. Is that right?"

"It's bad."

"I imagine it is, if it caused him to kill someone. Well, with two paramedics such as ourselves, we'll figure out how to help him," Li said.

"Do you really think so?"

"Who knows? Let's take a look at Casey and then we'll decide what to do."

"I have to warn you. He's not the Casey we knew back on Earth."

"I'm sure. Lead the way."

He pushed away from the bulkhead but waited for Li to lead the way.

CHAPTER 4

Li walked toward the door. It swished open and she stepped briskly through. Casey screeched when he saw her. It was a harsh, inhuman sound and it made Li shudder. She stepped back and bumped into Jon.

She was stunned. The naked body on the exam table vaguely resembled the man she had known, but the similarities only made him more grotesque. The man had fouled himself, but his face was the worst of all, eyes darting about, mouth open and teeth bared, as if possessed. It wasn't a man; it was a demon that was strapped to the treatment table.

When Li finally spoke it was the least of all that she mentioned. "Someone took off his com-collar."

Casey responded, his voice a rough whisper, "Spider, spider smile wider. Eat me! But bite quick, slick trick."

Li began to cautiously approach Casey; he responded by writhing against his bonds.

Jon grabbed her arm. "You better be careful. He might bite or scratch and, who knows, maybe this is due to some kind of contagious disease."

She backed away.

"Come on," Jon suggested. "Let's step out."

She didn't object; in fact, she led the way through the doorway into the passage.

When the door slid shut, Jon turned to Li. "What do you think?" he asked.

"I don't know." She shook her head. "I hate to say it, but it looks hopeless."

"I expected more from you," Jon said, nearly swallowing his words.

"Now just a minute! You've had as much training as I have. Don't you dare unload on me."

He took a quick step back. "I'm sorry. I had no right. It's just—"

"Damn straight you have no right!"

He cringed and covered his face with his hands.

She reached out and rested her hand on his arm. "I didn't

say I wouldn't try to help. It's just all so much to try to cope with. All the death, the ship malfunctioning."

He lowered his hands and looked at her with sad brown eyes.

"Buck up, Jon. We aren't going to give up without an effort. Who knows? We've had training. Let's see what we can do." It had its intended effect; she saw a trace of a smile.

"Li...there is one more thing."

She stared at him.

"You're not making it very easy, you know," he added.

She maintained her steady silence.

Though reluctant, he had to continue. "There's one other thing Slater told me we had to do." He stopped.

"Yes," she said dryly, "and what might that be, bring the dead back to life?"

He looked hurt again. "Li, please...."

"Get on with it. Give me the rest."

"He told me there was a thing in the control chair on the bridge and I was to dispose of it before the general meeting at sixteen hundred."

"Thing?"

Jon shrugged. "Actually, he said it was a monstrosity."

"A monstrosity? Well, it's almost sixteen hundred now. We'd better get a move on."

"But, what about Casey?" Jon asked.

"What about Casey? That's one problem we can postpone, at least for a while."

"That seems cruel." His face filled with imagined pain.

She took his hand as if he were a child. "Come on. He'll be all right until we get back." His hand was limp and sweaty. She was glad to release it when they arrived at the up-tube.

They exited the mouth of the up-tube on Deck One. There were a half-dozen gray-suited computer technicians working on the terminals, but there was a zone of emptiness around the control chair. Li and Jon walked toward it, with Li in the forefront. As they approached the chair, the comp-techs stopped their quiet discussions and turned to watch.

Li was not about to reveal her insecurities in front of this group; they already considered themselves better than the rest of them. She walked briskly around to the front of the chair. She was not offended by what she saw; it was more a sense of curiosity.

Jon began swallowing noisily behind her.

"Please, Jon, not now," she murmured to herself.

The figure in the chair was obviously the remains of a human. The flesh of the face had melted away, leaving behind a toothy, hideous grin. The eye sockets were empty. Patches of black hair clung to the skull. Li reached out and touched the hard surface of the chest. She brushed away white dust, all that the remained of the cadaver's uniform, revealing a corrugated chest wall, each rib plainly visible. She looked more closely and saw collapsed shadows, remnants of breasts. It had been a woman. There was a glint of silver on the seat next to the skeletal remains. Li picked it up. It was a laser-scalpel. She flicked the switch but it failed to light up.

Jon spoke in a squeaky voice. "What happened?"

Li ignored him. The white dust indicated they had discovered one of the missing guardian physicians, or at least what remained of her. But, as to the bigger question of what had happened, Li had no idea.

She was still inspecting the corpse when Slater entered the bridge. He was dressed in black and flanked by two colonists, also in black. Li didn't recognize the two men with him.

Slater walked directly over to Jon, ignoring Li.

"Yes, Commander Slater?" Jon asked, lowering his gaze to the floor.

Li was tempted to squeeze between them, to demand that Slater explain himself.

Salter pointed his finger at Jon. "I expect a full report, but for now get this carcass out of here. It's almost time for the meeting."

Jon stood there, looking blank and dumb.

"Do it now," Slater commanded and took hold of Jon's arm, propelling him toward the corpse.

Jon tripped and nearly fell.

Slater shook his head and said something to one of the men who had accompanied him. The man laughed.

Li whispered fiercely to Jon, "Get me a container from storage!" It was not a request; it was an order. She was furious at Slater's treatment of Jon and equally furious at Jon for his obvious lack of courage. To be associated with him was an embarrassment and her embarrassment made her angry with herself. She was not even aware that she was grinding her teeth while she stood with her eyes directed down at the deck, afraid to look up, afraid her anger would break loose without regard for consequences.

When Jon returned, she grabbed her end of the box with such force that it jerked out of his hands and fell to the deck. Her face flushed. She had no doubt that the comp-techs and Slater were enjoying her humiliation.

"Come on, Jon," she whispered, "help me."

"I am," he replied sullenly.

Turning his head away from the corpse, he took hold of one arm, while Li grabbed the other.

"Lift," Li ordered.

The corpse was unexpectedly brittle and light. The arms snapped off, sending a cloud of fine dust into the air. Jon fell onto his buttocks, still holding the cadaver's arm. One of the men with Slater laughed and Li could hear snickering from the comp-techs.

"Jon, damn it!" she said and then, after a cleansing breath, reached out and patted him on the arm. "It's okay, Jon. Let's get this job done."

They managed to get the grisly remains into the container without further mishap but, by then, the bridge was beginning to fill with guild chiefs. Jon took one end of the box and Li the other. They began carrying it down the passage toward the larger, equipment down-tube. As they passed Slater, he spoke to Jon.

"Just put it down in the passage for now. You don't have time to take it down and get back. I'm ready to start and I'm certainly not going to wait for you."

Jon nodded without comment. They placed the container in the passageway near the equipment down-tube and then returned to the bridge.

While they were gone, the remaining guild chiefs had arrived on the bridge. There was a low hum of conversation, but Li couldn't hear what they were saying to each other. It was plain they didn't consider either Jon or herself to be one of them. She looked around the bridge; all the important colors were present, with the glaring exception of white. The many colored uniforms gave the gathering a cheerful, almost carnival appearance, in sharp contrast to the underlying mood and grim faces.

Slater spoke. "Quiet please."

The bridge fell silent.

"I've asked you to be here in person so you can report to your individual guilds. I'm sure you've all heard rumors. Some of them are true. We've lost nine hundred and sixty-eight colonists, leaving only five hundred and twelve. Those who died included three guild chiefs which I've taken the initiative to replace." He paused. The room remained deathly silent. "In addition, we've lost our memory banks, but that's not all, we've also lost many valuable biologicals. Brita Baldus will fill you in on the details in a moment."

Slater's voice was somber, but his appearance was one of vigor. It almost seemed as if he was pleased with the disaster. "Despite these devastating losses, there is good news as well."

The crowd perked up, ready for good news of any sort.

"We have arrived at our destination and," Slater paused again, drawing out their anticipation, playing it, "it is like Earth itself."

Conversation erupted at once. It was a noisy, high-energy response. People were talking in loud voices and hugging each other. Jon wrapped his arms around Li, but she shrugged out of his embrace; her attention remained focused on the others in the room. Jon pulled back from the rejection, but Li didn't even notice.

The conversation level began to lessen and Slater spoke again. "Your attention please. I've appointed Jarmo Karna to replace Jon Sturm as Chief of Geology and Planetary Science. May Jon rest in peace. Jarmo will now give a brief report."

A slim man with blond-white hair began speaking in a monotone, belying the content of his message. "My remaining colleagues and I have completed a preliminary study of the planet we're orbiting and what we've discovered exceeds our most optimistic expectations. The planet is Earth-like in every aspect. Our probes have revealed a virgin planet, rich in mineral resources, with a hospitable climate and an atmosphere that duplicates that of Earth, prior to hydrocarbon pollution. We've located a number of advantageous landing sites, but I personally favor site 'C'." While he spoke a holographic projection of the planet materialized above the heads of the gathered chiefs.

Li was astounded, as were the others. It looked just like the blue planet Earth, with oceans and swirls of white clouds. She could easily make out landmasses. It looked so much like

Earth that she unreasonably expected to be able to pick out the familiar shapes of the continents but, try as she might, the landmasses had shapes of their own.

A bright red spot appeared on the globe and it stopped rotating.

Jarmo continued. "The marker is on what we've judged to be the most advantageous landing site. It's situated on a peninsula 1000 kilometers in length and averaging 300 kilometers in width. As you can see it runs parallel with the equator, but is far enough north to be temperate. The peninsula has a ridge of mountains stretching along its length. These mountains probably have snowy peaks most of the year and should provide a ready source of fresh water. It's currently the equivalent of spring on the peninsula. Incidentally, we've detected no sign of intelligent life."

He had concluded, but the bridge remained quiet.

Li again tried to put the pieces together and identify her home world. Her breath caught. How could she have been so wrong? It looked remarkably like Earth. She could even identify a continent that looked like Asia and a large island that looked like Japan. The most striking difference was the peninsula that Karna had pointed out. A strong tug of homesickness twisted her stomach, as it did for many of those present.

"Very good, Jarmo," Slater said with a cheerful lilt to his voice. "Now, if I can have your attention, Brita will give us a report on the state of our animal biologicals."

Brita Baldus turned to gaze around the room. She was a big-boned woman with an uninteresting face, except for her smile, which seemed to broadcast warmth and goodwill. She saw Li and Jon standing in the background and actually winked at them. Despite her optimistic nature, her report was depressing. When she announced there would be no horses, someone in the crowd moaned.

Li found that particularly disgusting. She tried to see who it was that would moan for a horse, but remain silent for the loss of friends and colleagues. It could've been Lisa Bouviet, dressed in communication pink, but she wasn't sure.

Brita's report seemed interminable. Slater began shifting his weight from one foot to the other. Finally, as Brita began to name insects that had survived the journey, he interrupted her.

"Thank you, Brita," he said. "We have to move along now.

We're confident that enough of the animal biologicals have survived to serve our needs. We'll leave the details to your capable staff."

She looked somewhat taken aback by the interruption, but she managed a smile. She wasn't one to take offense.

Gao Min then gave her report on the survival of plant and seed biologicals. Her report was mercifully brief as she summarized in sweeping generalities, in dramatic contrast to Brita's epic report.

"Now it's time for my report," Slater said. "I—"

"Before you begin, I have something to say." Aleksandr Protonov, Chief of Computer Science and Instrumentation, stepped forward.

For once, Li was pleased by Protonov's arrogance.

Slater glared at the tall man with gray eyes and black hair. Protonov was one of the few colonists who sported facial hair, a short-cropped, full beard that came to a point at his chin.

Slater added a smile, but the smile did not reach beyond his lips. "Why of course, Chief Protonov, we're all interested in what you have to say."

Protonov turned to face the gathering. He did not make eye contact with anyone but, instead, looked just over their heads. "As you are no doubt aware, there has been a computer failure. Obviously, the functionality of basic programming remains. Otherwise we'd all be dead. But, beyond that there is no content. Such an unusual and selective failure is unprecedented. We will continue to investigate but to date we've been able to retrieve very little of the missing data. The issue is that we cannot hope to survive as a viable colony without our database. Each of you must designate a portion of your resources toward the documentation of your particular fields of expertise. I demand it."

"I give the orders here!" Slater shouted and his face reddened.

Protonov slowly pivoted toward him. "Then give the order."

Protonov's leisurely response had given Slater time to regain his composure. "But, of course, Aleksandr. I whole heartily agree. It'll be the responsibility of each of you to ensure that our knowledge is preserved."

Slater paused, glanced down for a moment, and then back up, as if to signal that what he was about to say was difficult, yet, well considered. "Friends," he began, his voice now mellow, "we've each been trained in a primary and vital specialty. Mine, of course, was in administration and implementation. I was assigned the title of Commander so that there would be no question of who was in charge during planet-fall, but the planners could never have foreseen the terrible losses we've suffered."

He paused, to let them each dwell on their own personal losses, and there was not a colonist present who had not experienced loss first hand. He continued. "If we're to survive, we must function efficiently with complete coordination of our activities. For this to occur, there must be someone with the authority to make decisions. I am that person. It's what I was trained to do and I pledge to you that I'll do my very best for all." His voice was becoming louder, sweaty with fervor. "I'm the ultimate authority here and I will not shirk my duty. I will make the decisions. I will have the first and the last say. With the crisis upon us, there is no leeway for the finery of civilization. We're fighting for our very lives. Under my direction, we will survive and prosper, but I will not tolerate disobedience, simply because we cannot afford it."

He challenged them with an intemperate stare, beginning with Protonov, daring him to object, and then continued around the bridge, from face to face. There were furtive glances, but no one voiced an objection.

The diminutive Li Quon was clenching and opening her small hands. Jon reached out and grasped her forearm, as if that would be enough to restrain her. She twisted her arm out of his grip and ignored his whispered warning, as if brushing off a harmless pest.

"Slater!" She said it forcefully, but her voice sounded as small as that of a young boy, especially when compared to Slater's carnival-barker tones. "How dare you characterize democracy as a finery of civilization? You talk about it as if it's a bauble, as if it's only a gaudy decoration."

"Quiet!" Slater yelled and then returned his attention to the gathered guild chiefs. He smiled his broadest smile. "Don't worry, friends. I too look forward to the time when we will be strong. I too look forward to the time when I'll be able to step down and hand over the heavy burden of command to others, to a democratic leadership but, until that time arrives, rest assured, I will remain vigilant for the good of us all."

"For the good of us all?" Li shouted. "I can't believe what

I'm hearing. You have no right to claim total power and then dress it up——"

"I told you to be quiet!"

"I will not be quiet. History has much to say about unrestrained power. Power corrupts and absolute power corrupts absolutely. Even you must have heard—"

"Shut up, woman! You were not chosen to be a guild chief and you were not invited to be present at this meeting. I did not ask for your opinion. If I had wanted Humanity's opinion, I would have asked Chief Abdulahak Achik. He is mature enough to understand expediency. Your voice does not deserve to be heard."

Slater turned to a man dressed in the black uniform of administration and whose scalp was covered with a bur of short, blond hair. He spoke quietly to the big man. The man stood at rigid attention while he listened. He was a stranger to Li.

Li looked to the gathered guild chiefs. She found the maroon of humanities but, of all those present, Chief Achik was not looking in her direction. She gathered her courage and returned her attention to Slater.

"Slater, I will not let—"

"You will address me as Commander Slater!" He was like a coiled snake preparing to strike. His words erupted as a guttural growl from deep in his throat. "I am your leader."

"You're not my leader!"

Jon edged away from her.

The muscles bulged on the sides of Slater's jaw. He snapped his hand out and pointed a finger at Li.

The burly man who Slater had spoken to responded at once. He marched directly through the gathering, shouldering guild chiefs aside if they didn't move fast enough to suit him.

Despite her courage, Li felt the urge to run, but she couldn't get her feet to move. She stood alone, with a chill nibbling at her fingers and toes. The man walked toward her; she saw neither violence nor reason in his ice-blue eyes.

The guild chiefs watched while the man confronted Li. He reached with remarkable quickness and snatched the com-collar from around Li's delicate neck.

A cry of pain and surprise escaped her mouth. She grabbed her throat with both hands; her breathing was stridorous and tears spilled down her cheeks. The man did not offer assistance; no one did. She fought for each breath and dropped to her knees. Her assailant turned his back on her and walked back through the gathering to retake his position at Slater's side.

Slater spoke and all in attendance turned back to him. His voice was now soothing. "I'm sorry you had to witness this unfortunate scene. I'm grieved that colonist Quon does not have the foresight to understand the desperate position we find ourselves in and the difficult decisions that must be made, but do not doubt me. I will do my duty, regardless of unpleasantries."

They could all hear Li's noisy respirations.

Slater continued. "I can only say, thank you. Thank you for your selflessness and vision. Do not leave here thinking I'm an unreasonable man. I know you all have questions and concerns, and I will meet with each of you individually, when time permits. I do value your opinions." He nodded toward a thin woman dressed in communication pink. "Jane Veck has volunteered to assist me in our reorganization and I have appointed her Guild Chief of Communications."

"What? Hey! That's my—"

Slater swung his gaze to focus on Lisa Bouviet. She closed her mouth.

Slater continued. "If I'm not available, Jane will be happy to take your messages. For us to function efficiently, our communication needs to be coordinated. We cannot afford another demoralizing, general broadcast like that of Arnald Schmid during the tragic murder of Mitch Klaus by Casey Conklin. If Conklin's collar had been adjusted to our present frequencies, it may very well have resulted in an even greater tragedy. I find it regrettable, but necessary, that a minor adjustment be made to the com-collars so that all-call will be, temporarily, eliminated. You will, of course, be able to continue to communicate among yourselves on a one to one basis using your personal codes."

The chiefs began to grumble; offended by this new restriction, but Slater raised his voice to regain their attention. "I also yearn for a resolution of our crisis. We must be strong. We must be resolute in our commitment to function as a team and I will be captain of that team. In six days we will leave orbit for planet-fall. It's not much time to prepare but, before you return to your duties, my associate here..." He swung his arm around to indicate the man who had attacked Li. "…Mister Olson, has a few words to say. I thank you in advance for your cooperation."

Slater then walked around the edge of the group and they all watched him as he disappeared through the doorway at the side of the bridge.

They were still turned toward the closed door, when the sober man dressed in black called their attention back to the front of the bridge. "Guild chiefs, before you return to your duties, you will file past either me, or Mister Sabine." He nodded toward the other man dressed in black.

Jack Sabine was a thin, intense appearing man. He smiled at the assemblage with poorly disguised pleasure.

Sten Olson continued, his diction as crisp as his back was straight. "We will adjust your com-collars. It will be necessary to replace the all-call crystal with a null crystal to maintain the circuit."

There was angry mumbling from the guild chiefs.

Olson raised his voice so it had an edge. "This is not optional. You will do as I say." He pointed to Brita Baldus, "You first."

She hesitated only a second and then stepped forward. Olson popped out the ruby-red, all-call crystal and replaced it with a jade-green one. Brita turned, without facing the others, and quickly exited via the down-tube.

"Next," he ordered, and the crowd began to move forward, one at a time.

As Olson and Sabine adjusted the collars, Olson told them to expect to see the black uniform on other colonists who would be visiting their areas to adjust the rest of the collars. He told them he didn't want any trouble, but that disobedience of Commander Slater's orders would not be tolerated. There was very little talking as the chiefs made their way past one of the two men and then rushed over to the down-tube, relieved to escape the unresolved tension on the bridge, until only one chief remained. Olson motioned for Protonov to step forward.

"If you want to adjust my collar, you come to me," Protonov demanded. "You have no idea how difficult it is to keep life support functioning in particular cabins."

Olson smiled. This is language he understood. "I think we could become good friends."

"Not a chance in hell."

Olson, still smiling, walked across the bridge and changed

out the crystal in Protonov's collar. After which, Protonov walked slowly toward the down-tube, nose held high, and dropped out of sight.

All the chiefs had departed, leaving only Li Quon, still on her knees, and Jon Brent, who squatted next to her with his hand on her back. Her breathing was finally beginning to ease.

Jon looked up when he heard the "swish" that indicated a door had opened. His hand fell away from Li's back.

Slater walked casually toward them. He stopped when he was standing over them. "I can't say I'm impressed by your choice of colleagues, Jon."

Jon had to crane his neck uncomfortably upward to see Slater's face. "Li is very competent. She was the best of us all and is the only other paramedic to survive."

"I'll tell you what. Why don't you leave us and attend to your duties in the medical suite. Mister Olson will stop by and adjust your collar. In the meantime, I'll have a nice, quiet chat with Li. We need to discuss her new responsibilities. Don't you agree?"

Jon didn't move. He looked to Li and she met his look with the imitation of a smile.

"Don't you agree?" Slater asked in a louder voice.

"Go ahead, Jon. I'll be all right." Li's voice was raspy. She gave him a gentle push.

He slowly stood.

"Go on, Jon," Slater said without a hint of anger in his voice. "She just told you, she doesn't need you. She'll be down to join you in a few minutes."

Jon walked over to the down-tube. He took another look at Li; she forced a smile and waved him on. He stepped forward and disappeared into the mouth of the tube. When he disappeared, so did Li's smile.

Slater rested his hand on Li's fine, jet-black hair and began stroking it. She jerked away from his touch and glared up at him.

"What am I going to do with you?" Slater mused. "I certainly can't afford to have a minor player like you mucking up the works. I should've known that a humanity-tech would be the last to recognize expediency." He paused as if gathering his thoughts. "I know you find this difficult to believe, but I do have a duty to perform, just as you do. Why do you think I was included in the crew?"

"You were included in the crew to organize and coordinate the landing, not set yourself up as dictator."

Slater reached down and grabbed her jaw, snapping her head back. "It doesn't have to be like this. I find you quite attractive, but don't let that fool you." He released his grip and began to caress her hair again. "I'll do whatever needs to be done. I won't warn you again. Don't step out of line. We can't afford to lose another colonist, but I won't allow anyone to jeopardize our success. Don't force me to take action. That would be most regrettable."

"Are you actually threatening to kill me?"

"No, of course not." He brushed the backs of his fingers across her cheek. "Mister Sabine will supply you with a new collar. Come visit me when you get a chance. I'm sure we can work out an equitable arrangement. I can be quite generous to those who are willing to give in return."

He patted her on the head and smiled before he walked across the bridge to reenter his suite of rooms. Li watched him leave and then turned her gaze to Sabine.

Sabine sauntered over and held out the collar, dangling it from his bony fingers. When she reached out for it, he let it drop to the deck. He grinned while he played with the ring on his left long finger, a black cross with wings, and then squatted so that he could come face to face with her. As he did so a swastika on a thick gold chain swung into view.

"I don't suppose that yungdrung you're wearing around your neck means you're a Hindu," she said as she glowered at him.

"What?"

"Didn't think so."

"You're a strange one, but I like strange, if you get my drift. Just remember, honey, if you need help, you can always come visit old Jack. We'll have some fun."

His greasy laugh grated on her ears, but she remained perfectly still until he stood and swaggered off, down the passageway.

Li was mortified by her treatment. It was as if she had been transported back in time. She picked up the com-collar from the deck, quickly stood, and rushed for the down-tube, afraid that even worse things would happen to her if she remained on the bridge. Just before she dropped into the tube, she saw a giant man standing in the shadows, also dressed in black. He was such a hulking figure that he made Olson look normal in comparison. She shivered with dread and jumped into the tube.

By the time she exited on Deck Two, her fear had transformed into a smoldering anger and a hostile resentment of Slater and those uncivilized ruffians he called his assistants. Where had they come from? If they had been in any of the training groups, she definitely would've remembered them. These were not the kind of people who could walk around without being noticed. She looked ahead and saw Jon staring at her approach. The passage was busy with colonists, walking purposefully on their individual missions, but no one paid any attention to Li.

Jon waited until Li stood next to him before he spoke. He looked her up and down. "Are you okay?"

"I'm just fine," she answered, biting off each word.

Jon hung his head. "I'm sorry I left you alone up there. It's just...well...."

"Forget it. You did what I told you to do." She rubbed her hands on her jumpsuit, as if to wipe off the filth of her experience. "How is Casey?"

"The same," he said dully.

"Jon, we need to salvage him. He's the only physician to survive. He must know something about what happened to the ship and the dead colonists. He may be our best hope to work our way out of this Draconian society we've awakened to. Come on, let's go to the lab."

She started down the passage, not waiting to see if Jon was following, but he was. After a few strides he was walking at her side. The medical suite stretched along thirty meters of the curved passage. The last door was that of the instrumentation lab. The door sensed their approach and opened with a "whoosh" of air as it slid into the wall. They entered without breaking stride, confident it would open, and then came to an abrupt halt. Although the interconnected treatment rooms occupied most of the space allotted to the medical suite, the instrument lab was the largest single room, with an overhead that was a full ten meters off the deck. Cubbyholes lined the walls, filled with row after row of strange devices, each with its own custom-fitted slot.

"Jon, we need a diagnostic kit and a molecular synthesizer.

Any idea what they look like and where they might be?"

He had an empty look on his face, arms dangling at his sides.

"Snap out of it! Don't just stand there. Take some initiative. Think!"

"Find it yourself," he said bitterly. "You've had as much training as I have. Does that sound nice to you? Because it didn't to me when I asked for help."

They stood glaring at each other, not a blink between them. Then Li shrugged and began walking along the instrument packed walls, peering through the transparent door of each recess, hoping that the sight of the right instrument would stimulate its own recognition. After looking at dozens of devices, ranging from an irregularly shaped blob of silver metal with purple spikes, to a deceptively simple gray cylinder, she began to lose hope.

She noticed a preservation chest and walked over to raise the lid. It was filled with new, white uniforms. She looked down at her own beloved maroon. After all, she thought, I'm a historian, not a doctor. What could she really expect of herself? She looked over at Jon, who leaned listlessly against the bulkhead. The fatigue of new-awakening was visible in every aspect of his appearance, from his half-closed eyelids, to his slack jaw and bent knees. She walked over to him and reluctantly took hold of his hand to lead him into the passageway.

"Jon, I think it's time we get some sleep. Maybe we'll be able to think more clearly after we've rested."

He nodded agreement and shambled off to find his personal storage locker. The corridor was already littered with bodies, sprawled on their pallets, deep in senseless slumber. She looked at them with envy, but resisted and pushed back the heaviness of exhaustion. She felt a strong sense of urgency and had a plan.

CHAPTER 5

Li paused a short distance from the exam room. Even though she had a plan, it was still nebulous. It was obvious to her that to reverse Casey's psychosis she was going to need the assistance of a fully trained physician. The only physician available was Casey. Therefore, what she had to do was entice Casey to help himself. She felt confident that she could somehow get through to him. They hadn't actually been friends on Earth, but Casey had been her proctor during her secondary, and they had at least developed a respect for one another.

She committed herself to the effort and stepped through the portal into Casey's room. Despite the purifying system, the air was saturated with the sharp odors of urine and sweat. Casey remained strapped to the exam table. His struggles to escape had abraded his wrists and ankles to a raw redness. He was still and appeared to be asleep. She approached the table cautiously. When she was an arm's length away, his eyes flicked open, an automaton come to life. Li sucked in a quick breath and stumbled back a couple of steps.

His voice was weak. "So, Child Princess, you're the one they sent to kill me. I don't hold it against you. I guess it's fair. All I ask is that you tell me one thing. How is the Virgin of the Woods?"

"Who?" Her forehead creased with effort as she tried to recall a colonist with that nickname, but she came up empty.

"Don't toy with me, Princess. Did you kill her too?" He tried to reach her, straining against the straps, wide-eyed and fierce in his attempts to break free. His finger's reached toward her. Although there was no possibility he could grab her, she took another step back.

"Casey, my name is Li Quon. Don't you remember me?"

"I remember you, Princess. I remember all of you. I just want to know if the Virgin is well before I die. Is that too much to ask? Does that ruin the game?"

"Honestly, Casey, I don't know who the Virgin—"

"Her name is Britty, damn it! You know who I mean!

Everyone knows the Virgin."

She knew no one by that name. "I do want to help—"

"Do you think I don't know what you're up to?" He spoke with a growl. His dry tongue licked his cracked lips.

Li walked to the wall console and took out a squeeze bottle of water. When her back was turned, she heard a hissing and quickly looked over her shoulder. Casey's mouth was wide open in a hoarse, nearly soundless laugh. She shivered, but took a deep breath and suppressed it before she turned to face him.

"All right, Casey, you win. You always were too clever for us."

He nodded.

Li continued. "I'm here because the Virgin needs you, desperately."

He stopped moving and his stare seemed to bore right through her.

"She needs your help. She's been injured. She needs you, Casey, or she'll die. You're the only one who can help."

His eyes narrowed as he watched her take a sip from the water bottle. He licked his lips again. "That's a lie. You're trying to trick me." It sounded more like a question than an accusation.

Li pushed her extemporaneous fabrication, trying to sell it. She mixed in a little truth. "You know I was trained as a paramedic. You trained me. But Britty's injuries are too severe for me to deal with. She had a terrible fall and has suffered a serious head injury. I was afraid to move her and I can't decide what instruments to use. You know it's beyond my capabilities."

Li paused. Casey stared at her, probing for visual signs of truth or deceit. She kept her face blank. He seemed less savage. There was something about the way he held his head that made him look more human, more rational.

Fatigue blunted her alertness, but she knew she would never get a chance like this again. Slater would never give his permission, that was certain. The whole ship was asleep, except for the two of them. The thought of sleep made her feel like curling up on the deck and giving in. It was a powerful need and became stronger with each passing minute.

"Casey, we don't have much time. Britty needs your help. She's depending on you." Li sounded desperate, and was feeling desperate, fighting off sleep desire with pure will.

"Release me, Child Princess, and I will go with you."

Now that he had agreed, she was hesitant. He had already killed once. She was not at all certain she could handle him, even in his weakened condition. What she really wanted to do was lie down, even if just for a moment. When her thoughts returned to Casey, so did her eyes; his sparse hair was matted with a patch of dried blood where Schmid had struck him, his bright eyes were rimmed with scarlet, and he was smiling. Li's legs began shaking. Fear or just exhaustion? Or both? She could no longer tell. She approached him, watching for signs of attack, but he remained still and appeared to be in control of himself.

"Here, Casey, have a sip."

His eyes never left her face as she brought the water bottle up. He parted his cracked lips and Li dribbled in a few cool drops, and then a few more. When he next spoke, it was easier to understand him.

"What did you say happened to Britty?"

"She fell. I can't go into the details now. We don't have much time. I'm going to cut your straps, and then we need to get a diagnostic kit and molecular synthesizer from the lab."

While she talked, she used a laser-scalpel to slash the band holding his left wrist. He lay perfectly still. She walked around the exam table and cut the bands on his legs; he continued to remain motionless, except for his eyes, which followed her every move.

She cut the strap across his chest and then hesitated. Was she really ready to cut the last restraint of a psychotic killer? It was now or never. She severed it and jumped back, but he didn't move.

"Casey?"

"Yes, Princess?"

"We must be very careful. There are people on this ship who would stop us if they knew you were free. Do you understand? We must be quiet."

A wide smile spread across his face, causing his cracked lips to ooze blood. He snickered. "Of course, Princess. I know the game, better than you." A cacophonous laugh erupted from his widely opened mouth.

Li pressed hard against the bulkhead; an adrenaline surge awakened her fully and caused her heart to race.

"Casey, be quiet! Stop laughing. You'll get us both in serious trouble."

"Laughing?" he asked, his eyes searching her as if reassessing. "I'm not laughing. You know very well it's Mendoza."

"Now listen," she said sternly. "Britty's life depends on us. You must control the laughter from wherever it comes. Do you understand?"

"I understand everything."

"Well?" she asked.

"Well what?"

"Well, you're free to sit up. We need to move fast. Don't you remember?"

"Are you sure this is part of the game?" he asked.

"This is no game. Britty needs our help."

"Princess, you are so sweet. Why don't you come closer so I can give you a kiss?"

The thought of this filthy, sick old man kissing her made her nauseated.

He persisted. "Don't you want a kiss?" He pouted, his lower lip glistening with blood.

This was getting her nowhere. Her patience was gone. While she held the scalpel with one hand, she grabbed his arm with the other to pull him upright, but as soon as he felt her touch, he lunged toward her. He caught her arm and twisted it until the scalpel clattered to the deck. Then he grasped her other arm. He pulled her close and swung his legs over the edge of the table so he sat facing her.

His breath was a fetid odor and his whisper sounded sinister. "You don't play the game very well, Princess, but I do."

He slid onto the floor and pulled her down with him while he felt for the scalpel. He brought it up and reactivated it with a flick of his thumb. Li was breathing fast and deep.

"I'm skilled with this blade," he said. "Should I show you?" The wild laughter bubbled forth, until it was interrupted by a fit of coughing. When he recovered he spoke again. "Now, Princess, we're going to the lab, just like you suggested, and then you'll take me to Britty. Any questions?"

Li had no voice. She slowly shook her head.

"Very well."

He held her firmly as he opened a preservation cabinet

and brought out a roll of strapping. He tied her right wrist to his left and jerked her toward the portal. When they entered the passage, he stopped to look up and down the curve of the corridor. There were over twenty colonists visible in this short section of the passage, but none of them moved; they were all deep into their First Sleep. He tugged Li around so he could face her and bent his face close to hers, bathing it with his foul breath.

"It's my turn now," he said. "Even though you are a princess, if you try to warn the others, I'll punish you severely. You do believe me, don't you?"

He raised the scalpel for emphasis and touched it to her throat, drawing forth a drop of bright red blood. She began to swoon, the passageway appeared to darken, but her terror and the touch of the blade brought a measure of control back to her body.

"I understand," she managed to whisper.

"That's good, because it's fair if I cut off your head. It's not against the rules, you know."

"C-Casey, B-Britty needs us," she stammered. "I only want to help her."

He chuckled and withdrew the scalpel. He started down the passage without warning, causing Li to stagger as she caught her balance. Each time they approached a sleeping figure he would ready the scalpel to slash and kill, but each time the figure remained motionless in sleep and was passed over.

He paused for a moment outside the portal to the instrument lab, and once again looked up and down the passage, but seemed satisfied that there was no movement. He pulled Li with him, through the portal and into the lab. He dragged her about the room as if she were only an afterthought. It took him only a few seconds to locate a diagnostic kit and a molecular synthesizer and then he searched until he found a surgical kit. He turned to face her.

"Where is she?" he asked.

Li was desperately trying to think of a way to escape this psychotic maniac. She searched the room with her eyes, looking for anything she could use for a weapon.

"Don't stall," he commanded and activated the scalpel. "It's fair for me to slice little pieces off you. Perhaps I should start with your cute little nose."

Li's mind froze with the thought of being dissected alive. Casey grasped her left hand and held it firmly against the bulkhead. He brought the blade toward it, smiling all the while.

Li screamed and then sobbed as she spoke. "She's been taken to Deck One. You need me. I can show you where."

Casey's voice was soft. "Really? You don't think I know this ship? I've spent my life wandering around in it." He placed the blade against her little finger, drawing blood. "Now, where is she?"

"She's in the commander's suite! Slater's got her!"

Casey continued to apply pressure with the blade until the bone snapped and her severed finger fell to the deck. Li swayed for a few seconds and then crumpled, no longer able to cope with the terror, which was far worse than her pain. She dangled from the bond that bound her to Casey's wrist. Casey laughed and flicked the blade across the strap so that Li collapsed to the deck. Her dark skin was pale and her lips were tinged with purple; her breathing was shallow, almost imperceptible.

"Just kidding, Princess. No offense intended, none taken. Right?"

He turned from her and, without another glance in her direction, picked up the diagnostic and surgical kits with one hand and the synthesizer with the other. He lost all caution as he focused on Britty, a captive of Butt-Face Slater. He entered the passage and failed to notice the hulking figure waiting outside the portal. The blow was struck with such precision that there was no pain, only immediate blackness.

CHAPTER 6

Casey awakened. He opened his eyes and saw the thin light-lines in the overhead. Bizarre and chaotic memories filled his mind, bits and pieces, with a strong undertow of violence. A sense of place drifted upward from his fragmented memories but then evaporated. He started to sit up, but the movement was only begun when he was jerked back by his restraints.

He turned his head and vertigo made the room appear to tilt and twirl. Nausea arose and flooded his mouth with saliva. He squeezed his eyes shut and waited for the sickness to pass. Questions swirled in his mind, mixed with visions of blood and death.

He opened his eyes when he heard the "swish" of the portal. A petite figure entered and, when their eyes met, stopped cold, as if striking an unseen wall. They peered wordlessly at one another until Casey spoke.

"Who are you?" Casey asked.

"You don't know?"

"I'm so tired. I don't understand. Where am I?"

"You're onboard the starship Pinnacle."

"Starship? I don't feel well. I don't understand. Who are you? Why am I tied up?"

She didn't move and didn't speak. Her left hand was covered by the shimmering pink of a gel dressing. She slid it behind her back. Even that small movement brought a grimace to her face.

He stared at her. A memory reached upward and then skittered away before he could grasp it. He began to tremble.

"Do you know me?" he asked.

Her voice was reserved when she finally answered. "I know you."

"My name...what is my name?"

"Your name is Casey Conklin."

"Casey?" He looked to her for confirmation.

Li backed toward the portal.

"Don't leave. Don't leave me here all alone," he begged.

She rushed toward the portal. It opened and she ran into

the passage.

His head ached. He tried to free his hands from the restraints but the effort only made his headache spike. The light-lines seemed too bright, the room too white. It was all too much. The medicated disk continued to secrete drugs into his system. He was afraid to close his eyes but the drugs were potent and he fell into a restless state of partial sedation.

When he awakened he saw light and then the light came into focus as lines in the ceiling. A sense of place coalesced. He was aboard the starship Pinnacle. He turned his head to the left and saw the regeneration tank. He knew exactly where he was, in the primary treatment room of the medical suite. He turned his head to the right and saw a small woman with silky black hair standing motionless just inside the portal. Their eyes met.

"Hello, Li," he said.

"You know my name?"

"Of course I know your name."

"I'm sorry I ran away and left you alone," Li said.

"What are you talking about?"

She said nothing.

"Li, why am I strapped to this table? I remember attending to my duties, and then...suddenly, I wake up and find myself tied to an examination table. Am I your prisoner for some reason?"

Li focused on the cobalt-blue, transdermal patch stuck to his chest.

Casey followed her gaze and saw the disk; blue meant a psychotropic drug. Odd. "Did you?" He bobbed his chin toward the blue disk.

She nodded.

"Why did you medicate me? I have one hell of a headache, but we both know this isn't an analgesic patch."

She remained silent.

"There is absolutely no reason for me to be tied up like some kind of wild animal. I am filthy and need to get cleaned up. Remove these restraints."

"No."

"No? Did you say 'no'? What the hell is going on? I want to consult with one of the other doctors. Contact one for me, perhaps Grace."

She shook her head.

"Why not?"

"I can't."

"You can't, or you won't?"

She lowered her gaze to the deck.

"At least tell me this. Have we arrived?" he asked.

"Yes."

"Thank God. Did we choose well? Is it habitable?"

She looked to him and actually smiled. "It's all we could hope for...more."

"Truly amazing. I have to tell you I had my doubts. Tell me all about it."

Li retreated into silence.

When it was obvious she wasn't going to say any more. He focused his attention on her gel-dressed hand.

"What happened to your hand?" he asked.

The mere mention of it made the pain flare and she cradled it with her good hand. "Don't you remember?" she asked, the tone of her voice indicating that she did not believe his claim of continued memory loss.

"Remember what? Release me and I'll take a look at it."

Li touched her com-collar and spoke briefly into it. Casey couldn't make out her words, but within moments the portal whisked open and admitted a giant. Li looked tiny in comparison; her head came to just above the man's waist, the largest and the smallest. The comparison was almost comical, but Casey felt fear, not amusement. His gaze fixed on the barrel-chested giant. The man's pate was completely bald and shined with lines of reflected light. His eyes were small. His ears were nubs on the sides of his head and the skin of his face was as smooth as a baby's. His neck was so short and stout that his head seemed to rest directly on his torso.

Casey recognized him. He was one of the colonists that had been housed on Deck One, but he was a mystery. He was one of a few that Casey had found scattered among what he considered the legitimate colonists who had no personal file, no history to review. He was a blank. He had a name, but only one, Yamaguchi. While Casey studied the man, the man studied Casey with equal thoughtfulness, and then another name came to Casey's mind, the Unsmiling Buddha. It seemed to fit, but he couldn't recall why it seemed so right.

With unexpected suddenness, the nausea flared up. Casey turned his head to the side and retched repeatedly, until he felt like his stomach was being pulled inside out. He was unaware of Li's cautious approach and didn't feel the soft touch of sedative and anti-emetic disks being applied to his shoulder. Warm relaxation spread through his body. Without noticing it, he floated off into a thoughtless state of sedation.

CHAPTER 7

Li massaged the painful tension in the muscles of her neck and shoulders with her good hand as she cautiously approached the sleeping man. She was more surprised than pleased that she had managed to coax a disk from the molecular synthesizer that actually seemed to be returning a balance to Casey's rampant insanity, but she'd had enough of playing doctor. His attack had pushed past her resilient exterior and had penetrated her core. She felt no comradeship with the still pitiful-appearing man. Her most fervent desire was to be rid of him. He was no longer the key to a solution; he was just another problem.

She touched her com-collar and spoke, "Connect me with Jon Brent."

"Hello?"

"Jon, this is Li. Casey has awakened and...although it's still early, it appears he may be sane."

There was no response.

"Jon, are you hearing me?"

"Are you sure?"

"No, of course I'm not sure, but I need your help, now."

There was no answer.

"Jon, you are the Chief Medical Officer. Get your ass down here!"

"All right, Li," he said, reluctantly, "I'll be there as soon as I can. But you don't have to talk to me like that."

Li waited impatiently for Jon's arrival. She couldn't really blame him. After all he was a librarian, not really a chief medical officer. As time passed, her mood changed again, if she could deal with it, then so could he. When the portal finally opened and he walked in, his shoulders were raised and his head bent. He reminded Li of a turtle.

"Sorry I took so long. What can I do?" His voice was soft and his eyes avoided the motionless figure tied to the exam table. The strong stench of vomit and body odor was nausea provoking. Jon's Adam's apple bobbed as he gulped and gagged.

Her anger faded again, to resignation. She led him into the

passageway and fresh air.

"Jon, I can't handle this alone."

"I know." He laughed at himself in self-deprecation. "I'm sorry—"

"Don't be sorry, just do your part. I told you what Slater said after he found out I'd let Casey loose on a sleeping ship. I really think Slater could've killed me, to say nothing of Casey."

Jon eased away from her.

She shook her head. She hadn't even told him that Slater had struck her with his fist and knocked her to the deck. How is it possible that only the weak, power hungry and insane had survived?

"Jon, listen to me. Neither of us had our primary training in medicine. It was secondary. We were trained as paramedics. We know how to do that, but that's not what Salter is demanding of us. He's demanding that we be something that we're not."

"I can't be Chief Medical Officer. I can't."

"I know that, Jon. That's what I just said."

"But, he's going to hurt me."

"Then help me, damn it! Do your part and maybe Conklin will resume his duties and we can get the hell out of this mess. God damn it, Jon! Do you have to be such a wuss?"

"Why do you talk to me that way?" He began twisting one of his hands with the other.

"All right, Jon. I apologize. I'm exhausted. I gave Conklin a strong sedative. Can you at least sit with him until he awakens? I need to rest. When he awakens, all you have to do is call Veck and then call me. You can do that, can't you?"

He nodded.

Li brushed past him but Jon followed and reached out to catch her by her shoulders.

She shrugged away from his touch and turned to face him. "What now?"

"Can we talk for a few minutes?"

"I need sleep. What don't you understand?"

"I'm only asking for a minute, please."

"All right, Jon, what is it?"

He looked down at the deck and shifted his weight from foot to the other.

"I don't have time for this bullshit." She started to turn away.

"Wait...please. I feel...Li, this isn't the way it was supposed to be. We were supposed to be on a glorious mission for all mankind."

"All that remains of it anyway."

"Don't be that way. You know what I mean. And now, the library is gone. All the video and audio and the writings." He looked down at the deck. "We've lost our culture, the richness that makes us human. What am I supposed to do? I'm useless."

Li was tempted to agree but his face was constricted with grief. She reached out and grasped his hand; he responded with an almost spastic clenching.

"Jon, you're hurting my hand."

"Oh, I'm sorry." He released his hold. "I'm so sorry, Li."

"We've all lost a lot, not the least of which is the nearly one thousand colonists who died. At least we're still alive."

"I want to go home."

Li sighed. "We have to come to terms with reality, as difficult as it is. You know we can't go home, right?"

He said nothing.

"We'll talk about this again, but I really need to get some sleep. Okay?"

He nodded, but wouldn't meet her eyes.

She waited a moment more and then walked away.

CHAPTER 8

Li moaned and rolled over when she heard the persistent chime of her com-collar. "This is Li." Her voice was thick with sleep.

"He's waking up!" Jon yelled.

"Calm down." She didn't attempt to keep the irritation out of her voice. "He's completely restrained, you know."

"But...but he's waking up! What should I do?"

Li rubbed her face.

"Li, are you there? Can you hear me?"

"Yes, Jon," she said with resignation, "I can hear you. I'll be right there."

"Hurry, please!"

She cut the connection.

Within ten minutes, Li approached from down the passage. Her feet felt heavy. She felt so sluggish.

Jon walked toward her. "What took you so long?" he asked.

"Long? I urinated, brushed my teeth and washed my face. Anything else you want to know?"

"Li..." He leaned toward her and whispered. "There's somebody with him."

She ignored him and walked on by to enter the room, but stopped as soon she entered. The giant was bending over Casey. When he straightened and turned, he didn't speak to Li, or acknowledge her presence in any way. It was up to her to dodge out of his way as he passed through the portal and into the passage. Li turned her attention to Casey. He had a new com-collar around his neck and appeared fully awake, though still restrained, still dehumanized by his filth and involuntary nakedness.

"Li, allow me a moment before snowing me again." His speech was clear and his attitude reasonable beyond expectation.

Li was quiet as she thought. Her hand was less painful than it had been at her last visit. She smiled, but it was with a sense of accomplishment, not joy.

Casey answered with a lopsided smile of his own. "So, I

presume, in view of these restraints and the visit by the Unsmiling Buddha...." He paused and then picked up from where he'd left off. "I gather I was out of control in some way." Li's silence confirmed his suspicion. "Why have none of my colleagues been by? I want to talk with Grace N'duforchu." He raised his hand against a restraint. "I'm having technical difficulties using my com-collar. Contact her for me."

She shook her head.

"Why not? This is ridiculous. You've medicated me with a psychotropic and I haven't even been attended to by a physician. I'm not trying to denigrate you, but isn't this a bit out of your scope of practice? What the hell is going on?"

"It's not for me to say."

He raised his voice. "Then who *is* going to tell me what's going on?"

Li backed away until she was near the portal.

"Are you afraid of me? You aren't afraid of me are you?"

She nodded, causing waves of light to reflect from her black, silken hair.

"You are?" His bloodshot eyes opened wide and he stared at her, waiting, but she didn't elaborate so he continued. "I frankly admit, I'm not eager to find out why you'd be afraid of me, or what I've done that could have resulted in me being placed in hard restraints, but I need to know. My memory...there's something wrong with my memory." He shivered. "But I assure you, I'm not a violent person. You know that. I want you to release me so I can get cleaned up. Is that too much to ask? You have my word; I'll be on my best behavior."

Li stood there without answering. She was amazed to find herself actually considering his request when she heard the soft "swish" of the portal. Expecting to see the seemingly ever-present giant, she was surprised to see a pleasant appearing man with an engaging smile, punctuated by dimples on both cheeks. He wore the same black suit that she had come to detest, but his carrot-red hair seemed to deny that he was one of them too.

He extended his hand in a friendly greeting. "Hello, my name is Padraig Glancy."

Li responded automatically by placing her small hand in his. He ignored the bound figure on the table and focused his entire attention on her.

"Commander Slater has instructed me to assist you," he said.

The mere mention of Slater's name made Li feel that the warmth of the stranger's hand was just another trap. She extricated her hand from his.

Glancy chuckled. "Slater is rather a wanker isn't he?"

She lowered her hand but didn't step away.

Glancy continued. "For the present, it seems to me, the most sensible approach is to maintain a low profile, but don't feel alone in your concerns. I too have grave doubts about his ambitions."

The words were reassuring. They were the ones she wanted to hear, yet, they came too easily. His bright blue eyes sparkled and seemed full of good humor. Li felt neutralized, suspicious of such immoderate charm, but reluctant to reject outright the first potential ally she'd met.

She smiled. "Pleased to meet you, Padraig."

"His real name is Gingersnap."

She had forgotten all about Casey and jerked when he spoke

"Sorry, don't know where that came from," Casey added. "But seriously, don't be too pleased. He's one of the blank people, added to the list of colonists at the last minute. He has no personnel file. You don't remember seeing him around the training facility at Copper Mountain, do you?"

She frowned at Casey, irritated by his unasked for advice, which ran contrary to her wishes. When she turned to face Padraig again, she caught a flash of coldness, but then his smile returned, bigger than ever.

"It's true," Padrig said. "I was added at the last, but that's no reason for you to take it as an indictment. You'll have plenty of time to form your own opinion. For now, all I have to offer is my assistance. You don't resent that do you?"

"No," she answered, "not at all. Would you release Casey so he can attend to his personal needs? We don't have much time before planet-fall."

"But of course." He withdrew an electronic key from his waist pouch and used it to remove Casey's restraints. He walked around the table with confidence, in control.

His manner allowed Li to relax. Finally, she thought, someone to share this burdensome responsibility with. Jon, for all his good intentions, had proven himself to be a worthless partner.

Casey kept his eyes on Glancy as he circled the table, meeting his smile with a bland look.

"Come on, ol' boy." Glancy reached out to assist Casey, but Casey ignored the offer and struggled to a sitting position on his own.

"My, aren't we contrary today," Glancy said, treating the rejection as of no consequence.

Li shifted her weight as Casey stared at her. It seemed like he was trying to communicate something, but it only made her uneasy.

Casey looked down at the blue, transdermal patch on his chest, but he didn't attempt to remove it. He was forced to lean on Glancy while he was led to the cleansing cabinet in the personal room. Glancy allowed no privacy and stood watch over him. When they emerged from the personal room Casey looked less frightening to Li. As if in recognition, he answered her look with a smile, bringing out unnoticed laugh lines at the corners of his eyes, but his smile retained a sardonic quality.

Glancy tossed him a new, white uniform, but Casey's reflexes were still slow from the sedative and it struck him on the chest, falling in a heap on the deck. Casey spent a sober moment staring at Glancy, but his obvious dislike rolled off the man like water being shed by any well-oiled bird.

Glancy smiled benignly. "Here, let me get that for you," he said, but remained where he was, with a twinkle of self-appreciation in his eyes.

Casey took hold of the edge of the table and with painful slowness retrieved the uniform. While he struggled into it, he kept his eyes on Glancy.

"Thank you, Padrig," Li said.

Glancy turned toward her. "I'm glad I could help. I think you've been carrying more than your fair share."

Casey took advantage of the opportunity and entered Grace N'duforchu's code into his com-collar.

"You do not have authorization. Get off the circuit," the voice said.

"Prissy? I mean Jane Veck? Is that you Jane?" Casey asked in surprise. "What are you–" The connection went dead.

"Ah, Ah, Ah," Glancy said and wagged his finger. "Now don't be naughty. Come on. Someone wants to see you."

"Who?"

"You'll find out in a few minutes."

"Why am I not authorized to use my com-collar? I never heard of such a thing."

"So many questions. Let's see if we can get you some answers."

Glancy took hold of Casey's upper arm and walked him past Li.

Li kept her gaze directed at the deck and felt some guilt at allowing her patient to be led out of the room by a stranger, but Padrig was well-mannered. Casey would be okay. It was the first time since his care had been entrusted to her that she could look to her own needs and it felt good.

It was less than twenty-four hours until planet-fall, a new planet, a whole world to explore, filled with its own wonders and mysteries. It was an exhilarating prospect. Her skin tingled with undefined expectations as she walked the passage to find a quiet place and wonderful sleep.

CHAPTER 9

Casey permitted the man to hold onto his arm without comment, and was taken to the up-tube. The stranger's grip was not uncomfortable, but he suspected, like a Chinese finger trap, it would only tighten if he resisted. He entered the mouth of the tube freely and a moment later bobbed out of the shaft and onto Deck One.

Immediately, two men grabbed his arms. He looked to his right and saw an unpleasant smile and above the smile the flinty eyes of another blank. Casey recognized him, Jack Sabine, but a more appropriate name also came to mind, the Shrew. On his left was Sten Olson, hair clipped short, efficiently completing a task. It was Mister Attention. They squeezed his arms much harder than was necessary and propelled him toward the control chair in front of the empty screens. The chair slowly swiveled, revealing its occupant. Casey wasn't surprised. It was Geoffrey Slater, also known as Butt-face, at least to Casey.

"Hello, Geoff." Casey smiled. "Long time, no see," he added flippantly.

Slater's lips thinned to a threatening snarl. "I can see you have some lessons to learn, the first of which is, I'm in charge here. What I say goes. From now on you will address me as Commander Slater."

"Okay, Geoff," Casey replied, and at the same time shook his head. "Whatever you—"

Sabine punched him in his flank and he dropped to his knees. Slater waited patiently until Casey was able to breathe again.

"Casey, you're a psychotic killer. It is only by my mercy that you're still alive."

Casey ignored Slater's ridiculous assertion. He pressed his hand against the pain in his side, but didn't attempt to rise off his knees. "Commander Slater. Has a catchy ring to it, doesn't it? On Earth, you were a self-serving prick—" Sabine was about to kick Casey, but Slater restrained him by raising his hand. "—and now you're a flaming sociopath. Commander

Slater, that isn't really how you think of yourself, is it? In your twisted mind, you're god Slater, lord and master of the universe. You were Mitchell Mason's pet and he twisted you...but then, you didn't really require much twisting, did you?"

Slater's voice was ominously calm. "Are you finished?" He waited a moment and when Casey didn't reply, he continued. "I'm not going to defend myself to the likes of you. I'm going to ask you one question, and you better answer it, or I'll teach you what disobedience means. What were you doing when nearly two-thirds of the colonists died in stasis?"

Casey was stunned. He sensed Slater was telling the truth. The loss was staggering. All those beautiful youths he had tended to so diligently, spent his life watching over, dead. His eyes began to shimmer with tears.

"Dead? How did they die? How is that possible?" Casey asked.

"That's what I want to know. You were supposed to be their guardian. What kind of a fucked-up, incompetent guardian would allow a thousand colonists to die?"

Casey was speechless with grief.

"Nothing to say?"

"What about the other guardians?" Casey managed to ask.

"You tell me."

"I don't understand. Mendoza and Bezdicek were with me and then there were the three who took over for us."

"There are no other guardians, Casey. You're it, the one and only."

Casey shook his head. "No, that's not possible."

"They're all dead. Actually they're missing, which is as good as dead. Unless, of course, you think they're hiding in a closet somewhere on the ship, waiting to pop and say, 'surprise'."

"Dead?" Casey whispered.

"Don't play dumb with me. Did you kill them, too?"

"Wait...what? No...no, please...it can't be."

"Is that your answer?"

Casey closed his eyes. All those beautiful youths. All his colleagues, his friends. Dead. The pain escaped his mouth as a whimper.

Slater smiled and snapped his fingers at Olson. Before Casey could react, Olson kicked him in the ribs, knocking him to the deck. Sabine snorted with pleasure and cocked his foot to kick Casey in the back, but Slater again raised his hand. Sabine shrugged and stepped back. Casey lay on the deck moaning.

Slater spoke again. "You will answer any question I ask, promptly and fully. There will be no more of this sophomoric bravado, will there?"

Casey rolled onto his side, struggling to breathe.

"You probably need a few minutes to regain your composure. When I ask questions, you will answer them, or I won't be so gentle. Think about it, Casey." Slater swiveled the chair and called across the bridge to communication specialist Veck, who stood just outside the portal to his suite. "Jane, contact that good for nothing Jon Brent and tell him he has some work to do." He nodded toward Casey. "Tell him to come patch up this defective creature, if you think that dimwit can find Deck One without a guide."

Sabine laughed.

Slater arose crisply to his feet and, without another glance at Casey's sprawled form, walked across the bridge and entered his suite, followed by Veck. As soon as the portal shut, Sabine kicked Casey repeatedly in the back and ribs, and then purposefully walked around and kicked him square in the face, breaking Casey's nose. A puddle of bright red blood began spreading across the gray of the deck beneath Casey's face.

Olson looked with disapproval at his partner; it had not been ordered. Sabine ignored the unvoiced criticism and swaggered non-nonchalantly down the passageway, smiling while he entertained himself by whistling a discordant tone.

When Jon arrived, he found Casey lying face down on the deck, perfectly still, with Olson standing nearby. He approached Casey in a crouch, hesitant, as if he didn't want to arrive and see confirmed what his mind imagined.

"What happened?" Jon exclaimed with horror. He glanced up at Olson's hard face and then back down at Casey.

"Fix him," Olson ordered.

With an extended index finger, Jon gingerly nudged Casey on the shoulder, but Casey didn't move. He slowly stood and began backing away.

"No! No, I can't! I need Li Quon." He reached for his com-collar, but Olson stepped forward and grabbed his wrist, forcing it down without any sign of effort. Jon let his arm fall to his side.

"Fix him," Olson repeated.

Jon just stood there and stared at an empty spot on the deck.

"Do it!" Olson shouted.

Jon flinched and watched Olson out of the corner of his eyes as he reluctantly stooped to examine Casey. He rolled Casey onto his back.

Casey groaned and his eyes flickered open. He saw Jon's face close above.

"Teddy Bear," Casey said. It was a one-word plea.

"Casey, this is me, Jon Brent," he whispered. "I don't know what to do."

The glaze was beginning to clear from Casey's eyes. "Get one of the other doctors. Get Ishak or Gupta."

"I can't. Their capsules failed. They're dead."

"Oh, please...no." Casey closed his eyes as he tried to cope with the unending tragedy. "Talking hurts," he finally said. "You know what to do." A fit of painful coughing took his speech away.

Jon held Casey's hand, helpless, as he waited for the flare of pain to recede.

Casey opened his eyes again. "Don't worry. I'll be all right." He tried to smile but couldn't. "Get a molecular synthesizer."

Jon looked at him without the least sign of comprehension.

"Get Li, will you?" Casey gasped.

Jon glanced up at Olson, but the big man shook his head.

"I can't," Jon said in a small voice.

"You can get it." Casey had to pause for a moment. "It's a small, gray cube with green crystalline corners—" He paused to catch his breath. "—in the lab. Please, go now, and bring back some gel."

Jon let go of Casey's hand and laid it carefully on the deck. Then he looked up at Olson.

"Get it," Olson ordered, "but don't talk with anyone on the way."

Jon stood and rushed to the down-tube, disappearing into its mouth. When he returned, he had the cube clutched in his hands and a tube of gel in his pouch. He knelt next to Casey, whose face was now so puffy, his eyes were only slits. Jon wasn't even sure Casey was conscious, until he spoke.

"Good, Jon." Casey mumbled. "Put the synthesizer next to my hand." Casey pressed in a code and then let his hand fall back to the deck. Shortly, a green disk slipped out of a slot in the top of the box. "Take the patch and apply it to my chest."

Jon hesitated when he saw the blue patch, but then stuck the new one next to it.

After a few minutes, Casey's breathing came easier. "Very good, Jon. Now apply the gel. I'll tell you where."

It wasn't long before Casey was able to sit, with his back propped against a bulkhead.

As if on cue, Slater returned to stand in front of him. "You may go now, Jon," he said, without looking at him.

Jon backed away and dropped into the down-tube.

Slater tilted his head as he studied Casey. "You look like shit, but don't think that means you've paid your debt to the colony, not even close. But I am curious. Why did you kill Mitch Klaus? He was kind of a stupid oaf, but why kill him?"

This time Casey remembered more. He remembered defending himself against a...dangerous fish and an evil giant, and then a struggle, followed by the terrible weight of a body crushing him. He remembered being smothered.

Slater saw that his statement had its desired effect. "So, you do remember."

Casey didn't deny it.

Slater continued. "I'm an understanding man. Compassionate, really. If you were to help the colony, say by making a record of your knowledge as a physician and by providing me with answers, I believe I could arrange a modicum of amnesty, but I'll need a commitment from you. That's not too much to ask, is it?"

"You have all the information you need in the memory banks."

"Afraid not. The memory banks have failed. They are completely empty."

"That's impossible. There was a failsafe...." The words "fail-safe failed" echoed in his mind.

"You were about to say?"

Casey remained motionless. Something had happened. What was it?

Slater continued. "Yes, there were many fail-safe mechanisms. It's enough to make a person wonder. The medical database was erased."

"Erased?"

"One can only assume it was erased. It can't just disappear. The computers are fully functional otherwise. That technology wasn't new, unlike the cryo-capsules. Chief Protonov has been investigating this anomaly and, although he can't be certain, he did come up with one interesting tidbit. There are indications that around Midpoint the cryo-capsules were opened. I don't remember awakening at Midpoint and neither does anyone else. Did you open the capsules, Casey? You had the codes."

"All I did was my duty."

"Did you do something to us? Did you do away with the colonists you didn't like?"

"That's absurd! That's—" Bad children came to mind. "Impossible."

"Is it? You sound a little confused. Did you cause the capsules failures and all the deaths?"

"If I had you would have been at the top of the list."

Slater nodded. "Interesting. And who else was on this list?"

"There was no list. I didn't do anything except my duty."

"So you say. I wish I could believe you. The point is, as a result of the deaths and equipment failures, you are now a valuable man."

"What about the other physicians?" Casey whispered.

"God damn it! Weren't you listening? Must I repeat myself? There are no others. They're all dead. Dead! Did you hear me that time?"

"That can't be. That's impossible."

"You can't possibly believe we'd be having this discussion if there was an alternative. Why do you think that feeble minded Brent was attending to you?"

Casey was devastated. His friends were truly gone. "How can that be?" he mumbled.

"How indeed? Who would benefit? Let's see. We have no stored data. We have no physicians…that is except one. You. Who has suddenly become indispensable?"

"Shut up, Slater. Not everyone is like you. Thank God."

"Do you need another lesson in manners? Have you forgotten already?"

Casey lowered his gaze to the deck. "No."

"As long as we're having this friendly little tête–à–tête, I do have another question. Why did you build a cryo-capsule in the land-shaper?"

"It was part of…the game," Casey concluded lamely.

"Game? A thousand colonists were dying and you were playing some kind of game?"

Casey had nothing to say.

"I can barely stand to be around you. You disgust me beyond words. The next time we have a question and answer session, you better be a hell of a lot more forthcoming."

Casey continued to stare at the deck.

"Well?"

"I will," Casey whispered.

"And you'll do whatever I tell you to do. Won't you?"

"Yes."

"Do I have your word? Or do you require more convincing?"

Casey nodded agreement, his shoulders sagging.

Slater leaned forward and cupped his hand behind his ear. "I can't hear you."

"I'll do what you want."

"Your word of honor, for whatever that's worth."

"Yes, my word."

"I'm so glad we've had the opportunity to have this little chat. I knew I could count on you. I'm the best person to guide us through this crisis. Don't you agree?"

Casey remained mute.

"Don't you agree?"

Casey nodded again.

"From time to time, I may ask you about a colonist, and there will come a time when I will insist that you tell me what you know about ship's failure, but we can leave that alone for now. I can see you're tired. In the meantime, Mister Yamaguchi will attend to your needs." He smiled down at Casey and then walked over to drop into the down-tube, with Olson and Sabine following.

Even though the giant remained, Casey was alone. There was no one left alive he could call his friend, not Jon, not anyone.

CHAPTER 10

The colonists were safely tucked away in their cryo-capsules for the descent from orbit. They didn't feel the jolt as the Pinnacle separated from the massive star engine and accelerated toward the waiting planet. They didn't feel the vibration or deceleration as the ship entered the atmosphere. Nor did they feel the final shock as the ship came to rest on the planet's surface. By the time the cryo-capsules opened, the ship had cooled and all was quiet.

Casey's capsule opened and he regained consciousness. The slightest movement caused him pain, but he wasn't about to remain in the capsule, a helpless invalid, while the others were out and about, not on this day. It had been theory and now it was fact; they had successfully traversed interstellar space and had arrived at a habitable planet.

When he finally managed to place both feet on the deck, he had to pause, his forehead moist from the effort and pain. After a moment, the pain eased to a level that the analgesic patch could suppress. He opened his still puffy eyelids and looked about. By this time there were only a handful of colonists left in the passageway. All the others had scurried off to prepare for departure from the ship to the planet's surface.

Casey turned to gaze in the other direction and was surprised to see the hulk of Yamaguchi, staring stoically back at him, not offering help, not expressing joy or comradeship, merely watching.

"How courteous of you to wait for me and to provide such invaluable assistance," Casey said with a wry grin. "As long as we're going to be bosom buddies, we may as well be on a first name basis. Don't you agree?"

There was no response.

"Oh, I'm so sorry," Casey continued. "I just remembered. You don't have a first name, or maybe you don't have a last name. Kind of confusing, isn't it? I guess you're only half there. You can break in anytime you want." Casey paused but Yamaguchi remained silent. "Let me think. You know, back at Copper Mountain there was a doctor from Kyoto who tried to teach me some Japanese. Yama Kuchi. I believe that means mountain entrance. Impressed?"

Yamaguchi said nothing.

"You look like a mountain. Is your mouth actually an entrance? Is that why no words come out of it?"

He remained silent.

Undaunted, Casey continued. "It's been my experience that good buddies like you and me always have nicknames for one another. How about Unsmiling...?" The moment Casey said it, something deep inside felt like it twisted and was about to reveal a truth, but then it was gone. "To hell with it. Unsmiling Buddha it is."

"My name is Yamaguchi."

He was an intimidating figure, but Casey was riding high on the excitement of planet-fall and drugs. He clutched his ribs and laughed. "All right, Yamaguchi, have it your way, but you really know how to bring a person down. Get it?"

The giant remained impassive.

Casey shook his head in disbelief. "At least lend me an arm will you? I'd like to find out what's happening. Aren't you even a little curious?"

After a short pause, Yamaguchi extended a trunk-like arm, which Casey leaned heavily on. Together they slowly made their way to the up-tube and then exited onto the bridge. When they arrived, Casey was breathless from the exertion and eased down to the deck, resting his back against a bulkhead. He asked for no further help and his bigger than life shadow offered none.

Casey dozed, fatigued from even this modest effort, but soon awakened to the murmur of voices. He knew all the men and women present, either personally, or from his long years of study while they slept. He saw a tall, buxom blonde and his heart thumped. Virgin of the Woods. The essence of Britty flashed across his mind, leaving in its wake an ache of impossible longing for her, left behind on Earth and now dead of old age. Lisa Bouviet only resembled Britty superficially, yet, he couldn't bear the sight of her. He lowered his gaze and focused on his deck-slippers. When he again raised his attention to the gathered guild chiefs, more heads than not were turned in his direction.

Casey tried to stretch his swollen lips into a smile and waved lazily, causing the group to move a small, but perceptible distance farther away. No one returned his wave. He saw Jon on the other side of the bridge, studiously avoiding his eyes. Within moments, no one was looking in his direction, as if by ignoring him, he would cease to exist. His head drooped forward and he closed his eyes, as he tried to cope with his newfound infamy and isolation.

The crowd became silent and Casey glanced up, just in time to see the entrance of Commander Slater, flanked by black-suited assistants and followed by the slim form of Jane Veck, wearing communication pink. She walked with her chin raised, her narrow face radiant with self-importance, and her thin lips pursed. Casey's attention was drawn back to Slater. He was now standing on the control chair, demanding that he be seen, as if simply hearing him wasn't enough.

Slater began with a grand smile. "Friends, we've arrived. Although you've been invited to be on the bridge, my message is being broadcast to all the colonists." He nodded toward Jane Veck who seemed to stretch even taller.

There he was, elevated above the rest, surrounded by his black goons and speaking in condescending tones to those he had demanded to be present, most of whom were his superior in intellect and attitude. If the scene hadn't been quite so grotesque, Casey probably would've laughed, a comedic parody of every dictator who had ever existed, but the reality of their plight, as represented by the silent man in black at Casey's side, allowed no such levity.

Slater continued with his well-rehearsed message. He raised his arms, "Let us rejoice, on behalf of all humanity for we, the Pinnacle, the best of all mankind, have arrived. I've spoken with the landing assessment team and their instruments confirm we've found a home. No, not just a home," he raised his voice yet another notch, "a perfect home. And I guarantee you we will match that perfection with the perfection of our own gifts and skills. Mankind's gamble was not in vain. We've discovered a new Earth!"

There was a restrained display of joy as the chiefs congratulated each other. They were excited, but subdued. Slater waited for this small ripple of response to pass. He tipped his head back, as if waxing philosophical, and then continued. "The universe is truly a more wondrous creation than we ever imagined. The very existence of a place such as this, ripe for our arrival, begging to be shaped, confirms that we are indeed the chosen. We have an opportunity to create a society unknown on Earth, a perfect society. We are superior to those we left behind. Let us grasp this opportunity and create a true utopia!" Slater extended his arms as if in benediction, and then bowed his head. In a quiet voice he said, "I know I will do my best. You have my word. Please, my friends, join me in this great quest."

There was movement toward the control chair on which Slater stood, but it was cut short when Slater's men stepped forward. The crowd seemed confused by the conflicting signals and bumped into each other as some advanced and others retreated. The smile on Slater's face faltered. He jumped off his perch and pushed past Olson, glancing sideways for a fraction of a second with a gritty glare. He managed to replace it with a friendly twinkle as he joined his flock, but the moment was lost. As he walked among the guild chiefs, a circle of space opened around him. When he pivoted, he saw not enough loyalty and too much fear.

Casey could withhold his amusement no longer and began to chuckle; all attention was immediately focused on him. Slater snapped his fingers and Yamaguchi stepped forward to stand over Casey, like the face of a cliff. Casey became quiet at once, not able to cope with this obvious intimidation. With Yamaguchi standing between Casey and the gathered chiefs, their attention again focused on Slater.

"Friends," Slater said as he turned in a circle to view them all, "today, this very day, we shall place the mark of humanity on this new world. We will join hands and together be a part of this, the greatest accomplishment of mankind. Join me."

He extended his hands again, but this time directly toward two members of the group. It was too personal, too strong of a gesture to be easily rejected. Brita Baldus grasped one of his hands and Jarmo Karna the other. Slater raised their joined hands overhead, his smile now a broad grin. The others moved forward, touching him, patting him, none wanted to be left out, and Jon Brent was in the thick of it, but for Casey there was only Yamaguchi at his front and the hard bulkhead at his back.

Casey heard the sound of people leaving and the number of voices dwindled until the bridge was once again quiet. "Well, Yamaguchi," he said, "aren't you going to hurry off to be one of the chosen too? Don't worry, I promise I'll save your place and I give you my word, I won't jump up and take over the ship, or is it planet now?"

Yamaguchi remained in place.

"At ease, Yamaguchi!" Casey ordered in a mocking tone, but Yamaguchi still didn't respond.

Casey slumped back against the bulkhead. "Great," he said to himself, "fifty years of solitude and now I'm stuck with a mute jailer." That thought brought with it a grim smile.

"Yamaguchi, I don't know about you but I'd like to see this biblically inspired melodrama play itself out. Help me get down to Storage."

CHAPTER 11

All the colonists were assembled on the Storage Deck. Slater, with the help of two of his assistants, managed to be at the forefront, ensuring that he would be the first to set foot on the new world. He signaled the technician and the storage bay door began to open. A shaft of sunlight broke into the cavernous hold, making the illumination from the light-lines appear dim by comparison. There was a profound hush, broken only by the soft whine of the mechanism as the window on the new world opened farther. They stared in wonderment. It was sunlight, but not of the sun. The sight brought tears to some and opened-eyed rapture to even the most restrained.

All attention was on the opening. A blue sky with fluffy white clouds was revealed, and still the opening grew, revealing the peaks of snow-capped mountains along the distant horizon. As the huge door lowered and extended to become a ramp leading to the planet's surface, the crowd surged forward. There was no stopping them.

"Stay back!" Slater shouted, but no one, not even his two associates, responded. All eyes and all minds were focused on the outside. Even before the leading edge of the ramp touched the ground, colonists pushed past Slater and climbed onto it, to step outside, to breath fresh air, to sense the new world all around them. By the time the ramp "clanked" to a stop, people were streaming past Slater as if he were an inanimate object.

Li Quon was among the first, running down the slope of the ramp with abandon. She continued running until she was beyond the others and then stopped with her back to the ship. The tall grass rippled in waves as a gentle breeze brushed across the prairie that stretched toward the distant mountains. There were clumps of red and yellow flowers and, farther out, clusters of trees, their branches thick with green leaves, but her eyes were continually drawn back to the distant mountains, purple at their bases, snowy white at their peaks. It so reminded her of the mountains near her home on far distant Earth.

The colonists stood silent in awe, seeing the Earth as it might have looked millennia ago. The air held just a hint of salt, suggesting the presence of a nearby sea. And the sun! It could have been Sol itself, bright with warm yellow light. This was Earth as Earth should have been.

There was a spontaneous outpouring of brotherhood, hugging, holding, and finally words, exclamations of wonder and thanks, growing until they became one sound, the sound of many voices raised together in exaltation. It was sometime before Slater's shouts for attention were heard, but slowly, person-by-person, they began to grow quiet and turn to hear what he had to say.

From Slater's vantage point, still standing on the ramp of the ship, he could see the entire crowd of five hundred colonists, and it was they that he focused his attention on, hardly noticing the panoramic view of the prairie and mountains.

"This is a proper place for what we are about to do!" Slater shouted. "We will take this gift onto ourselves and improve upon it!"

Still, there were many of the colonists who ignored the man who demanded their attention, absorbed in the wonder of the vista and the miracle of having arrived; trying to reconcile what their hearts told them with what their minds knew. This was not Earth. This was someplace else in the universe.

But Slater would not be denied. "People, people!" he yelled. "Let us not lose ourselves!"

Reluctantly, the majority of the crowd turned to hear what the man was shouting about, but Li Quon, and a few of the others, would not be distracted from the intoxicating view of the world around them.

Finally, Slater had enough of their attention that he no longer had to shout in such a shrill voice. "People, this is the day those we left behind dreamed about. We are children of Earth and we have saved mankind from oblivion. The Death and the devils that brought it cannot reach us here. We are the chosen. Let us behave like the chosen. I know this place plucks at a primordial string to our past, but don't allow yourselves to become lost. We have a sacred mission to perform. We are the safeguard of humanity. It is our duty to succeed and succeed we will!"

Slater lowered his voice again, causing the crowd to gather closer to the ramp, closer to him. "I have no doubt we will fulfill the scared trust placed in us. No, more than that, we will surpass expectations, just as our destination has surpassed our expectations. We are the strongest, brightest, and most determined men and women who have ever existed. We will make our distant mothers and fathers proud to claim us as humanity's beacon for the brotherhood of all mankind, but we must keep our focus." He paused for effect. "If the mundane is to be our first task, then let us be heroes of the mundane, gladiators of the everyday, explorers of duty, but, before we attend to our duties, there is a piece of business that cannot be postponed. We need a name for our new world!"

A small voice arose from the edge of the crowd. "I suppose you think Slater's World would be a good name."

An uneasy silence, with scattered pockets of nervous laughter, answered Li Quon's suggestion. Petite as she was, she was not visible to many in the crowd, but Slater could see her, challenging him with her hands on her hips.

Slater didn't answer her directly. He bowed his head, as if both hurt and offended. When he looked back up, the crowd had become stone silent.

He nodded. "I agree with you, my brothers and sisters. This is exactly the kind of attitude we must guard against. We cannot afford to be our own adversaries. We are partners. We all have vital duties to perform, duties that fit our particular aptitudes. I am aware that there are a few among you who feel I have overstepped my authority, but I am also aware that at the root of these feelings is a lack of trust. I trust you, completely, every single one of you. I trust you to do what needs to be done and I need your trust in me so I can do what needs to be done. Without this belief and trust in one another, we will not be able to survive."

There was a murmur of approval from the crowd.

Slater brought his fist up to rest against his chest. "Believe me; it's not for my benefit that I take on this heavy responsibility." He opened his hand and extended his arms to the crowd. "I give myself to you."

"We're with you, Slater!" someone in the crowd shouted, and another, "You can count on us!" and then more shouts of support, until the individual words were lost in a noise that signaled a pledge of fealty.

Slater smiled and raised his arms again. The crowd quieted, but he waited patiently until there was once again silence.

While he waited, his eyes searched the crowd for signs of dissent. Then he looked out to the edge of the assembly and saw Li Quon, standing by herself, until a mid-sized man broke through the edge of the crowd and walked over to stand at her side. Slater recognized him. It was Simon Weiss, wearing the yellow of a geology technician. Slater watched as Li faced Simon and they exchanged words. Li extended her hand and Simon took it in his own.

Slater redirected his attention to the crowd and began again. "A name is important. It will help define our goal and attitudes. Are there any suggestions?"

A rich baritone called out from somewhere in the crowd. "There is one man who had the vision to construct the Pinnacle and the wisdom to bring us together, Mitchell Mason. We should name our world Mason's World." The man was dressed in the maroon of humanities and had an easy smile and a likable face. No one standing near him recognized him, but his red hair identified him to those who did know him, Padrig Glancy.

The colonists remained quiet. Slater recognized that this was one promise he wouldn't be able to keep.

"I appreciate the thought," Slater said. "As many of you know, he was like a father to me. I knew him well and, if he were here, he'd never have permitted such self-aggrandizement." Slater ignored the scattered laughter. "Are there any other suggestions?"

"Let's call our world Eden," yelled a blond woman dressed in the pink of communications.

The crowd took up the name and it could be heard being passed around, lips and ears getting a feel for it.

Slater bent toward Olson. "Her name is Lisa Bouviet. She came to the bridge uninvited. Seems to think she's still chief of communications. A troublemaker. Add her to the list."

Olson smiled. "My pleasure."

Slater waited a few more seconds and then spoke. "Yes, my friends, I think that is exactly what we've found, Eden. We are the chosen and I've been ordained to lead us into the Promised Land. Does that agree with you?"

In answer, from scattered areas in the crowd, the word "Eden" was shouted, and repeated until it became a chant, shouted in unison by the assembled colonists. Then someone slipped in Slater's name and it became, "Eden! Slater! Eden!

Slater!" It was a moving moment of complete agreement and a shared sense of belonging to one another but, even at that moment Slater scanned the crowd, adding to his mental list those who refused to join in the affirmation of support. After his visual survey, he bowed his head humbly, as if unworthy of the adoration he'd so carefully orchestrated. When the chant began to weaken, he raised his arms and the assemblage became quiet, but attentive.

"Friends," Slater said, "I'm deeply touched." He wiped his eyes, brushing away nonexistent tears. "And I vow to you that I'll do my utmost to be worthy of your generous support. I will give you all I have. It's my solemn oath to you. And, although we've left our mothers and fathers behind, think of me like a father. If you have a problem, come to me. My door will always be open."

He paused and beamed at the assemblage. "Friends, we need to start today, no, not today, this very moment in preparing our new home. Report to your guild chiefs. It is time!" he shouted. "Let us begin!"

He raised a fist overhead; the crowd responded with cheering and their fists arose over their heads, a salute. He bowed slightly at the waist before standing tall and turning with well-paced dignity to reenter the ship and disappear from view. As soon as he was out of sight, Jane Veck stepped onto the ramp and began, in her reedy voice, to direct the various guilds to their respective chiefs.

CHAPTER 12

Casey sat in the relative darkness of the storage bay and watched Slater stroll past. He intended to keep a low profile, to stay the hell out of it. It wasn't his affair any longer but, even as he had these thoughts, he struggled to remain silent. It was only a few seconds before the impulse to speak overwhelmed his good sense.

"I sure wish I could be a hero of the mundane," Casey said.

Slater stopped and turned to face him.

Casey continued. "That was very impressive, Commander Slater. God, King, Daddy. It's so hard to keep track of all your titles. Should I be calling you Daddy Slater now?"

"Shut up, Casey" Slater snarled. "You never did know when to shut up. Always pushing."

"I was deeply moved, really touched. In fact, I might have voted for you myself, that is, if there had been a vote."

Slater walked with a strong stride to stand over Casey and glare down at him.

Casey met Slater's eyes while he sat with his back against the land-shaper that had been his home for so many unremembered years. Yamaguchi stood motionless, a few steps back in the shadows.

"Sorry I can't stand to kiss your hand. The beating you gave me has left me a bit under the weather. I'm sure you can understand."

"Now you listen to me, you limp-spined scum, piece of shit!" The words rained down on Casey along with a fine spray of spittle. "You failed at your duty and a thousand of your fellow colonists died. A thousand! You're a failure. You miscreant. Weak, worthless, hiding from responsibility behind a wall of faked insanity. You're a menace to the community, a cancer. It would be better for all of us if I disposed of you. And believe me, I could. I'm sure no one would object. Everyone hates you."

"I can't be certain, but I'm beginning to think you don't like me."

Slater leaned down and grabbed the front of Casey's uniform, twisting until the pressure seam opened, revealing the transdermal patches on Casey's chest. "You're nothing but a sick cripple and I will not tolerate your disrespect."

Casey's smile was deformed by his facial swelling, but nonetheless he managed to express his contempt for Slater with eloquence beyond speech.

Slater drew back his arm and, passing through a sweeping arc, slapped Casey's face. That slap brought on another and then another, until, in a moment, Slater was slapping Casey's head back and forth, from one side to the other. He seemed unable to stop once he had started.

Yamaguchi stepped forward.

It brought back a measure of control to Slater. His breathing was fast and his was face flushed from the excitement and exertion. He laughed, mildly embarrassed to have lost control in front of one of his men. He turned away without another word and walked over to climb the stairs to the up-tube.

Blood dripped from Casey's nose and mouth onto his white uniform, appearing as black spots in the dim light of the Storage Deck. He raised his eyes to the sun-filled portal of the landing door and saw a childlike silhouette walking in his direction. She avoided eye contact as she walked past on her way to the up-tube.

"How convenient," Casey said, his voice muffled by his increasingly swollen lips. "First a visit from our glorious leader and now my personal physician. Don't neglect your duty, Li."

She stopped. "What do you want?"

"Are you afraid, Li?"

She walked over and bent to get a closer look, but kept her weight well balanced, ready to jump away from any suspicious movement. She tried to keep her face neutral, but failed.

"Well, how do I look, Doctor Li?" Casey asked, knowing full well he looked terrible.

She answered in a controlled voice, professional in her assessment. "You've sustained considerable soft tissue damage, but I see no evidence of permanent injury."

A dry laugh accompanied Casey's reply. "No permanent injury? How would you know, you charlatan. You're no more qualified to be a physician than that mousy, former friend of mine, Jon Brent."

She stepped back, her eyes sparkling with anger. "Then

why did you ask, Casey? To bait me? You get yourself beat up and then wallow in self-pity. Has your memory been returning? Or, perhaps it's your conscience. Is this the way you deal with your guilt?"

"You guessed it. You understand perfectly. I've been beating myself up for wasting my life watching over you and the rest of the colonists, while you slept in your blissful hibernation. I squandered my youth on you and the others, and for what? To be beaten by your chosen leader and his goons? Is that what you think, Li?"

His words made her look away from him, down toward her boots.

"What about you, Yamaguchi?" Casey asked. "What do you have to say?"

In his quiet, motionless way, his presence had fallen from Li's awareness, but with the mention of his name she turned her gaze upward and peered at his expressionless face. "You heard him. What do you have to say? What is going on between Slater and you and those other goons? I demand an answer!"

She impulsively reached for the giant's arm and pulled on it, but it didn't budge. All she accomplished was to cause sharp pain to shoot up her arm from her still-healing hand.

Yamaguchi said nothing. It was as if he hadn't heard her questions, or felt her touch.

She put her throbbing hand behind her back and again focused on Casey. "You have few—" She paused. "No, that's not the truth. You have no friends. If you reject me, and I don't claim friendship, you'll also be rejecting the only person left who is still willing to talk with you, leaving only Slater and his men. Is that what you really want?"

Casey studied her, but didn't answer.

"Think about it." She returned her gaze to Yamaguchi. "And you, you big bastard, you're no better than the rest." She turned away but, instead of going to her personal locker as she'd intended, she went back outside.

When she had gone, Casey turned to his jailer, or attendant, as circumstances warranted. "Surely you'd like to get a look at our new world. Why don't you go and take a quick peek? I promise I won't crawl away."

The man's small, dark eyes shifted toward the sunlit doorway, but only for a moment before they were back on Casey.

"Suit yourself," Casey said. "If you aren't even curious, then help me return to the medical suite. I need to attend to my wounds. Did you ever hear that old saying, 'Physician, heal thyself'?"

Yamaguchi remained mute as he effortlessly lifted Casey to his feet.

"Well, it doesn't mean what you think it does. Surprised?"

Yamaguchi remained expressionless.

"I can see you're shocked, as well you should be." Casey paused, but there was no response. "Damn it! If you can't speak, even an occasional grunt would be appreciated. Is that too much to ask?"

He remained silent.

While Casey was being lifted into the up-tube, he continued his one-sided conversation with the silent giant. "All you do is talk, talk, talk. How can you expect a man to think with all that constant chatter?"

When Casey disappeared into the tube, the Storage Deck became quiet.

CHAPTER 13

The following day, Casey had Yamaguchi position him at the top of the ramp. Yamaguchi stood by while Casey settled his sore bones onto a pad so he could take a look this new Earth, or Eden as it was now called. It had made him smirk when he first heard the name they had chosen, but when he saw the bright morning sun and the vista of the grassy plain bordered by the rugged beauty of the distant mountains, he didn't feel quite so smug. Eden indeed.

Most of the colonists had been pressed into service by the engineers to assist in building the base camp. Mounds of steel-foam were scattered across the grass, with a cluster of colonists near each, deciding exactly where each structure was to be located. It wouldn't be long before the first structure would be inflated and then crystallized by a burst of high-powered energy.

The transformer was being attended to by two red-suited power-techs. As the morning wore on, the main building was expanded to its proper dimensions, rising like a giant marshmallow. Casey had seen this demonstrated on a number of occasions during training back on Earth, but this was for real and took on a new significance. Despite his cynicism he felt pride and wonder.

He let his gaze wander and saw Li talking with Jon, who was sitting with his feet resting on a metallic crate. Li was gesticulating while shouting something. Jon shook his head and looked down at the ground. It seemed to be his characteristic pose since the Awakening. He shook his head again, and then stood and walked off.

Casey remembered how Jon had been back on Earth, gentle to the point of absurdity. Specifically, he remembered when Jon had chased a roach around their room, trying to capture it in a plastic cup so that he could let it go free outside, rather than kill it. The last thing Earth needed was more insects. The memory brought a smile to Casey's face.

Casey's com-collar came to life. "This is Commander Slater. The Main Dome is now ready for energizing. I want all you spectators to move at least a hundred meters away. We can't afford any foolish accidents."

The scattered groups of colonists responded leisurely, but soon there was a wide space cleared around the big Main Dome.

Slater spoke again, "I'm now going to turn control over to Chief Power-Tech, Mika Ishida."

"I'm surprised you're willing to turn anything over to anybody," Casey murmured.

The next sound he heard was the soft, feminine voice of Mika. She directed the final preparation with confidence and efficiency and then gave the order to energize.

Everyone's attention was on the dome as a line of incredibly bright, sparkling light worked its way across the surface. When it had completed its path a cheer arose from the on-lookers.

Casey's attention left the now solid dome when he saw blue-black smoke out of the corner of his eyes. He turned. It was the transformer. One of the red-suited techs had already seen it and was running over to investigate; it was an important piece of equipment. When the tech got within twenty meters of the smoking machine, he went rigid and fell to the grass. Another tech wasn't far behind and started to go to his comrade's aid, but he too suddenly arched his back; his arms shot out from his sides and he collapsed motionless on the grassy plain. Others were beginning to converge on the scene.

Casey punched in Slater's code. "Cut off the power from the ship!"

"Get off the beam whoever you are!" Came Slater's reply, but even as he heard Slater's remark, he saw the power beacon from the ship go dead.

The crowd approached the two fallen men, but the closer they got, the more hesitant they were to close the final distance.

Slater's voice came over all the com-collars. "Li Quon and Jon Brent, respond. The rest of you keep your distance."

Casey saw Li running toward the nearest body. She rolled him onto his back, but then seemed uncertain what to do.

Casey turned to Yamaguchi. "Quick. If we're going to be of any help, we've very little time. Go to the lab and bring me the gray box with yellow stripes. You'll find it in row 'A', slot four."

Yamaguchi immediately sprinted toward the up-tube. If Casey hadn't seen it for himself, he would never have imagined a man his size could move that fast.

Casey struggled to his feet and managed a step before his injuries brought him to his knees. He punched in Veck's code.

"This is Conklin. I need help to get to those men. Now!"

"Stay off this beam," was Veck's shrill reply. "This band is for emergency use only until further notice."

But, within a few seconds, two sturdy power-techs came running to Casey's position on the ramp and lifted him. They managed to carry him, all be it painfully, to the two victims.

When Casey got closer he saw Li was applying an archaic resuscitation technique to one of the men. Although he was too injured to assist physically, within a shorter time than he would have thought possible, Yamaguchi was at his side with the kit. Casey flipped open the lid and quickly withdrew two needleless syringes. He touched Li's shoulder and ordered her to stop. When she heard his voice she sat back on her heels, breathless and sweaty. He shoved the syringes at her.

"Take these and inject one into each man at the occipital tuberosity."

She looked glassy eyed at him.

"Now!" Casey shouted.

She regained her focus, took the syringes, and did as she'd been instructed. She placed a syringe firmly against the back of each victim's head and squeezed it off.

Next Casey turned to Yamaguchi. "I need to get these men to the medical suite at once."

Yamaguchi pointed at a few colonists and pulled them forward as if they were attached to his finger by an invisible wire. Then he picked Casey up and began running with him toward the ramp, his footsteps smooth and solid. Abruptly, they were on the ground, Yamaguchi on his back and Casey sprawled across him. Casey looked over at Yamaguchi's face and saw that his eyes were big with surprise, causing a set of parallel creases to run across his forehead. Seeing Yamaguchi display human emotions couldn't have amazed Casey more than if the man had shouted obscenities, but the moment passed like the edge of a cloud and, before Casey could speak, he found himself once again in Yamaguchi's arms, moving at break-neck speed up the ramp and into the ship.

When the victims arrived at the medical suite, Casey could only care for one at a time, while Li followed his instructions. She was remarkably skilled once she knew what to do. As he watched her, he recalled training her back at Copper Mountain. At the time, he hadn't appreciated how competent she was. The man Li had tried to resuscitate responded to the life stimulation cabinet, but the other remained as he was, dead.

"Li."

She turned and her black eyes fixed on him.

"Where was Jon? We could've used him."

She looked away.

"I guess that pretty much answers the question. On the other hand, you did a really good job. Would you consider taking further training?"

She looked back to him. "I'm a historian."

"If you change your mind, I—"

"I won't change my mind."

"As you wish. Help me transfer Tabor into the regeneration tank and then you can return to your usual duties with my deepest gratitude."

By the time the final task had been completed and Li had been dismissed, Casey was utterly exhausted. He entered the passageway, leaned against the bulkhead for support, and informed Mika Ishida and the other power-techs that Erik Lindh was dead, but that Tabor Klampor had an excellent chance of recovery, although it would require a prolonged convalescence in the regeneration chamber. Mika and the others appeared stunned. They had lost so many in cryostasis that the loss of another was almost too much to bear.

"Have you tried everything?" Mika asked.

Casey nodded. "Absolutely everything." He felt the loss as well; he knew everyone to a greater or lesser extent. After a period of mutual silence, he continued. "I hate to bring this up at a time like this, but do you have any idea what happened?"

Mika shook her head, and then made eye contact with each of the techs in the passage, but no one even offered a theory.

Casey sighed. "You can take Erik's body and make ready a farewell as you deem proper, but prepare yourselves. He is quite badly burned. I'm afraid you won't be able to talk with Tabor. He's in the tank and will need to remain that way for about six weeks."

The red-suited group filed past Casey into the treatment room. Soon they exited, carrying a wrapped body that smelled of burnt flesh and hair. Casey watched them until they disappeared around the curve of the passage and then re-entered the treatment room. He made one last check of the life support equipment and then slumped to sit on the deck. His head was so heavy he could hardly hold it up, but his eyes opened when his com-collar came to life.

"Conklin, this is Commander Slater. I want you in my office. Now!" There was no further communication.

Casey didn't move. It was an impossible request. His eyelids drifted shut, but then opened a crack when he felt himself being lifted by powerful arms, almost tenderly. He drifted into a light sleep like a babe, confident in the arms that held him. He was too tired to even consider what Slater had in mind.

He was shaken awake with a pinching grip on his shoulders. He looked blurry eyed into Slater's hawk-like face.

"Wake up, you worthless piece of trash! You're not going to desert your duty while I'm in command."

Casey lifted his head to look more closely at the flushed face, shouting at him from only centimeters away.

Slater exhaled and then withdrew to sit at his desk. He continued. "I understand only one of the two injured men survived. What kind of an incompetent doctor are we cursed with? Just what the hell do you think the rest of colonists will think when they find out there's been a death on our second day on Eden?"

Casey watched the man through red-rimmed eyes.

Slater took a swipe across the top of his desk and sent a sheaf of printouts fluttering to the floor. Then he grabbed a plastic glass and threw it at the bulkhead; it bounced back and hit him in the chest. There was something about the man's extravagances that struck a chord of amusement in Casey.

Slater bolted to his feet and stormed back over to Casey, who was still in Yamaguchi's arms. "You think this is funny?" He took hold of Casey's face and squeezed it until his mouth looked like that of a fish. "Laugh at me, will you? You lunatic! I'll pinch that stupid little head right off your neck," he added through clenched teeth, but then let go, pushing Casey's head back with the palm of his hand.

When he continued he had regained a degree of control. "I presume you at least saved the man's testicles and an adequate tissue sample."

When Casey failed to answer, Slater threw his arms up in

the air. "Do you still think this is a game?" His voice was hoarse with frustrated fury. "How the hell do you expect us to survive as a viable colony without everyone's genetic material?"

Casey's eyes searched the room: the overhead, laced with light-lines; Slater's desk, with the built-in monitors; and finally the rear bulkhead, which contained an array of computer screens.

"Damn you! Look at me! You're so spaced you aren't even hearing a word I'm saying. Damn it to hell!"

Finally, in utter disgust, Slater ordered Yamaguchi to remove Casey from his sight before he killed him. While Casey was being carried out, onto the bridge, Slater was already issuing orders to someone via his com-collar.

When Casey awakened, he was on his sleeping pallet in the instrument lab. He struggled to a sitting position and gathered his thoughts. He thought about the accident the day before and the unusual injury pattern the men had suffered. It had been on his mind ever since he had examined the victims. It appeared that both men had come into contact with a powerful electrical current. Their lower extremities had third degree burns, but there were also severe burns on their backs and arms. In fact, every surface that had touched the ground had been charred. Yet, neither man had come into contact with the malfunctioning transformer.

A cheerful salutation, too cheerful, interrupted his thoughts. He looked at a pair of legs standing next to him, dressed in the maroon of the humanities. His eyes followed up the uniform until he saw a smiling redheaded man with electric-blue eyes.

"Top of morning to you," the man repeated in a pleasant voice. "You are Doctor Conklin, I presume."

Casey continued to study him, but said nothing.

The man ignored Casey's cold reception and continued as if Casey were responding favorably. He stuck out his hand. "I'm Padraig Glancy, formally of humanities, music is my primary, but I've been assigned to you as your student. I'm to be a doctor in training, so to speak," he concluded with a warm, self-effacing laugh.

"Shove it up your ass," Casey said in an even voice.

The man withdrew his hand.

"I know you," Casey continued. "You're no more a humanity-tech than Slater is a leader. Didn't think I'd remember you, did you? My mind wasn't that foggy when you delivered me to Slater and your cronies so they could beat the hell out of me, but I remember you from even further back, when you were sleeping peacefully in your cryo-capsule. You're another one of the blanks."

Padraig spread his fingers and studied them before looking up. "I don't know what you mean by the term 'blank', but I guess I may as well admit I'm not a humanity-tech by training. No use in trying to fool a smart, old codger like you." He smiled with youthful innocence, his beautiful teeth flanked by dimples.

"Where are Li Quon and Jon Brent?" Casey asked.

"Ah, well," Glancy said, "I've been told they've been reassigned to the agri-techs. Seems they're short-handed and need personnel for the test farms. I know I can never replace the likes of Li Quon. As for Jon Brent...well, enough said. I assure you, I'm only here to learn, not to cause you aggravation."

Casey scowled at the sunny-faced youth.

The man stopped his beaming smile and put on a face of pained earnestness. "Doctor Conklin, let's face facts. I've been ordered to be your assistant and student. Orders are orders. I have no choice, just as you have no choice. I'm sure you can use an assistant, even an untrained one. So, let's make the best of a difficult situation." He extended his hand again.

Casey ignored it and pulled himself painfully to his feet. He stood face to face with the man, who looked at Casey out of the tops of his eyes, as if he were nothing more than a small and vulnerable boy.

"Please, Doctor Conklin," the man implored.

Casey shook his head. "What the hell," he said under his breath, and then more audibly, "Where's my buddy, Yamaguchi?"

Glancy shrugged his shoulders.

Casey didn't pursue it. As they were about to enter the treatment room, Casey paused and turned to face Glancy. "By the way, if I were you, I'd save that phony load of crap for someone else. I'm not impressed."

Glancy smiled, and Casey added, "In fact, if I see much more of that idiotic smile, I may be forced to jam it down your throat."

Glancy's smile faded. "Doctor Conklin, are you threatening

me? What're you going to do? Give me a serious tongue-lashing? Did you really say 'Jam it down my throat'?" He laughed. "You've got ballacks, I'll give you that."

Casey stared at him.

Glancy laughed again. "Whatever you say. You're the boss."

"Right," Casey replied sarcastically and hobbled into the treatment room.

He ignored Glancy as he studied the monitoring output from the regeneration tank. When he had completed his assessment, he was satisfied the man would survive, thanks to Li's quick thinking. He wondered where she had learned that technique. It certainly wasn't taught anymore. He wished Li was here to help, instead of this self-serving dandy.

"What could possibly have happened?" Casey muttered as he studied the man in the tank. His reverie was interrupted by Glancy clearing his throat. He turned to look at the man.

Glancy spoke. "I took the initiative to interview the power crew and they told me the transformer must have been defective. Its circuits were fused. Water, or some other conducting liquid, had seeped into it. My theory is that, when the short occurred, it must have allowed an energy build up that discharged as an arc into the two approaching men." He looked down at the instrument counter and rubbed his fingers across the surface, as if he spoke in all modesty.

Casey watched his performance for a moment before he answered. "You know, Glancy, you're not even real shit. You're fake shit. A rubber turd."

Glancy looked up sharply, fire in his eyes.

"Finally, an honest reaction," Casey said. "I was beginning to think you were just one facade on top of another. If I peeled away all your various personas, I expect I would see the wall behind you."

Glancy eased back and leaned against the bulkhead; the flush faded from his face.

"All right, Conklin, why don't you set me straight?"

"First of all," Casey said, "I saw the whole thing and I guarantee you, there was no arc. Secondly, even if there had been an arc, the distribution of the burns would've been much different. These men were burned as if the energy came up from the ground. And thirdly, how do you explain water damage to the transformer? Do you think, perhaps, it rained in the Storage Deck while we were in deep space? I suggest you begin your brilliant investigation over, but this time ask them how the current was transferred to the victims and ask them how they can explain the water damage."

For once, Glancy's face was expressionless, but Casey wasn't about to let up. "I guess Slater won't need a more official report than the one you'll provide for him and, when you see his imperial majesty, you can tell him to send me someone a bit more forthright than you and I'll be more than happy to begin training."

Glancy began to object, but closed his mouth without voicing his thoughts.

"You better get a move on, Mister. You have no idea how dangerous this place can be if you don't know the equipment. The results could be a lot more serious than a tongue-lashing."

Glancy turned to leave, but then stopped. "Conklin, there'll be a time when your usefulness won't be quite so vital. If I were you, I'd try to be a little more civil, that is if you expect to survive."

"Get the hell out! I've already survived more years than I expect you will." Casey smiled coolly. "What more could a man want?" He turned his back on the stranger and heard the portal swish open and shut.

"So this is Eden," he mumbled as he returned his attention to the unconscious power-tech.

CHAPTER 14

During the following week, the community blossomed, like
mushrooms in an over-watered lawn. Tabor Klampor continued
to improve and Casey was beginning to feel much better. His
face was still discolored a sickly yellow, but the swelling was
gone and he was able to walk with only mild discomfort and
stiffness.

The problem with the transformer had not been
satisfactorily resolved, so the power-techs had switched to a
more direct transmission of energy from the ship. Power
channels snaked through the grass to the various domes.
The fiber optic cables glowed brightly, even in daylight.

Most mornings, as on this particular day, Casey could be
found sitting in the gaping mouth of the ramp, like a lazy cat,
soaking up the warmth of the sun and watching the activity
below. Occasionally, he would spot Yamaguchi's unmistakable
physique, but he had yet to see the tiny form of Li Quon.

Casey's attention focused on Jim Wheeler, chief nutrition-
tech, who stood in the doorway of the Main Dome. There was
something strange about the man. He rubbed his elbows
incessantly and had a smile that appeared to be plastered on
his face. In space school he'd been known as Wacky Wheeler
because of his penchant for playing practical jokes. Casey
recalled a time when Wheeler had spiked the punch at a
reception with an emetic. It was kind of funny. The
distinguished faculty had run around looking for containers
and vomited into anything they could find. No one officially
pointed a finger at Wheeler, but there was little doubt in any
student's mind who was responsible. But now the man, who
had been so gregarious on Earth, ducked back into the dome
whenever a colonist approached.

Casey decided the next time he saw Slater he would
recommend an evaluation of all the colonists. There had to be
much suppressed, and as yet, unresolved emotional trauma.
Likely, everyone suffered from PTSD to some extent.

He tilted his head back. The morning sun shone with its
usual warmth and the deep blue sky had its usual assortment

of cumulus clouds, drifting slowly along. "Eden is it?" Casey asked himself. Perhaps so. Perhaps Slater was right. Perhaps he was always looking for the dark side of good fortune. That thought caused a mental grimace. But, there was something about this place that just didn't seem right. It was too quiet. Where were the animals and the insects? The flora didn't appear primitive. Where was the fauna? Slater insisted that this place was created so that mankind could meet its preordained destiny. If that was the case, who created it? He nodded. That was the root of it. Chance events do exist but, at least in this one respect, he agreed with Slater. This was no chance event. It was too perfect.

Casey arose stiffly to his feet and walked down the ramp and across the grass to the second largest dome in the colony, the Agri-Dome. He wanted to talk with an agricultural-tech, maybe even Min. She was perhaps the closest thing to a friend he had left.

He walked up the gentle incline of the ramp that led to the dome, through the air door and into the humid interior. He took a deep breath of the fragrances; some of the flowers had already bloomed. The dome was brightly lit by sunlamps that hung from the curved ceiling. Within the dome, Casey could see a handful of agri-techs tending to the plants. If there were others present, he couldn't see them through the already tall vegetation, rich with leaves, displaying vital shades of green.

While he stood there, Gao Min walked toward him along one of the aisles created by hydroponics tanks that stretched toward the rear of the building. The rush of nutrient fluid through the tanks caused enough background noise that she didn't attempt to speak until she had come to within arm's reach of Casey.

"Why are you here?" she asked without preamble.

Casey was taken aback by the sharpness of her greeting. She had always been even-tempered when they'd spent time together back on Earth.

"Nothing special, Min. I just thought I'd stop by and see how you were getting along."

Her voice softened. "I'll tell you, Casey, I never saw anything like it back on Earth. We've already begun field-testing. Our initial results indicate that our vegetation will not only survive here, but will flourish. You can't see it from here, but in the rear of the dome we've planted directly into the soil and the plants are growing even faster and more luxurious than they do in the hydroponic tanks. It's all so wonderful! It's a miracle!" she gushed.

"It's a miracle all right." Casey's voice sounded flatter than he'd intended.

Min's smile vanished. "I don't expect to be made fun of, especially by a person like you."

"Like me?"

"You know what I'm talking about."

Casey sighed. "I...I wasn't myself when I...."

Her expression hardened.

"If I've offended you, Min, I apologize. You only have my respect. You know that. I was just wondering what your evaluation of the local flora revealed."

Min looked back at him, her mouth slightly agape. "Local flora?"

"Yeah, you know, stuff like that grass we've been walking on." Casey regretted his sarcasm as soon as he said it.

She looked stunned for a moment, as if the thought had never occurred to her, but whatever uncertainties she may have felt quickly faded. "Since when do you tell me how to do my job? We've had more pressing matters to attend to. If that's all you want, get out of here and stop bothering us."

"You mean you haven't even begun to evaluate the native vegetation?"

"What's here, is here," she replied, and began to turn away.

Casey reached out and grabbed hold of her arm. "I can't believe what I'm hearing. You of all people. What's wrong with you, Min?"

She stared at Casey's hand on her arm as if she could hardly express her distaste at his touch and jerked her arm out of his grip. By now, other agri-techs had begun to walk toward the two of them.

Min's usually mild voice was strained with anger. "What's wrong with me? How dare you say such a thing? Look to yourself, Conklin. If I ever need your advice, I'll ask for it, but don't hold your breath waiting."

"Min, this is—"

"You're interfering with important work. If you do not remove yourself at once, I'll personally contact Commander

Slater and see that you're removed."

"This is me, Casey, remember?" He patted himself on his chest. "Don't you remember those evenings we spent in the Arboretum Cafeteria drinking beer and eating pizza? I'm the one who listened to you rhapsodize about the special beauty of roses while we—"

Min became enraged. "Get out!"

Casey backed up a step. "All right, I'll go, but I want to talk with you again, when you have the time."

"Get out!"

Casey walked out into the sunlight, but felt the heat of hostile glares. He hurried down the ramp and walked with his gaze downward, seeing the grass pass beneath his feet. He couldn't understand Gao Min's reaction, or that of the entire guild. Was it all because of Klaus' death? Didn't they realize that he'd been mentally ill at the time? As he passed the Main Dome, he saw Wheeler standing in the doorway, but when he angled in that direction, Wheeler disappeared back inside.

Casey was filled with confusion while he stood in the grassy yard of the compound. Were people watching him, he wondered, or was he being paranoid? Perhaps his age set him apart. Perhaps they were all afraid, on some unconscious level, that if they associated with him, they'd catch it.

He turned toward the ramp of the ship and began trudging toward it, a humorless smile on his face, generated by loneliness and rejection. While he walked, he made up his mind. Slater needed to be informed of the glaring lack of basic research he had uncovered.

When Casey exited the up-tube on Deck One, he came face to face with Glancy, who now wore a black uniform. Glancy placed his hand against Casey's chest.

"The saints be praised, if it isn't Doctor Conklin. What can I do for you?"

"For one thing you can take your damn hand off me and, for another, you can go dimple somebody else into a stupor." He tried to push past Glancy, but was restrained by a firm grip on his arm.

"Whoa there," Glancy said. "Where do you think you're going?"

"I'm going where I choose."

"I don't think so. If you have a message for Commander Slater, you can give it to me. He's much too busy to be bothered by you."

Just then the portal to Slater's suite swished open and Slater exited with Jane Veck in tow, a respectful two-steps behind. He spotted Casey and approached him.

"You look upset, Casey. Is there a problem?"

"There's a problem all right. I've just returned from the Agri-Dome and I've discovered that there has been no evaluation of the native flora. None. It hasn't even been started."

"Really?" Slater said dryly. "How typical of you to get the priorities all screwed up. We must look after first needs first, and that means food and shelter. Do you dispute that?"

"Yes," Casey answered hotly, "I dispute that! We know nothing—"

"Casey, I have no time for this. As you're well aware, we've enough instrument readings taken while we were in orbit to last us for years. Don't you trust our tools? You know, and I told you this many times while we were in training together, you're always looking for the worm in the apple. Now I've changed my mind. You are the worm."

Slater laughed at his joke and was joined with a titter from Jane. He walked away.

As he was about to drop into the down-tube, Casey called out a warning. "Slater, wake up! There is something terribly wrong here."

Slater shook his head and laughed again before disappearing into the tube. Jane looked smugly at Casey for a moment, as if she needed to express her own contempt, and then followed Slater. Glancy and Casey were left standing in the quiet of the bridge.

"Conklin, there's something you should think about. The higher a monkey climbs the tree the farther up its arse you see."

"What?" He stared at Glancy for a moment. "Am I completely surrounded by crazy people?"

"You should talk."

Casey glared at the too-handsome man before dropping into the tube himself.

CHAPTER 15

Casey went directly to the medical suite to check on Klampor, who was floating motionless in the bubbling regeneration tank. Satisfied Klampor's progress was as expected, he went into the lab and began inspecting the equipment.

In the rear of the room, he noticed a rectangular box. Curious, he walked over and lifted the lid to peek in. It was a moment before the contents of the box registered in his mind. He flipped the lid completely back, aghast at what he was seeing. It contained a corpse. Nestled among the bones was a laser-scalpel. He reached in and pulled out a mummified arm with a hand still attached. It was light and dry.

"What the hell?" he said out loud. He emptied the contents of the box onto the deck. He examined the skull-like face, with a still sparkling diamond set in one of the central incisors, and sat down with the recognition of whose corpse this was. He held the skull in his hands and remembered.

His vision blurred with tears. He remembered her so clearly. Her beautiful ebony skin, her unmatched zest for life and cheerful optimism. He looked again at the diamond and remembered when she had come back to Copper Mountain with it, flaunting it as a minor rebellion against conformity, smiling widely at the instructors to make sure they saw it. She was to have been Casey's replacement, one of the guardians assigned to the remaining fifty years of the journey. What had happened to her? How could a person with so much life end up in a box tossed in a corner?

He tried to remember those last days of his tour as guardian of the ship, but his mind skidded around the memories until they were once again beyond reach. He didn't attempt to pursue the fragmentary bits and pieces left hanging in his mind. He was reluctant to remember; afraid of what he might recall, willing to postpone it. Instead, he touched his com-collar.

"Veck, this is Conklin, I need to speak with Li Quon about an important medical matter. Give me her code or connect us."

"Conklin, this channel is for official communications only." There was a pause, then Veck's thready voice returned. "Make it brief."

Casey found himself connected to Li Quon.

"This is Li. You need to speak with me?"

"Yes, Li. It's important. Can you come by the ship today?"

"Why?"

"I have some questions," Casey said.

"Then ask them."

"I'd rather do it in person."

Li delayed for a moment before answering. "This is a critical time for Simon and me. We've just planted our first test crop and I don't think it'd be responsible for me to leave the farm at this time."

"For crap's sake, you can't be more than three or four kilometers away. Oh, forget it. I'll come to you. What radius are you on?"

"If you must. North north west, four and a half kilometers."

"So, Simon Weiss is stuck out there with you, huh?"

"He's not stuck with me. He chose to be with me."

"Sorry, I didn't mean.... I'll be there shortly. Jane, I'm sure you're listening. You can have your official beam back now." The statement was confirmed by an abrupt disconnect.

After checking Klampor one more time and making a few minor adjustments, he started down the passage and was surprised to see Yamaguchi standing near the down-tube.

"Hello, Yamaguchi, back on guard duty I see."

Yamaguchi spoke. That alone was enough to capture Casey's full attention. "What is reality?" he rumbled.

"Come on, Yamaguchi. I appreciate you opening up like this, but couldn't you start with something a little less cosmic? Like, how are you?"

"Words are special. If they are overused their meaning fades. They should be used with careful consideration."

"Maybe I can buy that, to a limited extent, but the truth is, I'm not really prepared to discuss the essence of reality. I'm about to visit Li Quon at her test farm. Perhaps we could discuss it on the way."

Casey waited for Yamaguchi to respond, but he didn't. Casey shrugged and slipped into the down-tube. Yamaguchi followed after him.

When the two men entered the brightness of sunlight,

they paused for a moment to take in the vista, and then descended the ramp. There was a smattering of colonists passing across the yard, going from one dome to another.

Casey stopped to watch. They all seemed to be walking faster than they needed to and had an enthusiastic spring to their step. The excesses of youth, Casey thought, and felt envy. Although he could hardly have remained unnoticed, none of colonists met his gaze or offered a greeting. He couldn't remember much, but he did remember the loneliness he felt during his vigil on the ship. He sighed. The loneliness he felt now, with all these people about, seemed even worse.

He looked toward the Main Dome. Wheeler was standing in the doorway, a plastic smile plastered on his face while he massaged his elbows. Casey imitated the movement. It was awkward and uncomfortable. When Wheeler saw Casey watching him, he darted back into the interior. For a moment Casey considered confronting him, but the impulse passed.

Yamaguchi stood by, patiently watching and waiting. Casey glanced up at the big man and then began to walk out of camp, with Yamaguchi at his side. It wasn't long before the domed encampment was at their backs and before them, across the prairie, the smoke-gray mountains with bright, white summits.

There was a breeze ruffling Casey's uniform, bringing with it a sense of freedom and a measure of expectation. Someday, Casey vowed to himself, he would hike to those distant mountains and meet them in person. If only there were buzzing insects flitting from flower to flower and birds soaring through the sky, but there was only the soft swishing of wind caressing the grass and the rhythmic sound of their feet.

While they walked, Casey considered Yamaguchi's question. He began to think aloud.

"I think the debate about what constitutes reality is an over-rated one, complicated by semantics. I mean, is there really any doubt about what's real? The grass under our feet is real. The planet under the grass is real. The sunlight overhead is real. I can feel them, and hear them, and see them. If I can sense them, then they are real. One has to trust something, if not ourselves and our senses, then what? Do you doubt that, Yamaguchi?"

"Do you believe, if your senses perceive something, it is undeniably real?" Yamaguchi asked.

"Of course I believe it. It has a very real and definite impact on my existence, an undeniable effect."

"If you see a ghost lurking in a shadow, it has an impact on you. Is it real?"

"Come on, Yamaguchi. You know what I mean."

"Is reality a matter of statistics? If most people see the ghost, in fact, if everyone sees the ghost, does that make it real? Does majority rule?"

Casey was silent for a moment and then replied. "I don't know."

"I've been taught to question and to observe. Does reality require everyone to sense the same thing?"

"I believe there is an ultimate reality," Casey said.

"An ultimate reality. So, if everyone senses the same thing, it is not sufficient to call it reality."

"Why in the world would you not believe what you see, hear and feel? It's not rational."

"Do you consider emotions and beliefs to be real?" Yamaguchi asked.

"Now don't play with those precious words of yours," Casey said with a chuckle. "Certainly beliefs are also real, in a sense, not like our physical sensations, but they exist because they have a real impact on our existences."

"Then you believe there are two categories of reality— those that you directly perceive with your senses, which may or may not be something you call ultimate reality, and those that you conjure up in your mind. Is one more real than the other?" Yamaguchi asked.

"I'm not going to rank order reality for you. It's a meaningless exercise. It's not necessary to put everything in a list from biggest to smallest, but there is a difference. The physical world, the one I sense to exist, does not require my existence, but for beliefs and emotions to exist, I must also exist."

"So, if you ceased to exist, then there would be only one class of reality. Is that correct?"

"I guess so."

"What if two individuals sensed two different physical worlds? Which would you say existed then?"

"Are you saying that you don't see that red bunch of the flowers over there, or feel the wind on your face?" Casey asked.

"I am merely asking questions, as I have been taught, but

I feel resistance. I am able to remain true to my duty in life only by the most pure exercise of my will, without reason to support it." His words became halting, each one requiring a special effort. "I am fighting."

Casey stopped walking when he noticed that Yamaguchi was no longer at his side. He turned back and looked up at Yamaguchi's face. Yamaguchi's brow was furrowed and, despite the cool breeze, his face was glistening with perspiration. Seeing this man, who Casey had come to believe was impervious, showing physical distress during a casual stroll in the countryside, made Casey shiver with dread.

Yamaguchi's small, dark eyes met Casey's. "I do not fall," he said.

"You don't fall? What the hell does that mean?"

"There was no reason, yet I fell. I do not fall for no reason."

He said it with such utter certainty that Casey too believed it as a statement of incontestable fact, yet he had fallen. Casey turned from the man and looked ahead. He could see a white spot on the horizon that marked the location of Li's farm. He returned his gaze to Yamaguchi.

"All right," Casey said, "I too feel a wrongness. My senses tell me one thing, but my mind tells me there are discrepancies. There are cracks, as if reality doesn't quite fit together. I've spent years studying the colonists and knew many of them personally. At first, I thought they were only reacting strangely to me," he lowered his voice, "because of what I did. But now I'm beginning to believe that some kind of change has taken place in them, not me. Thank you, Yamaguchi. You have no idea how much this means to me. I was beginning to have serious doubts about my sanity. Especially after…well, you know."

"If you believe you are different, you are right. There is something special about you."

"Is it my deodorant?" Casey waited but Yamaguchi didn't respond so he continued. "You don't have much of a sense of humor, do you?"

"No."

"All right then. What the hell? I'll bite. What's special about me?"

"Being around you makes a person want to hurt you, to expel you. When I am with you, I have the urge to reach out and crush you."

Casey began backing away and glanced toward the farm dome, wondering if he could make it before Yamaguchi caught him.

Yamaguchi continued. "I refuse to be governed by the lower qualities of instinct or unfounded emotionality. I choose to be governed by intellect and duty. I observe and seek to know."

Casey stopped his retreat. "Does that mean I don't have to worry about you crushing me?"

Yamaguchi stood silently.

"I'll take that as a 'yes'."

Casey began walking toward Li's farm, but kept his head partially turned so he could see Yamaguchi in his peripheral vision. After a hundred meters, he gave up. He turned to face Yamaguchi.

"If you're going to crush me, then to hell with it. Do it."

"I choose not to."

"All right then." Casey nodded. "I'm good with that."

He pivoted away from Yamaguchi and began walking. The small white dome of the farmhouse was easy to see against the verdant green of the plain. He came to a sudden stop. There was something beyond the farmhouse. As he stared at it, the fogginess around the object cleared. It was a huge structure, sleek but with sections missing, as if it were crumbling. It looked like a derelict starship, but its patchy amber coloration and exaggerated curves looked nothing like the Pinnacle.

"What do you observe?" Yamaguchi asked.

Casey slowly turned away from the incredible structure until he was focused on the face of the giant. A shiver passed through him and he pointed toward the gigantic artifact. It had to be ten times the size of the Pinnacle.

Yamaguchi looked in the direction Casey indicated and then returned to stare at Casey.

"Don't you see it?" Casey asked.

"I see the plain. I see the mountains. I see the sky."

Casey swiveled and saw only the lush, flower speckled plain and the distant mountains. He slipped his hand into his jumpsuit to feel the medicated patch, to ensure it was still there. Had he forgotten to replace it on time? Briefly, he considered returning to the Pinnacle, but there was likely enough medication being released into his system, even it was at a reduced dosage.

"What did you observe?" Yamaguchi asked again.

Casey shook his head. "Nothing. I saw nothing."

He turned away and began walking with his attention focused on his feet and the grass. There was no excitement, no wonder, only doubts about himself. The emptiness hurt. He was a fraud, a hypocrite, to talk about reality as if he deserved to have an opinion.

They walked toward the small dome without further discussion.

As they closed the distance, Casey saw two figures bent over in the age-old tableau of humans tending to the soil, hoes in hand. How different it will be, he thought, when they roll out the machines and tear up the floor of the plain in giant swathes.

It was not until the two men were near enough to hear Li laugh at some comment made by Simon, that Simon chanced to look up and see them. He said something sharply to Li and she too looked in their direction. They stood straight, hoes in hand and grim faced while Casey and Yamaguchi walked the last few steps.

"Hello, Li. Looks like you're not exactly overjoyed to see me," Casey said.

Simon spoke. "Why have you come here, Conklin?"

"Simon, what has happened to your manners? I've come all this way on foot, just to make a neighborly visit. Aren't you at least going to invite us in for some refreshments?"

Li and Simon's eyes met in a brief, wordless conversation, then Li turned to walk in the direction of the small dome.

"Come along, Casey," Li said, "and you too, Mister Yamaguchi, if you want to." Her tone was one of resignation. Simon brought up the rear.

The door to the simple dome was an old fashioned one; it swung open on hinges. Li held the door open for Casey and Yamaguchi to enter the cool interior of her home.

Casey looked around. It was plain but clean. It consisted of one round room, with a foam-steel table and four chairs, a reconstitution unit and two sleeping pallets, flanked by their small preservation chests which were being used as bedside tables. There were a few personal touches. There was a plastic jug, decorated with twisted cord that was being used as a vase for a bouquet of yellow flowers and on the back wall there was a nearly completed mural of a mountain scene. It was skillfully done and obviously depicted the mountains on the distant horizon. He walked over to get a closer look.

"Do you like it?" Li asked with evident pride.

"Yes, it's beautifully done. I didn't know you were an artist."

"I'm not. Simon painted it for me. It's one of the reasons I like it so much out here. Those mountains are remarkably like the mountains near my home, back on Earth. It's one of my strongest and most vivid memories, of being with my family, and the mountains, always the beautiful mountains in the distance." Her voice was velvety with remembered contentment and love.

Casey walked toward the table and noticed the shine of tears in Li's eyes before she turned to go over to the reconstitution unit. He pulled out a white foam-steel chair and sat down. Simon begrudgingly pulled out a chair to join him. After a few minutes of Simon staring at Casey and Casey keeping his eyes downcast at the tabletop, Li came over to the table with a steaming pot of tea, made from tea leaves she had brought in her preservation chest all those billions of miles from Earth. She placed fine porcelain cups in front of Casey and Simon and filled their cups before she sat down with her own cup. Yamaguchi had refused the offer and remained standing near the door.

The tea was hot and fragrant. Casey sipped at it. He felt at ease, despite Simon's constant stare. It was the first time he had been in a real home in a long time and it reminded him more of Earth than anything else he had experienced since awakening.

"The tea is excellent," Casey declared. "Thank you. And these cups are beautiful."

"They belonged to my mother," Li said.

Casey savored the warmth of the cup he cradled in his hands, as much as the luxury of tasting tea. His gaze settled on a crude candelabra sitting in the center of the table. It was constructed from salvaged pipes and had a certain rustic charm.

Casey nodded toward it and looked to Simon. "Did you make the candle holder too? I like it."

"It's a Menorah," Simon said.

"Sorry," Casey said. "How stupid of me. Of course it is."

"Simon is reintroducing the old holidays to the new world," Li explained. "He's beginning with a minor holiday called

Hanukkah."

"I think I could find some material in the medical suite that could be used for candles," Casey offered.

"We can manage," Simon replied.

Casey nodded and they sat in silence, until Li spoke. "Why did you come here, Casey?"

Casey was reluctant to get his business over with so quickly and ignored her question. "You and Simon have a nice place here. I can see why you haven't been coming by the ship. After seeing you, it seems unlikely, but I want to repeat my offer. If you ever want to train to become a doctor, I'd be pleased to take you on. I was very impressed with the way you handled yourself during that accident."

Simon put his hand gently on Li's arm, as if to remind her of what they had.

"Thanks, but no thanks," Li said with certainty. "How is Tabor doing?"

"He'll recover, in time." There was a lull, and then Casey spoke again. "I see you've turned in your maroon for the green of the agri-techs."

"Yes. Simon and I have found the beginnings of true peace out here. It's a simple life, but I never realized how satisfying it could be to plant something in the ground and help it grow. I feel useful. There was a woman I spent a couple of years with in Tibet before I moved to Copper Mountain. She used to tell me how much joy she got out of it, but I didn't understand at the time. Her name is…was Roxanne Wiley. She helped me get a position on the starship. Did you ever meet her?"

"She was rather famous at Copper Mountain. I knew of her, but never met her. Jack Nichols helped me get into the program."

"Casey, why did you come to see me? Did Slater send you?"

"No."

Her voice became hard. "You can tell Slater if he wanted Simon and me out of the way, he has succeeded. All I ask is that he leaves us alone. He can run his little kingdom as he wishes. Just tell him to stay the hell away from here."

"Slater didn't send me," Casey said.

"You must think I'm naive," Li said. "First you talk to me through his sacred com-network and now you show up with one of his," she paused, as if substituting a word, "one of his assistants."

Casey tried to change the direction of the conversation. "Have you heard anything from Jon?"

She nodded. "Lisa Bouviet and he are on a test farm about a half kilometer from here. We see him from time to time. He seems to be doing okay."

Casey raised his eyebrows in surprise. "Lisa Bouviet, huh?"

Li nodded and then they sat in strained silence.

Casey focused on the missing finger on her left hand. "When you were helping me with Tabor, I noticed that you had lost a finger. I can help you with that. What happened to it?"

"You've got to be joking," Simon growled.

"I'm not joking. After I rescue Tabor from the tank, I could put Li in and regenerate the finger in two or three days. What do you say?"

Li's olive-dark complexion paled perceptively. She hid her hand in her lap and eased back from the table, increasing the distance between Casey and herself.

Simon pushed back his chair and stood protectively over Li, massaging her shoulders. "It's time for you to go," he said in a steely voice.

Casey remained sitting. "Now just a minute, Simon. I didn't come here to fight with you and I don't have the foggiest notion what's getting you all riled up. I was just offering to help."

"State your business now or leave. You are not welcome in our home."

"All right." Casey raised his hands in surrender. "All right. All I wanted to do was ask Li about a friend of mine, Grace N'duforchu. I found her body in pieces, stashed in a box in the back of the lab."

"Casey," she hesitated, searching for words, "it was right after the Awakening. Things were pretty crazy then." She stopped when she realized what she had said.

"Forget it, Li," Casey said. "Things were rather crazy then. I just want to know what you can tell me about her."

Li took a breath and released it before answering. "She was found sitting in the control chair on the bridge. She'd been dead for quite a while before the Awakening."

Quite a while indeed, Casey thought. Even most of her hair had disintegrated. "Was there any sign of violence?" he asked.

Li thought for a moment. "No, it looked like she had just gone to sleep and never woke up."

Casey hesitated before his next question. To even consider such a thing seemed like a betrayal of her memory and their friendship. "A laser-scalpel was in the box with her bones. Did it look like she might have killed herself?"

"I can't say. There was almost no soft tissue remaining. I found it on the seat next to her corpse."

"Is there anything else you can tell me?"

Li shook her head but then stopped.

"Did you remember something?" Casey asked.

"It's probably nothing, but I do recall seeing some scratches on the arm of the control chair."

"What did the scratches look like? Was it a picture or maybe words?"

"I don't recall."

"Was Vlada Bezdicek or Julio Mendoza—" Casey couldn't continue. It felt like there was lump in his throat, cutting off his windpipe.

"Are you all right?" Li asked.

He lowered his gaze to the tabletop. His friends, something terrible had happened. Was he somehow responsible?

"Casey, do you want a glass of water or something?"

He shook his head. "Were any of the other doctors found?" he finally managed to ask.

"No, at least I didn't hear of any other bodies being found. Only Grace." Li paused. "I'm sorry about your friend. We've all lost friends." She stopped, her eyes downcast.

"You have what you came for," Simon said harshly. "Now get out of here and don't come back."

Casey nodded. "As you wish. Thank you for your hospitality."

He meant it, but it was evident that both Li and Simon considered it just another one of Casey's sarcastic remarks. Holding onto the table, he shoved himself up and slowly straightened his back, which had become sore. He walked stiffly to the door and Yamaguchi opened it. Casey looked back into the room. Simon and Li were holding each other. Casey felt bitter regret and envy; they had each other and they had their youth. What did he have?

CHAPTER 15

Casey walked out into the sunlight and started the hike back with Yamaguchi at his side. In the distance, the shape of the Pinnacle arose, a soaring tower, bringing to mind the magical castles of a children's story, but its dull gray coloration suggested malevolence. To Casey, it simply looked like a long way to walk. His joints and muscles were aching from the unusual exertion and he was exhausted. He didn't look to see if there was a derelict phantom starship. He didn't even look toward the mountains. He would never see them up close, he admitted to himself. He was tired and old. He glanced over at the big man who walked beside him and recalled what Li had said those many days ago in the Storage Deck. If it weren't for Slater's men, he truly would have no human contact at all. He thought about the companionship that Li and Simon shared.

"What did Simon mean about Li's finger?" Casey asked. "He seemed to think I knew something."

"You do know."

"The hell I do! If I knew, I wouldn't ask." He was exasperated, but Yamaguchi said no more.

They walked in silence until Casey spoke again. "I've been doing some thinking. As difficult as this was to accept, the truth is I have no friends, and those I left behind on Earth are long dead. No one gives a damn about me."

Casey paused, hoping Yamaguchi would object, even if he didn't mean it, but he said nothing so Casey continued. "Obviously it's my duty to pass on my expertise to someone. Don't know who. But, after that, who cares?" He sighed. "I haven't told anyone else this, but I think of the colonists as my children, my poor suffering children. If I could have one wish granted, it would be to free them from whatever has taken them. If I could do that, I'd die a happy man."

"You are the One."

Casey stopped and turned to face him. "I'm the one? What the hell does that mean? Shit, when you do speak it sounds like…like I'm talking with a fortune cookie." That made Casey smile.

"When my Sensei was about to die, he told me his work was not yet done. He told me that he would reach into the future through me and, through me, he would talk with the One. I asked how I would recognize the One and he told me I would know. You are the One." With that Yamaguchi bowed to Casey.

Casey touched him on the shoulder. "Please don't do that. Although I do have to admit I prefer it to being crushed."

"You are the One."

"Enough of this 'one' bullshit. I'm just an old, lonely man who is tired. Let's get going."

By the time they arrived back at camp, the mountains were casting purple shadows across the plain. Casey wanted nothing more than to return to his pallet on Deck Two and collapse onto it but, midway up the ramp to the storage bay, he changed his mind.

He stopped and turned to Yamaguchi. "I need to talk with Slater. Will you help me?"

Yamaguchi nodded and led the way into the ship. When they exited on Deck One, Casey's attention was immediately drawn to Jack Sabine, who was lounging in the control chair. Sabine leisurely arose to his feet with a big grin on his face.

"What a pleasant diversion, I do declare," Sabine said. "What brings you boys up to the higher levels? You need me to work on your ribs a little, Casey?" He cracked his knuckles as he spoke.

Casey tried to ignore the man's jibes, but seeing Sabine made his courage falter. He could not help but recall the pain in his ribs and back after the beating. He still felt stabbing pain if he moved too quickly. Casey began to edge his way toward Slater's cubicle, but kept his eyes on Sabine.

Suddenly, Sabine jumped forward and interposed his body between Casey and Slater's portal. He shot out a stiff finger and jabbed Casey in the chest.

It felt like a stick had been poked into his ribs, but Casey managed to keep the pain from his face.

"You're really pushing me, man," Sabine said with a sneer.

"I have business with Slater," Casey said.

"You mean Commander Slater, don't you?"

"All right, I have business with Commander Slater. Get out of the way...please."

"Please?" Sabine chuckled. "Sorry, old man, there is no

way you're going to get in to see him. He told me he wasn't to be disturbed."

"I have to see him."

"Gee, things are really tough, aren't they, old man?"

"You stupid—" Casey caught himself, but too late. He reflexively closed his eyes as Sabine's fist flew toward his face, but felt only a whisk of air. He opened his eyes in time to see Sabine sliding across the deck on his back, to lay motionless near the console screens. Yamaguchi withdrew his hand from where Sabine had been standing a second before. Casey studied the prostrate body of Jack Sabine to confirm that he was still breathing. Then he looked up at the face of the big man who stood at his side, but could perceive no meaning; it was as empty as ever.

"Can I take a look at the control chair before we see Slater?" Casey asked.

Yamaguchi looked toward the chair but said nothing.

Casey was beginning to interpret his non-responses as "yes", so he walked over to the chair. There were some scratches on the upper surface of the left armrest. Grace had been left-handed. The armrest was made out of a titanium alloy. It would have taken something powerful to even scratch it, such as a laser-scalpel. He looked at it and then changed his position and finally sat in the chair. It wasn't words or even a single word. It was a picture...of something. It kind of looked like a bird's eye view of a canoe with lines across it that could be the ribs of the canoe. There were scratches that led away from the canoe that could be stems topped by flowers. Overall, the lines of picture were not smoothly drawn but jerky and jagged. Grace was the most skilled surgeon Casey had ever known. She'd been masterful with a scalpel. If she was the one who had scratched this image into the armrest, she must have been stressed or somehow handicapped.

Casey looked up at Yamaguchi who had walked over to join him.

"What do you think this means? What is it?" Casey asked.

"You asked the question. It is for you to answer."

"Thank you so much. Such insightful comments are so helpful."

Casey glanced again toward Sabine, who still hadn't moved, and then pushed himself to his feet to walk across the bridge. The door to Slater's office swished open to admit Yamaguchi and him.

Slater looked up with surprise at the unexpected intrusion but, in the brief time it took for recognition, he leaned back in his chair and smiled.

"Doctor Conklin, I suppose you've come to share more predictions of doom. I left orders I wasn't to be interrupted. Where's Sabine?"

"He's resting."

"Resting? I'll have to have a serious chat with him. Why are you here?"

"I've come to make a deal."

"A deal? What could you possibly offer that I might want?" Slater asked.

"I offer you two things. The first is my word that I won't oppose your running of this colony."

"Worthless, and what is the other?"

"I will train whoever you choose to be a fully qualified doctor."

"You'll do that anyway, but for the sake of discussion, what do you want in return? For such a grand gesture," Slater added.

"I want you to assist me in investigating ship's failure. I need your authority to get some cooperation from the colonists."

Slater ran his tongue across his teeth as he considered. "Well, I don't know. Ship's failure is a thing of the past. Why should I allow you to interrupt the important work of the colonists to investigate a problem that is no longer pertinent?"

Casey was tired and his patience had come to an end. "Not pertinent!" he shouted.

"I'm glad you were listening. With you it's a rare event."

"The difference between you and me is that you think any decision you make is the right decision. You believe you know everything. You—"

"And you believe no one knows anything. That is one of your many glaring weaknesses. You never did have the guts to come to a decision and stand behind it, always vacillating among the possibilities." Slater leaned forward in his chair. "Well, I make decisions, damn it, and it's a damn good thing I do!"

"The hell you say!" Casey shouted back. "You make decisions so easily because you really don't give a shit about any of the colonists. You only care about the exercise of power."

The silence that followed seemed just as deafening as the shouting. Slater tipped back in his chair. "You judge others pretty harshly, for a murderer. And, as far as ship's failure goes, there is a widespread belief among the colonists that you are the cause of ship's failure."

"That's a lie," Casey said.

"Far from it. Everyone knows you had plenty of time to study the computer hardware and plenty of time to accomplish a wipe."

"That's ridiculous. I did nothing of the sort. I did my duty."

"So you say. You think my associates are spying on you, but what they're actually doing is protecting you from the colonists. Don't you think it's remarkable that all the doctors died, except one? Makes you pretty important, doesn't it?"

"Those people were my friends, a concept you're unfamiliar with." Casey voice was choked with anger. He stared at Slater as if a blink would be an admission of guilt. "Slater, if you support my efforts, I'll find the cause of ship's failure. Are you afraid of what I'll find?"

"Casey, as far as you are concerned, I'm afraid of nothing, except that someone will do away with you before I have that information you're so carefully hoarding. Don't you have a conscience? Any concern for the welfare of the colony?"

Casey forced himself to remain silent.

"You've proven yourself impotent as a guardian and have been ineffectual since planet-fall, except for getting in the way." Slater threw his hands up in careless acceptance. "Sure, why not? I'm feeling generous today. You have my permission. Find out the reason for ship's failure, if you have enough guts to face your own guilt, but you will produce a permanent record of everything you know about the practice of medicine. I, at least, have the future of the colony to consider. Do you ever think about that?"

Casey's gaze dropped back to Slater's desktop. "I will find the answer."

"I'm sure you will. The question is, will you find the right answer? You have a real problem dealing with authority. How are you going to control that?"

"I don't have the problem, you do. Anyone who would demand a position of power over others has already proven himself unworthy of the trust."

"Aren't you the pure one?" sneered Slater. "Now get out of here before I follow my instincts as far as you're concerned."

Casey just stood there, temporarily at a loss.

After a moment Slater looked back up. "Are you still here?" He directed his eyes at Yamaguchi. "Take this human trash out of here."

Casey lifted his head. "Wait, I have some information for you."

Slater motioned for Yamaguchi to wait. "All right, what is it now? But please be succinct, you've already cost me much more time than you're worth."

"Before planet-fall, you said that I knew the colonists better than anyone, that you might consult me if you needed information about a colonist."

"Get on with it," Slater said, his lips drawn into a flat line of impatience.

"I have noticed something about the colonists, but it's not about any single individual, it's everyone."

"Right, everyone," Slater repeated sarcastically.

"No, wait! Listen to me."

Slater put his hands behind his head and leaned back in his chair. "Go on, Casey. This should be good for a laugh."

"I'm serious. Our colonists consist of highly trained and motivated people, but if there is one trait that is most characteristic, it's curiosity. Curiosity about everything, but now this trait seems to be universally missing. No one has gone to the ocean, though it couldn't be more than ten kilometers away. No one has gone to the mountains. No one has even dug a hole in the ground."

"Oh my gosh, I'm so worried," Slater said dryly. "The fact is my people have been analyzing the data gathered by ship's sensors since the first day of planet-fall. They've been diligently attending to their duties, admirably so, but you, now that's another story. Talk about missing traits. You have neither insight, nor self-discipline. What would you say if a paranoid schizophrenic told you the people around him were acting strange? Or, are you finally ready to admit it's all an act?"

"No, wait," Casey said earnestly. "I've run repeated diagnostics on myself. The therapy disk has returned me to normal."

"Normal?" Slater snorted with feigned amusement and then turned his gaze to Yamaguchi. "Get this pest out of here."

Before Casey could object further, Yamaguchi all but lifted him off the deck. Casey stumbled backward to keep his balance, nearly falling as he was pushed through portal and onto the bridge.

As he shook off Yamaguchi's hands and straightened, he saw Jack Sabine on his knees. Sabine had obviously just vomited and looked up at Casey, the whites of his eyes red with hemorrhage. He said nothing, but the vomit that was clinging to his uniform could just as easily have been venom. Casey trembled as he turned away and dropped into the down-tube, followed by Yamaguchi.

They were walking down the passageway of Deck Two when Casey stopped and turned to face Yamaguchi.

"Do you think I'm insane?" Casey asked.

Yamaguchi said nothing.

"To hell with you too," Casey muttered.

"No."

"No what?"

Casey studied the opaque face that stared back at him. He took a deep breath and sighed. It was all too much. He turned away from the giant and his shoulders sagged as he walked the final steps to the medical suite. He didn't care anymore. He didn't care if he ate. He didn't want to think. He looked forward to losing himself in sleep.

CHAPTER 17

The following morning Casey awakened with a renewed sense of mission. He was eager to begin his investigation, but first needed to adjust the regeneration tank. It required an inordinate amount of fine-tuning, as if it were in need of regeneration itself. As a result, it was early afternoon before he had satisfied his obligations to the unconscious Tabor Klampor. When he stepped into the passageway he found Yamaguchi waiting for him.

"Good afternoon," Casey said cheerfully, but Yamaguchi merely stood there. "I know," Casey added, "you're saving your precious words and you haven't yet decided if it's a good afternoon or not, right?" This time Casey could see a faint smile on Yamaguchi's otherwise blank face. "Come along if you want, we have work to do."

Casey walked down the passage to the lab and Yamaguchi followed. When they entered, Casey stopped; the sight of the dismembered corpse, still lying on the floor, gave him reason to pause. The excitement dissipated, leaving only a sense of determination. He walked over to the corpse and knelt.

"Grace, did you kill yourself? And, if so, what could possibly have driven you to such an act?" He carefully replaced his friend's well-preserved bones back in the box, except for her skull, which he cradled in his hands while he peered into the empty orbits.

"Forgive me, Grace," he mumbled, and took out a standard blade to scrape away the patchy remains of scalp and hair. Then he picked up a laser-scalpel, flicked it on and cut circumferentially through the dry, brittle bone. In a moment he had cut off the top of the calvarium. He held the bowel-shaped piece of skull and looked up at Yamaguchi, somehow feeling guilty, but Yamaguchi was as impassive as ever. He placed the remains of the skull and the other body parts into the box and stiffly arose from his squat.

He slipped the skullcap into his pouch and walked over to the wall of instruments where he selected a portable surgical kit and then exited the lab. Together, they walked the curve of the passage, past the tube mouths, and entered the Deck Two hall of sleep. Rows of cryo-capsules lined both sides. It looked like a giant crystalline mouth with most of the teeth gone bad. He suppressed a chill as he thought about the hundreds of colonists who had been vaporized to a fine white dust which had fused with the inner surface of the ceramic capsules, to become one with their capsules for eternity. It was a graveyard and had the feel of a graveyard, quiet and still.

Casey reached into the surgical kit and withdrew a sonic blade as he confronted one of the milky-white, failed capsules. Another one of those odd names that haunted Casey arose. Happy Beaver. He touched the capsule with the tip of his index finger. He not only knew the living, he knew the dead as well. This capsule had contained a marine biologist named Miguel Capucho. He had curly brown hair and had been smiling widely when he had entered cryo-stasis so that the space between his two front teeth had been clearly revealed. Casey had been looking forward to meeting this youth who had displayed such cheerful optimism.

"Doctor," Yamaguchi said.

Casey returned to the present and shook the memory from his mind. The outer release had opened at the time of the Awakening, but the inner lock was still active. He began working the blade along a nearly invisible seam until there was a sucking sound, as if the capsule was sipping air, and then the door popped open. He stepped back for a moment. Despite his sophistication as a scientist and physician, he felt the primitive fear of the unnaturally dead. He suppressed the feeling and set to work on the stasis crystal at the bottom of the empty capsule. He applied the blade at varying angles until, suddenly, the crystal cracked free along a cleavage plane. He briefly inspected the iridescent block, not much larger than his thumb, and then handed it up to Yamaguchi.

"Aren't you curious, Yamaguchi?"

The big man stared back at him.

"I'll tell you this," Casey said with unexpected intensity, surprising even himself, "you'll get nothing from me until you offer something. I need communication." Casey eased down onto the deck. When he continued his voice was soft. "I'm lonely. I need a friend, someone to talk to. Have you ever heard that old ditty that goes something like:

I feel the need to touch
With my hand
With word in hand
Often without meaning
The meaning is the touch

Yamaguchi turned his head once to the left and once to the right, an unequivocal "no", but then gently placed his hand on Casey's lowered head. "When I can ask the right question, Doctor, I will ask it."

After a short time Casey regained himself, accepting, resigned to his isolation, at least for the time being. He slowly stood and walked without enthusiasm farther down the passage until he found a clear crystal capsule. With sadness, he again recognized that not many had survived on this deck. He suppressed the ache in his heart and bent to work on the capsule. In a short time, he had liberated the stasis crystal and handed it also to Yamaguchi, instructing him to keep the two separate so they could later be identified.

Casey led the way back to the tubes and entered the down-tube to exit on the storage level. With unquestioned knowledge, he retraced unremembered steps, deep into the chamber and opened a preservation locker, withdrawing a new stasis-crystal. He stripped off the firm-foam with a laser-scalpel and placed this crystal in his own pouch.

By the time Casey and Yamaguchi entered the yard, it was dusk. Casey led Yamaguchi straight to the Geo-Dome but, once he arrived at the base of the incline that ended in the doorway, he stopped. It took a minute for him to firm up his resolve. He was dreading what he sensed would be yet another hostile confrontation. He walked up the ramp and stepped firmly through the air curtain, into the brightly lit interior of the dome. Yamaguchi remained in the yard.

He stood there for a moment, searching for the white-haired Jarmo Karna within the instrument-filled dome. At the same moment he saw the chief geology-tech, who was sitting in front of a computer console, one of the techs saw Casey and nudged Jarmo. The gray eyes of Jarmo turned toward Casey.

Jarmo swiveled in his chair and stood without haste. He walked toward Casey. "What is your business?"

Casey smiled ruefully at the deadpan expression on Jarmo's face. "Is that anyway to greet a fellow pioneer?"

Jarmo's face became even paler. "I am not amused. We have work to do here, Doctor Conklin. State your business or leave."

"I'm here at Commander Slater's behest." Casey pulled the skull fragment from his waist pouch. "You are to determine the age of this artifact. That is my business and now it is yours."

He held the skullcap out toward Jarmo, but Jarmo didn't reach for it, instead he turned to one of his techs that was standing nearby. She touched her com-collar and spoke briefly into it. Casey could read the surprise in the woman's face, even before she nodded to Jarmo.

Jarmo returned his gaze to Casey. "Put it on the counter."

Casey continued holding the piece of bone in his outstretched hand. "Take it!"

Jarmo reached for the object. When he had it in his hand he inspected it and, with sudden recognition, looked up at Casey. "This looks like a piece of a skull," he said, seeking confirmation, but Casey said nothing.

Jarmo tossed the skullcap onto a counter top; it clicked a few times before it rocked to stillness.

The disrespect, all be it unknowing, broke Casey's resolve to be tolerant. Unchecked anger flared in him and boiled out of his mouth. "You pompous asshole! You hibernate in this dome twiddling your thumbs while you diddle each other and call it science. I'll tell you this; if you find my presence disruptive to your precious stagnation, then you damn well better evaluate that bone fragment, because I'm going to come back here every day until you do. Do we have an understanding?"

Jarmo appeared unaffected by Casey's tirade. "If you have nothing more to say, then I would suggest you leave."

Casey felt like slapping a response out of the man but, instead, turned and stalked out of the dome into the purple light of early evening. Yamaguchi was standing at the base of the ramp. Casey walked past him and into the yard, filled with unspent anger. When he reached the center of the yard he was no longer angry, he was only tired. He had intended to go to the Chem-Dome and have the stasis crystals analyzed as well, but he no longer had the desire. He walked slowly toward the Main Dome, the light of its doorway irresistibly drawing him toward it like a moth to a fire.

Yamaguchi joined him and spoke, "What about the crystals?"

"That can wait," Casey answered in a subdued voice.

Yamaguchi reached out and stopped him in mid-stride. "You may be able to postpone, but I cannot. For me, each day is a test. What is it that you want done with the crystals?"

Casey looked up him. Yamaguchi's face was illuminated by the oblique light spilling from the nearby doorway, revealing the shadows of creases under his eyes and across his forehead. It was a picture of silent pain. Casey reached into his pouch and handed the third crystal to Yamaguchi.

"I need molecular thin slices and a topographic analysis of each of these crystals. The chem-techs have the equipment and the know-how. Be sure each crystal is carefully marked."

Casey watched Yamaguchi as he walked off into the night; his black uniform made him seem to evaporate into the darkness. Casey turned back toward the Main Dome and walked up the ramp. He stopped just inside to survey the crowd. Small groups of colonists were scattered around the spacious interior, generally sitting at tables with others of the same color, eating, talking and laughing. Casey's sense of isolation didn't lessen; it grew.

His feet felt heavy as he walked over to the nutrition counter and picked up a tray. Usually he ate in the ship, but this night he needed to be with people, even if it was nothing more than the appearance of being with others. He saw Jon Brent, animated while he talked with Lisa Bouviet, who appeared to be studying her nails. They were both dressed in the green of an agri-tech. Casey looked down self-consciously at his whites. He kept to the perimeter of the room and moved slowly, as if he could avoid detection simply by wishing it, but one by one groups of colonists turned to watch him as he eased along. He kept his eyes directed at the floor, avoiding the malevolent stares.

Jon and Lisa looked up as Casey approached their table. Jon left his last sentence unfinished.

Casey put his tray quietly on the table and stood with his hands on the back of a chair. "Hello, Jon," he said, and nodded a greeting to Lisa.

They both sat motionless, staring up at him.

"May I join you?" Casey added.

"Actually, we were about to leave," Jon said and saw Casey

glance at their plates of partially eaten food. His face flushed as he pushed back his chair and stood, but Lisa remained seated. "Lisa," Jon said through tightly drawn lips, "it's time we get back to the testing station."

"I'll be along shortly. You go ahead," Lisa said without a sign of concern.

Jon remained standing where he was, hesitant to leave her, but unwilling to sacrifice what remained of his pride. "I'll wait for you outside," he muttered and shoved the chair against the table. He walked through the center of the dome to the exit without a backward glance.

Casey pulled out a chair and slid into it. "I hope I'm not going to cause trouble between Jon and you."

"No, not in the least. Ever since I've been assigned to his agri-unit, he's assumed that he and I belong to each other. I have to admit, at first I thought his childish adoration was cute, but lately he won't leave me alone, even for a minute. I feel smothered. This will be a good lesson for him." She took a bite of food and chewed it thoughtfully.

"Thank you, Lisa."

"For what?"

"I think you know," he said, and began eating. He ate a few bites in silence and then spoke again. "How is it that the chief com-tech is wearing green?"

She put down her spoon. "It doesn't take much figuring. Veck and Slater are two of a kind. Can you imagine that blotchy faced Veck as chief?" Her hazel-green eyes were wide with incredulity, but then her eyes narrowed and she added, "That bitch. If she thinks she can get rid of me by ostracizing me to muck around in the dirt, with Jon Brent following me wherever I go and constantly staring at me with the eyes of a sick cow, she's got another think coming." Her full lips spread in a dazzling smile, totally contrary to the content of her words.

She took a bite of protein patty and chewed as she thought. She swallowed and met Casey's eyes. "Actually, I think Slater is afraid of me. I think he's afraid of women in general." Casey said nothing, but Lisa rushed ahead to prove her point. "All you need to do is look at Veck. She's more like a skinny teen-age boy than a mature woman. Or, take a look at his so-called assistants, not a woman in the group. I bet something happened to him when he was a kid. You may not know this, but his father was Roger Slater, the man who commanded the second mission to Mars. Maybe he acts the way he does because his father brought the Death to Earth. Maybe it's some kind of a freaky guilt trip." She paused and shook her head. "Naw, that's not the Slater we've all come to know and love. Do you know anything about his mother? I seem to recall something about her committing suicide. Do you know anything about that? Something I could use against him?"

Casey was caught up in studying the smooth, youthful skin of her face and the play of her facial features while she spoke. He glanced down at the shiny skin of his hands, blemished by brown splotches, and slipped his hands beneath the edge of the table.

"Casey, are you listening to me?"

"What? Oh, yeah, sure I am."

"Well?"

"Well what?" he answered.

"Well, for one, don't you want to know how I'm going to rescue myself from the oblivion of the farm?"

She had his full attention now. "Yes, of course I do," he said.

She leaned across the table and, in a soft conspiring voice, she whispered, "I'm going to publish a colony paper." She leaned back, speaking out loud again, "Unlike Veck I consider communication a sharing of information, not a controlling of it."

"I don't want to sound like a pessimist," Casey commented, "but wouldn't such a paper interfere with Slater's grip on the community? And, if so, don't you think he'd object? And when I say object, I mean he'd let loose those black-suited mercenaries."

"I'm sure he would. That's why I have to do it in secret, at least until it gets established."

Casey raised his eyebrows. "I wish you the best of luck. But why are you telling me about your plans?"

She laughed and the fullness of it made Casey feel like laughing too.

"To be honest, Casey, I've been wanting to talk with you because...well, I wanted to ask you if, maybe, I could use the computers and printers in the medical lab. There, I've said it." Her startling green eyes with their long, dark lashes blinked, proclaiming her innocence.

"Why don't you publish over the net?" Casey suggested.

"There's plenty of paper piling up as a byproduct of recycling. No one is using it. And, besides, it's too easy to track down the source if I use the net. I need anonymity, at least to start."

Casey chuckled dryly. "I guess you thought my life couldn't get much worse. Is that it?"

She looked hurt by the accusation, pouting her lower lip.

Casey continued. "You're probably right. I'll consider your proposition."

She reached out and stroked his cheek. "Somehow, I just knew I could count on you. And, if we're careful, which we will be, no one will find out how it's being done, or who's doing it, and by then it'll be too late for anything to be done about it."

When she withdrew her fingertips from his cheek, he could feel where she had caressed him. He resisted touching the spot with his own hand.

When Casey didn't respond, Lisa continued. "Does that mean you'll do it?"

"I'll need to know more," he said.

"Of course you do. Do you have some free time tomorrow? Perhaps later in the morning?"

Casey nodded, not trusting his voice.

"I've got to go now. I'll stop by the ship tomorrow."

She smiled with evident satisfaction and stood. As she walked past Casey she trailed her fingertips across his back. Casey turned to watch her long legs carry her through the dome, now nearly empty of colonists. She had such energy and youth in her gait. He watched until she passed through the door and into the night.

He sat for a while, playing with the remains of his food, but no longer had an appetite. He pushed himself to his feet, slowly overcoming the stiffness in his knees and back; it happened whenever he sat for any length of time. Usually he ignored it, but this night he felt old, even older than he really was.

When he walked toward the door, he saw Wheeler standing in a doorway at the rear of the reconstitution area and paused. Wheeler noticed that he was being observed and stepped back through the doorway to disappear from sight.

Casey was in no mood to pursue him. Let him remain a mystery. What was real? Perhaps he too should ignore the apparent inconsistencies. Perhaps they were only apparent.

Maybe Slater was right after all. As was becoming his habit, he checked to make certain the blue disk was attached to his chest.

He walked across the dark yard toward the ramp of the ship. The ramp's surface was a soft gray, illuminated by the light-sticks that lined its edges. He trudged up the ramp, entered the Storage Deck, and walked past the land-shaper to slide into the up-tube.

He exited on Deck Two. After examining and adjusting the equipment that contained the floating body of Klampor, he entered the lab and settled onto his pallet, quickly falling into a dreamless sleep.

CHAPTER 18

The following morning Casey was jolted awake, as if his pallet had been kicked. Through blurry eyes and a foggy mind he recognized the smiling face of Padraig Glancy, dressed in medical guild white.

"I find your uniform a bit presumptuous," Casey growled.

"You may as well get used to it. I'm here to stay. You haven't forgotten your bargain with Commander Slater, have you?"

Reluctantly, Casey sat up, rubbing his eyes, and then climbed to his feet. "Wait here."

He walked to the rear of the lab and opened his preservation chest. A few moments later he returned with a parcel. He showed it at Glancy, pushing it into his stomach, but there was no give to the man's abdominal muscles.

Glancy smiled at the feeble attempt to cause him discomfort. He looked down at the object in Casey's hands.

"And what do we have here?" Glancy asked cheerfully.

"I'm not surprised you don't recognize it. It's called a book. Until it gets scanned into the computer, this is all we have. You do know how to read, don't you?"

"You sure got up on the wrong side of the bed. So cranky."

"It's an anatomy text. I brought it with me as part of my personal allotment. Study it and, when you think you know it, perfectly, then come back and we'll talk."

Glancy took the book from Casey, but remained standing as he had been.

"Are you deaf?" Casey shouted. "What do you expect me to do, read it to you? Earn those whites! I won't let you make a mockery of my profession."

Glancy stood at attention and saluted. "Aye, aye, Sir." He turned smartly, mocking Casey with each move, and marched through the portal and into the passageway.

Casey followed him out and watched him in exasperation until he was out of sight around the curve. When he turned to reenter the lab, his com-collar came to life.

"Attention, all colonists," Jane Veck said in her stilted

voice. "It has come to Commander Slater's attention that equipment is being used for unauthorized purposes. We have neither the time nor the resources for such irresponsible waste. It cannot be condoned and will not be tolerated."

When Casey heard the click-off, he immediately entered Veck's code.

"This is Veck."

"Jane, this is Casey. I had a deal with Slater. He agreed to support my efforts in my investigation. Are you telling me the deal is off?"

There was a pause, then Veck's shrill voice returned. "Not at all, Doctor Conklin. Commander Slater has given his word that he'll support any minor inconvenience, as long as you reciprocate."

"Then what was that message about?"

"You heard it. It meant nothing less or more than was stated." Veck broke off the connection.

Curious, Casey thought, but then shrugged it off. Instead of returning to the lab, he walked the passage to enter the treatment room and attend to Klampor, after which he went down to take up his morning lookout, perched at the top of the Storage Deck ramp.

He watched another sunny morning unfold. The grass was as green and lush as ever, not showing the usual wear that inevitably occurs around human habitation. He let his gaze wander about the settlement until he caught sight of a woman approaching from the perimeter. Even at that distance he recognized the voluptuous figure of Lisa Bouviet. Her presence brought to mind their conversation of the night before and a puzzle piece unexpectedly fell into place. He eased his aching bones up and, as rapidly as he could, made his way back to the medical suite.

He entered the lab and immediately released the catch on his com-collar to take it off. He felt naked without the collar. He, in fact all of them, had worn com-collars during their entire time at Copper Mountain.

He placed the collar on the counter and directed his attention to the jade-green crystal that Slater had installed in everyone's collar. He attached it to a circuit analyzer and was almost surprised to have his suspicion confirmed. It was not a passive circuit as they had been told. It was fully functional and broadcasting. This could mean only one thing; Slater could monitor any conversation or, with computer assist, all conversations. Its functionality would be difficult to prove, but it was obviously true.

While Casey was considering the implications of his discovery, he heard the portal of the lab "swish" open. He turned and saw the well-manicured beauty of Lisa Bouviet. She was about to speak, but Casey brought his index finger up to his lips, indicating silence. She seemed amused, but obediently closed her mouth and raised a questioning eyebrow. Casey motioned for her to follow him over to the console where he tapped out a message on the temporary screen.

The text on the screen read: "Slater has bugged our com-collars. Jane Veck, or one of Slater's men, is monitoring everything we say. I guess that's what Jane means when she says she's busy."

Lisa's hazel eyes opened wider and she mouthed a silent, "Are you sure?"

Casey nodded.

Lisa bent over to punch out her own message. The softness of her breast pressed against his shoulder and he breathed deeply of her body fragrance. He felt guilty and it brought heat to his cheeks. He forced himself to focus his attention on her message.

"This is perfect," it read. "It's just the leverage I've been searching for to protect myself," and then belatedly added, "and you."

She straightened and unlatched her collar. Casey was taken aback by the ease at which she was willing to expose her neck to him, but he held out his hand to receive the collar, still warm from the heat of her body. He put both their collars in a preservation chest, closed the latch, and then turned back to Lisa.

"What do you mean, this is just what you needed?" he asked.

"Up to this point, there has been no hot button issue for me to promote that would result in real support from the colonists, but once I publish the information about the com-collars, I'll get all the backing I need. In fact, I predict I'll be able to publish the paper in an ongoing fashion, with impunity." She paused as she considered, and then asked, "Are you sure about the collar?"

Casey reflected a moment, considering the consequences;

they didn't seem quite as rosy for him. "Yes, I'm sure," he finally said.

Lisa nodded. "It makes sense. Among other things, it explains that bogus general communication this morning. I stopped by the Mitchell-Friedriche farm on my way in this morning and they never even heard it. It must have been directed at a select few. You heard it, I assume?"

"I gather you're referring to the directive on the proper use of equipment."

She nodded with a smile.

"I heard it. It's what tipped me off, that and seeing you. I guess Jane must have been up late last night and heard everything we had to say."

"She already knows what I think about her," Lisa said lightly, without a hint of misgiving.

"It also means one of Slater's men will be dropping in on us at any moment. I hate to say this, Lisa, but I can't go through with it. I can't risk another beating."

She leaned toward him, pressing her breasts against his chest and kissed him on the lips. "I understand," she said.

Tears came to Casey's eyes. He tried to hide them, but Lisa turned his face back to her and wiped away the tears with soft fingertips.

Casey cleared his throat so he could speak. "Britty...I mean, Lisa, you'll support me if Slater threatens me?"

She held his face between her warm hands. "Of course I will, dear."

"Come back this evening," he said. "There's plenty of paper. You do know how to use the equipment, don't you?"

She stepped back and rewarded him with a charming smile on her beautiful face. "I can manage. Remember, I was supposed to be chief of the communication guild, that is, before Slater gave the position to Veck and sent me to the farm."

"Okay. I'll keep their attention occupied elsewhere. In the meantime, we better put our collars back on and fill Jane's big ears with a little smoke."

Lisa nodded and her lips pursed as her mind raced along, making plans.

When they had their collars in place, Casey spoke. "Lisa, welcome. I was expecting you."

"Good morning, Casey. I'm ready to get to work."

"Just a minute. Didn't you hear that communication this

morning?"

"Yes, but come on, it's only a little newspaper. What harm could that cause?"

"No way. Unless Slater approves it, I'm afraid it's just not worth the risk. He's been fair and even generous in his recent dealings with me." When Casey said that he mimed sticking his finger down to his throat, as if to gag himself.

Lisa suppressed a giggle and then put on a long face. "I'm very disappointed in you. I had expected you to have more courage. Is there anything I can do to make you reconsider?" she asked seductively.

Casey leered at her and nodded his head vigorously. It was done as a joke but, on a more honest level, it wasn't. Verbally he said, "No, I'm afraid not. My mind is made up."

"All right, Casey, but think it over. If you change your mind, you know where to find me."

With that she bowed and, with a beaming smile, passed through the portal and hurried down the passageway, nearly bumping into Sten Olson, who was approaching from the opposite direction. She excused herself and continued down the corridor to slip into the down-tube. Olson's ice-blue eyes watched her until she was gone.

As evening approached, Casey wandered out of the ship and strolled over to the Geo-Dome. He paused at the base of the ramp and tried to appear undecided, letting his gaze wander aimlessly about the compound. After a moment, his searching eyes were successful. He spotted a figure standing beside the base of the ship. From his size and the way the light lit his head, it could be none other than the bristle-haired Olson, Casey's escort for the evening.

Casey walked up the ramp and into the dome. Jarmo Karna approached him at once, his back straight and rigid.

"Good evening, Jarmo. Did you have an opportunity to complete that little job I left for you?"

Jarmo reached into a nearby drawer, retrieved the skull fragment, and handed it to Casey who slipped it into his waist pouch. Jarmo's lips were downturned and his nose was wrinkled, as if Casey was not only malodorous, but his appearance was distasteful as well.

When Jarmo spoke, his voice was tight. "Why did you bring a fossil with you if you didn't know its age? This is an outrage. An inexcusable waste of time and resources."

"What do you mean?"

"You know very well what I mean. Get out of here before I report this poor excuse for a practical joke to Commander Slater."

He turned to walk away, but Casey reached out and touched his arm. Jarmo paused and, with evident disgust, his eyes focused on Casey's face. He looked as if he was about to spit. Casey let his arm fall to his side.

"I'm not leaving until you tell me what you found," Casey said.

"Very well, if it'll make you leave. As you well know, this skull fragment is approximately two thousand years old. Our business is concluded." He presented his back to Casey and walked toward a group of techs that had been watching the exchange from the center of the dome.

Casey felt so many conflicting emotions that he was momentarily immobilized. "How certain are you? Could it be a mistake?"

Jarmo turned and shouted, "My only mistake was allowing you into the Geo-Dome! Our business is through! Get out!"

Casey stumbled out of the dome, into the cool of early evening and the quiet of wind brushing across grass. He didn't remember walking toward the Chem-Dome, but soon found himself at the entryway. "Two thousand years." The words just wouldn't digest. How was it possible? Accelerated aging?

While he was standing there, Neomi Lung exited the dome. When she saw him, she took two quick steps back.

Casey recognized her as well. "Neomi, I've come to get the micrographs you were to prepare. Are they ready?"

She nodded and, backing up, re-entered the dome. In a moment, she returned with a small packet of micrographs and a bag containing the crystals. Wordless, she handed them to Casey. As he slipped the micrographs and crystals into his pouch, he studied her: cropped, black hair; flat, broad nose; and her eyes. Her eyes were moving about as if to detect the slightest movement. He saw fear. She was actually trembling. He turned away and descended the ramp.

What could he possibly say or do that would change their feelings about him, he wondered as he approached the ship, and then remembered he had agreed to decoy Slater's attention away from the medical suite. Light was flooding out of the doorway of the Main Dome and he headed toward it, without enthusiasm. The dome was crowded with colonists, but when he walked toward the nutrition counter a space opened for him, like a bubble rising through water.

He made his way to an empty table at the rear of the dome, ignoring the muttered comments aimed at him, keeping his eyes fixed straight ahead. He sat with his back to the room and stared at the white wall that arched upward and then out of sight over his head. He let his food grow cold without touching it. He wished Yamaguchi was with him; though Yamaguchi rarely spoke, they at least exchanged ideas, at times anyway. He continued to sit and the evening crawled slowly along, until he detected a significantly lower volume of conversation. He twisted in his seat to take a look. There were only a few colonists left in the dome.

He placed his palms on the table and pushed himself to his feet. He walked by the recycling bin, dumped the untouched contents of his tray, and then walked out into the dark of the yard and searched for Sten. He didn't see him, so he continued toward the ship. He hoped he had given Lisa enough time.

The ramp and Storage Deck were empty. Few of the colonists lived on the ship anymore; most lived in personal domes scattered about in the rear area, near their primary domes, as if the domes were an affliction and spreading but, to Casey, the ship was home. Perhaps it was the many years that he had spent in it, more years in fact than he had lived on Earth.

First he checked Tabor and the regeneration unit, both were doing better. Then, although reluctant and apprehensive, he entered the lab. He was relieved when he saw that it was empty. When he glanced over at the console, he saw a sheet of hard copy. It had something written on it by hand in flowing and looping lines. He stared at it for a moment before he recognized what it was; it was cursive script, used when people used to write things out by hand, an affectation that didn't surprise him.

Casey sat in the chair near the printer and was increasingly irritated while he deciphered the message. Finally, he was able to make out the words: "Thanks, Casey. It turned out great, if I do say so myself. You get the first copy. You've been a dear." It was signed "Lisa". It had hardly been worth the effort.

He turned the paper over and in bold letters across the

top it proudly proclaimed, "EDEN GAZETTE". The text consisted of one article, an editorial and news story rolled into one. The article described how the com-collars had been converted from lifelines into spying ears and concluded with the suggestion that there was a need for freedom of communication and that privacy was an inalienable right of all, but the body of the article also contained conciliatory statements directed at Slater. The gist of it was that Slater had done a good job, and that the colony did need a strong leader but, as in all governments, some rights had to be reserved for the people who were being governed.

After he had read the sheet, he laid it down and leaned back to stare at the overhead light-lines. He was disappointed by the mild tone Lisa had taken over the outrageous invasion of privacy that Slater had perpetrated, but he could understand her motivation. She wanted to make the paper as palatable as possible for Slater. She didn't want to push him into a corner without a face saving exit. After all, he did control the mercenaries, regardless of public opinion.

Casey reviewed in his mind Slater's "fete accompli". Slater seemed to have had access to a hidden agenda, while the colonists had merely been fed a plausible agenda. The presence of the mercenaries meant that the end result would've been the same whether the tragedy of the deaths had occurred or not. It was disconcerting to think that the World Space Agency had acted in such a unilateral and underhanded fashion, but the proof was hard to ignore. The probable architect of this dictatorship was Mitchell Mason. Even though Mason was undoubtedly dead, long dead if Jarmo's dating of Grace's skull bone was accurate, his conspiracy lived on and there was little he or anyone else could do about it.

He had to learn to live with reality, as onerous as it was. He walked over to his pallet to lie down. He tried to go to sleep, but it didn't come easily. Worries about the next day swirled through his mind. He hoped Lisa had been sincere when she said she would protect him, should worse come to worse. He had been careful. Slater would never discover his involvement, he told himself.

CHAPTER 19

The following morning, after attending to Klampor, Casey rushed down to his usual spot at the top of the ramp. He'd been sitting there for only a few minutes when he saw a contingent of grim faced comp-techs marching toward the ship, their drab gray uniforms reinforcing the overall impression of grave determination. Aleksandr Protonov strode in the forefront, with his sharp, black beard pointed toward the ship like the tip of an arrow. He was carrying a rolled sheet of paper in his fist, like a club.

They took no notice of Casey as they marched up the ramp and into the ship. Casey stood as rapidly as his stiff legs would allow and followed after them. By then they had disappeared into the up-tube, but there was little doubt of their destination. Casey exited the up-tube to find the squad of comp-techs gathered around the entrance to Slater's cubicle, being confronted by the improbable hulk that was Yamaguchi.

Protonov's voice was raised in anger. "I demand to see Commander Slater and I mean now! Get out of my way, you mute gorilla!" Though Protonov was no small man in his own right, compared to Yamaguchi he was insignificant.

Protonov's normally pale complexion was fiery red. "I know you can hear me, Slater! I'm warning you, get out here, and get out here now!"

While he was still yelling, the portal opened and Slater stepped out. He walked around Yamaguchi and smiled. "Chief Protonov, what an unexpected surprise. Is there a problem?"

"Unexpected my eye! You know damn well why I'm here! You can play your silly game of innocent ignorance with the others, but don't try it with me." He shoved the rolled paper at Slater.

Apparently Slater hadn't seen a copy yet. His eyes flicked back and forth as he quickly skimmed the article. His jaw muscles bulged and his lips pressed together. Even before he had finished reading, Protonov spoke again.

"Spying and the loss of personal privacy are intolerable. It is a despicable act. In Russia, there is a strong prohibition against spying. It is strictly proscribed, criminal! It's worse than murder. It is murder!" For emphasis he detached his collar, slammed it onto the deck, and ground it under his heal until it "hissed" and "popped' and released a tendril of blue smoke from under his boot. As if that was a signal, all the comp-techs dashed their collars to the deck and crushed them so that it sounded like popcorn, and filled the room with the acrid odor of fused circuitry.

Slater's eyes were now a bit wider and shifting back and forth, searching for a response.

Protonov continued. "Don't even try to deny it. We're not gullible agri-techs. It took only a few minutes to verify that the new crystal was a broadcast unit."

Casey smiled until he felt his cheeks were being stretched out of shape.

Slater appeared ashen under the heat of Protonov's self-righteous indignation. His upper lip and forehead glistened with the sheen of perspiration. Finally, he found his voice.

"Brother Aleksandr, please come into my office so we can discuss this unfortunate misunderstanding." His voice sounded small.

"If you have anything to say, say it now," Protonov ordered.

"Certainly I have something to say," Slater said. Yamaguchi provided a still and silent backdrop to Slater's moving hands and shifting weight. "You have to understand my position. I'm sure you're aware there are dissidents among the colonists that I had to monitor. Surely you don't think I was gathering intelligence on loyal supporters such as yourself."

Casey couldn't see Protonov's face, but from his rigidly upright posture, hands planted firmly on his hips, it didn't appear that Slater's explanation had much of a salutary impact. It was pure pleasure to Casey, the most enjoyable moment he could recall since planet-fall.

"This is a warning," Protonov declared with a growl. "Your one and only warning. If we detect any further evidence of spying, you may consider the dome of the comp-techs a house of dissidents." Slater tried to speak, but Protonov brushed away the effort and continued, "This is not an empty threat. We've had to continually rebuild the computer hardware since the Awakening. If you think you can manage without your computers, then ignore this warning. Furthermore, I intend to invite colonist Bouviet to join my section. You can expect a regular publication of this paper and if you dare harass any of my people, you'll find out what computer wipe really means!"

As Slater tried to reassure Protonov, the comp-chief turned his back on him and marched with the other comp-techs to the down-tube to disappear, one by one. Casey slid farther into the recess between two cryo-capsules in the hall of sleep. This was no time to be noticed by Slater, with his anger and frustration crying out for a target.

From his hiding place Casey continued to watch. Abruptly, Slater turned to Yamaguchi, snapped a brusque order and re-entered his suite. Casey remained perfectly still, crouched in a crevice between two capsules, quieting even his breathing, but in a moment Yamaguchi was standing over him.

"Commander Slater wishes to speak with you," Yamaguchi rumbled.

"I suppose he does, but can't we delay it for a while, until he can get things into a better perspective?"

In answer Yamaguchi reached down and pulled Casey into the passageway. He began walking steadily across the bridge toward Slater's suite, effortlessly pulling Casey along.

Desperation stimulated Casey's mind. "Just a minute, I have some information that will interest you."

Yamaguchi released his grip and turned to face him.

Casey continued while he rubbed the circulation back into his arm. "We need to go to the medical suite." He started walking toward the down-tube, half-expecting to be jerked back toward Slater's office, but dropped into the tube unmolested.

When they arrived on Deck Two, Casey first inspected the regeneration tank and then, finding Klampor's condition stable, walked with Yamaguchi down the passage to the lab. He went over to the counter and with exaggerated care picked up each micrograph in turn, held it carefully between his index finger and thumb, and then carefully replaced it on the counter. He glanced over at Yamaguchi, who stood stolidly by the portal, unimpressed by his theatrics. He shrugged, picked up the micrographs again and tossed them on the work counter next to the stereo-magnifier. He slid the first micrograph into place and the molecular field jumped onto the screen.

Casey could make no sense of it. In a way Slater had been right. He had not spent all those years idly awaiting midpoint, but he had not studied computers; he had studied cryo-stasis.

The matrix of the crystal was in such disarray that at first he was unable to get his bearings. Then he recognized what had happened; the heavy metal molecules had migrated out of the crystal lattice in an apparently random fashion. He slipped in a second micrograph, and then one after another, until he had studied them all.

He rubbed his eyes and then sat back while he considered the implications. All the crystals showed the same deterioration. The wonder was that any of the crew had survived. Even that short hop from orbit had been extremely risky. He shuddered as he thought once again about the dead colonists. It had all been a matter of chance; if the random distortion of the crystal allowed a short circuit through the lattice, then they were exposed to the unfiltered energy of the star engine, vaporizing in a flash.

Casey considered what he knew about the crystals. No such changes had been detected during the years of testing. There had not even been a suggestion of such entropy. Perhaps they hadn't been tested long enough. Perhaps if they had been tested, say for a few thousand years.... Casey felt cold. Jarmo had not been wrong. He sat silent and still, until he had stretched even Yamaguchi's patience. Yamaguchi walked over and touched his shoulder.

Casey felt weary, tired of trying to put the pieces together. Yamaguchi nudged him again, this time with more force.

"Okay, okay...I hesitate to tell you what I think. It seems so unbelievable, even to me."

"What is real?" Yamaguchi asked.

"What indeed?" Casey mused. "I have two pieces of information that both say the same thing. The evidence indicates that we have not been in stasis for a hundred years, but rather, for *thousands* of years. I am convinced this is reality and, if so, how did we arrive at our destination?"

"At whose destination?" Yamaguchi asked.

Casey looked up and met the man's obsidian eyes, opaque to interpretation.

"I don't know what you're suggesting," Casey said, "but if you're implying that the World Space Agency selected a new destination, many more light years from Earth, I cannot agree. That's so improbable, it's impossible. Maybe we arrived on time and then remained in orbit for thousands of years but, if that's the case, then how did we finally awaken and why weren't there additional expeditions from Earth? I just don't know. What do you think?"

Yamaguchi took hold of Casey's arm, more gently this time. "Come. It's time for your meeting with Commander Slater."

"A minute please. I need you to contact Lisa Bouviet. I don't think Veck will let me do it. It's important. Please."

Yamaguchi touched his collar. "Veck, this is Yamaguchi. Connect me with Lisa Bouviet."

Casey couldn't hear the directed response of Yamaguchi's collar.

"Yes, I have him," Yamaguchi said and, after a brief pause, "I will bring him now." He turned his attention to Casey. "Lisa Bouviet's collar is off line."

"She's probably at the Comp-Dome, right across the yard. It would only take a moment."

"I am to take you to Slater's office now."

"But, Lisa said she would help if I got into trouble because of her gazette."

"Lisa Bouviet?"

Casey sighed. How stupid.

"Now."

Casey nodded, resigned. Yamaguchi assisted him to his feet and Casey shuffled along beside him. There was no way this was going to be pleasant.

When they arrived at Slater's office, the portal swished open and revealed Slater, who was sitting at his desk. He looked up. "Come in, Casey," he said softly.

Visions of being caught in a web sprang into Casey's mind. For a moment, he seemed to remember being attacked by a big black spider, but then the memory was gone.

It was impossible to ignore Jack Sabine who was leaning against the bulkhead. Sabine's smile revealed canines that looked too long and too sharp. He was a predator and couldn't have appeared more eager to get his hands on Casey than if he had actually been licking and smacking his lips.

"Sit down, Casey," Slater said.

"I'd rather stand."

"Sit down!" Slater ordered.

Sabine pushed away from the bulkhead.

"All right," Casey said, and sat in the chair, but did not lean back.

Slater folded his hands and rested them on his desktop.

He began with quiet, well-spaced words. "I've encountered a serious problem today and I know you're the cause. You and a certain nymphomaniac named Lisa Bouviet. You know what I'm talking about, don't you?"

"I'm sorry, Commander Slater," Casey replied respectfully. "I'm afraid I don't know what you mean."

Without warning Casey was slugged on the side of his head. It made tears come to his eyes and caused a burning pain to spread across that side of his face. His hearing in that ear was replaced by a high-pitched ringing. He pulled his head down between his shoulders and looked in the direction the blow had come from, into the smiling face of Jack Sabine.

Slater continued in a steady tone. "I thought you were smarter than that. You behaved yourself quite well after we had that brief discussion in orbit, at least for a while. Did you forget?"

Casey began to shake his head, but was overcome by waves of nausea. He was instantly soaking with sweat. He touched his fingers to his injured ear and came away with blood.

"Some people need to be reminded from time to time. I guess you're one of those people. The next time you consider doing something that you think I might disapprove of, take a moment and remember and, Casey, don't ever remove your collar again."

"Please, Commander Slater. I didn't take off my collar. I didn't do anything. I wasn't even in the ship. You can ask Mister Olsen. Please, ask him."

Slater nodded to Sabine.

"I'm telling the truth!" Casey yelled.

Sabine pulled on Casey's left arm until it was fully extended. Casey tried to pull away, but Sabine was too strong, wiry strong. Casey watched speechless with horror as Sabine pried out his thumb and pulled it back until it snapped audibly and protruded at a queer angle from his hand.

Casey heard himself beg, he was willing to do anything, to offer anything, but Slater only smiled, and nodded to Sabine again. One by one, Sabine broke the fingers on Casey's left hand.

Casey screamed. There was unbearable pain and then it became something else. The color faded from his vision and then his field of vision shrank, until it was a tunnel with Sabine's face at the other end, and then there was nothing.

Slater motioned with a flick of his hand for Yamaguchi to remove Casey from his cubicle. Yamaguchi gathered up the limp form and carried him down to the medical suite, where he placed him with care on his sleeping pallet.

When Casey awakened, he was alone. He had a pounding headache and throbbing pain in his hand. The light seemed painfully bright, but he managed to produce an analgesic disk out of the synthesizer. He waited for pain relief before raising his head to inspect his hand; it was a swollen ball of flesh, purple with bruising. His fingers extended oddly from his hand, like crooked sticks. He was exhausted.

He reflected about himself as a person and judged himself lacking. He found cowardice. He remembered begging, pleading with Slater, offering his soul, surrendering every shred of pride. He hated Slater, but underlying that hate was fear, fear that Slater would inflict still more pain.

CHAPTER 20

It was four days before the swelling had subsided to the point that he could reduce the dislocations and fractures. He anesthetized his hand by using a depolarizing ring around his forearm and, after aligning the bones, immobilized his hand in a glove of firm-foam.

The pain persisted, but gradually required less potent analgesic disks. He learned how to manage his daily needs with one hand, rather than commit himself to a day of unconsciousness in the speed-healer; there was no one he could trust to watch over him.

For the next two weeks Casey stayed in or near the medical suite, not feeling well enough about himself to face others. He didn't believe he'd be able to tolerate their anger. His only contact with the outside was his copy of the "Eden Gazette", surreptitiously left outside his portal each morning.

The day he finally ventured out was a special day. He had read about it in the "Gazette". The bio-techs had succeeded in reviving the first of the animal species to join humanity on the new world. It was appropriate that mankind's oldest friend in the animal kingdom would be the first. The occasion was Dog Day. Casey had read that two breeds were to be presented, the Miniature Schnauzer and the German Shepherd.

When he entered the Storage Deck, he paused to look around and was relieved to find that no one else was there. He approached the sunlit doorway of the ramp with care and stopped just inside, using the edge of the doorway to partially conceal himself.

The Bio-Dome was just to the right of the main bubble and that morning it was the center of activity. A large crowd of colonists milled about, a rainbow of jumpsuits, representing all branches of the colony. The loud conversation and laughter carried easily to Casey's hiding place and reinforced the festive atmosphere of that bright, sunny morning. He felt a strong desire to be with them, to be one of them, but he was beginning to believe that would never happen. His gaze dropped to the gray of the ramp as he thought bitterly about what he had given up for these youngsters and what they had given him in return.

Casey looked up as a cheer arose. A figure dressed in the chocolate-brown of a bio-tech appeared in the entryway of the dome, holding a furry, squirming bundle under each arm. Above the buzz of the crowd, Casey could hear the high-pitched yelp of a puppy. The bio-tech carefully held his precious bundles aloft, one light gray and the other with tan legs and a dark face. The crowd responded enthusiastically, cheering and clapping.

Casey turned away from the joyous scene. He could no longer tolerate watching without being a part of it. He retraced his steps back to the medical suite. When he entered the lab, he stopped. There stood Padraig Glancy, smiling and leaning nonchalantly against the work counter, book in hand.

"Doctor Conklin, how nice of you to join me this fine morning," he said cheerfully.

"What do you want?" Casey replied gruffly.

"Your star protégé has returned to learn at the master's side."

"We'll see about that."

Casey tested Glancy's depth of knowledge and understanding and had to admit that the man had done a respectable job of learning the material in an astonishingly short period of time. Despite himself, Casey became interested in the prospect of training Glancy. The rest of the morning passed quickly and, when Glancy tipped his hand in a mock salute as he left, Casey was unable to muster any honest irritation. He might even have allowed a smile to escape.

As the day wore on, Casey received a second unexpected visitor. Having just finished a meal, prepared on his small reconstitutor, he was sitting on his pallet when he heard the swish of his portal and glanced up to see Yamaguchi.

"Hello, friend, and I do use the term loosely," Casey said.

In answer, Yamaguchi reached into his pouch and withdrew a ball of active gray fur. He held the frisky puppy out toward Casey.

Casey looked into the Yamaguchi's still unreadable face, although it was now marked with easily visible lines, and tried to get a sense of the man. A man who would stand by and watch another be tortured without interference and, yet, a man who could see Casey's desperate need for companionship and respond to it. It didn't make any sense.

Casey reached out with his good hand to take the puppy and hold it against his chest. At first it tried to wriggle free, but then it curled up against his body heat and became still.

"Thank you," Casey said. "I—" His voice caught, filled with unexpressed emotion. It seemed to Casey that he saw a hint of a smile on Yamaguchi's face before he turned to leave. Casey looked down at the puppy nestled in his lap and began stroking the soft fur.

CHAPTER 21

The next week was one of healing for Casey; he began to recover from both the mental and physical trauma. The mornings were spent with his pupil, who was proving himself to be especially adept. The afternoons were spent in mindless relaxation as the puppy and he forged a bond of mutual affection. Casey named his dog Marta, after his mentor back on Earth, Doctor Marta Barken. He didn't think she would've minded, if she were here, instead of back on Earth and long dead. Casey sighed. Britty and Doctor Marten. He wished they were with him now. He thought about them while he stroked the luxurious fur of the puppy.

By the end of the week he had begun to once again venture into the community, but it was on an impulse that he decided to take his evening meal with the others in the Main Dome. He carried his puppy in his pouch until he arrived at the Storage Deck and then put her down. She ran around in circles, a fuzzy ball of energy. Marta followed Casey as far as the light-stick lit ramp and ran back and forth across the opening, but she would go no farther. It was with some reluctance that Casey continued across the yard, hearing Marta barking out her objection at being left behind, but he decided that it was just as well the dog didn't accompany him; he expected it to be crowded in the dome.

While he walked, he thought about the difficulty he was having enticing Marta out of the ship. When he set her on the ground she would shiver and shake, her eyes turned upward in supplication while her ears and tail drooped. The thought slipped from his mind as he walked up the ramp of the Main Dome and was met by two orange-suited mech-techs. When they saw him, they stopped talking, moved as far to the side as possible, and then walked past without speaking. Casey scowled at their backs and pushed ahead, through the air curtain and into the interior.

The dome was noisy with loud conversation and boisterous laughter. Casey almost turned around and left, but then decided he was through running. He forced himself to pick up his meal and walked the perimeter of the dome without drawing much attention. He found a small, empty table at the rear of the dome and sat with his back to the wall, so he could watch the colonists enjoying themselves and imagine he was one of them. It was a difficult fantasy to maintain; soon after he took his place, the colonists sitting at the tables around him began to pick up their trays and move away. It was not long until he found himself sitting alone, amidst empty chairs and tables in an otherwise crowded room. There were a few dogs present, but Casey was glad he had left Marta behind.

The colors appeared to be mixing more and it seemed to Casey that there was a lot of hugging and even less subtle sexual activity. He spotted the yellow-blond hair of Lisa Bouviet and next to her the unmistakable profile of Aleksandr Protonov, both in comp-tech gray. They were leaning heavily on one another. He was offended and amazed when he saw Protonov reach inside Lisa's jumper and fondle her breasts, in plain view of the others at the table who were laughing uproariously.

Casey was disgusted by such immodest behavior. He was outraged that Lisa would allow such an obvious sexual advance in public and, even though he couldn't admit it, he was jealous as well. He stared at them and saw Lisa was touching Protonov under the table. He couldn't bear to watch, but as he looked around the room, he saw that Lisa and Protonov were not alone in their outrageous behavior.

Fewer women than men had survived what had become known as the Death Sleep, so many of the women had more than one male competing for their attention. They were all so young, so virile, and so undisciplined, that it made Casey feel sick. It's possible he might have felt differently if he could've joined them, but there was little chance of that.

Without thinking, he suddenly stood, knocking his chair over, and then threw his tray on the floor so that it clattered loudly. Like a ripple across a pond, most of the less deeply involved colonists turned to see what had happened. The room became noticeably quieter while Casey walked through the middle of the dome, his anger and disdain evident on his face.

Perhaps to demonstrate their manliness, a group of male colonists formed a semi-circle in front of Casey's path. They stood there breathing deeply, with wild energy in their eyes. Casey could see they were only posturing for the females, but he could also see it was to be at his expense.

A small man with black, curly hair and deep brown eyes was the first to speak. He was dressed in the yellow of a chem-tech. Casey knew his name, Giuseppe Marciano. He knew them all.

"You are scum," Giuseppe began. "You killed our friends and got away with it and you wiped our computers and got away with it. It's time you pay the price. Commander Slater has been protecting you, but I'm not afraid of Slater."

"Me either," said another in a loud voice and stepped forward.

By this time the entire room was watching, some colonists standing on tables to get a better view, and the young men knew it.

Another man, not to be outdone, stepped forward. "You're not welcome here. Murderer!" he yelled.

The others took up the word. "Murderer, Murderer, Murderer!"

None of the young males wanted to be excluded, each elbowing the other aside to become more visible.

Casey began to back up but discovered he was completely surrounded. He turned in a circle. There wasn't enough air! He couldn't breathe! An agri-tech spat at him; the viscous glob landed on his cheek and ran slowly down to his chin. Casey was shocked. It was Jon Brent, with hate in his eyes.

They began pelting Casey with food, throwing it as hard as they could, from no more than an arm's length away, and then cheering each other on. Casey brought up his uninjured hand to protect his face. He backed up against a body and was shoved violently forward, coming up hard against a well-muscled lad in the maroon of the humanities. The man put his fingers under Casey's jaw and with painful pressure lifted Casey's face, held it there for a grinning moment, and smashed his fist into Casey's mouth, sending him sprawling onto his back.

Casey was dazed, not sure which way was up. The metallic taste of blood was flooding his mouth. He heard the hooting and yelling, but couldn't make out any of the words. He tried desperately to get to his feet, but couldn't find his balance and fell back to the floor. He didn't see his assailant jerked aside and was confused as to his whereabouts when Yamaguchi lifted him off the garbage-strewn floor.

Yamaguchi carried him back into the ship without interference and laid him on his pallet in the medical lab. Casey was awake, but dull-witted. His puppy whined and licked his face, but he only responded with a dazed look. After a short while, he fell into a fitful sleep interrupted by unconscious moaning.

CHAPTER 22

When Casey awakened the next morning, he was groggy. He lay there for a moment, aware of a bundle of warmth curled up against his side. Slowly, his mind pieced together the fragmentary memory of the night before until it had meaning.

He tried to turn over and his puppy hopped out of the way, but his entire body was stiff and he slumped back against the pallet. It was not long after that Casey heard his portal open. He tried to move, as if he were one inflexible piece, cringing within, fearful of yet another attack, but relaxed when he heard Glancy's voice.

"Top of the morning to you, Doctor. Heard you were out brawling again last night. Looks like you came up a bit short," he said, laughing.

Glancy took a firm hold on Casey and without hesitation pulled him to a sitting position, causing Casey to gasp in pain. A reddish tint passed across Casey's vision.

"Sorry about that," Glancy said in an airy way.

When Casey's vision cleared, he responded, mumbling through thick lips. "Glancy, I have no doubt you'll become a doctor of considerable skill, but you lack an important attribute and I doubt that I can teach it to you."

"Oh, yeah? What's that?" Glancy asked without real concern.

Casey thought about himself and the young man standing over him. Perhaps even Glancy's attitude will add to his proficiency. He'd known a few doctors who lacked the ability to feel for others and, in ways, they were superior; they were able to act with aggressive precision, unencumbered by compassion. In the end it was results that people valued, not attitudes. It was a disquieting thought.

"Get me the molecular synthesizer," Casey ordered in a flat voice.

Glancy looked at him blankly.

"The cube on the counter by the portal," Casey elaborated with exasperation.

Glancy leisurely walked over, picked it up, inspected it,

and finally placed it on the deck next to Casey's pallet.

"You asshole," Casey muttered under his breath. He entered the code for an analgesic disk. At this rate, he thought, it would make sense for him to carry a batch of them in his pouch, ready at a moment's notice for his next beating. The blackness of the thought struck him as humorous and he smiled. Shortly, his pain began to wane and, although still stiff, he was able to move.

Glancy watched Casey with curiosity as he struggled to his feet, without attempting to help the aging physician, and then spoke. "When are you going to teach me the real secrets, or are you afraid once I learn the instrumentation, you'll no longer be of value?"

Casey studied the young man, who for once was not smiling and apparently earnest.

"I'm not afraid of that," Casey said. "The truth is it'll be a relief to have someone else take on the responsibility of being the colony's doctor. I don't belong here and I'm more ready with each passing day to accept whatever fate is in store for me. But, know this; if you're to be the embodiment of my profession, you can damn well be sure you'll be the best I can make you. I will withhold nothing. You'll become a first class physician, or nothing. Is that understood?"

The brightness and smile returned to Glancy's face. The moment had passed. "Sure, Doctor Conklin, sure. I was just wondering. That's all."

Casey sighed and hobbled into the personal room to inspect his latest damage in the mirrored bulkhead. His lower lip was worse than his upper. It looked like a tight, purple sausage, but at least it hadn't burst. He gingerly pulled his lip down and noted a number of small lacerations on the inside. He decided that his injuries appeared worse than they actually were.

While Casey was inspecting his wounds, he heard Glancy talking with someone in the outer room. It sounded like a woman's voice. Although Casey realized it was simple vanity and ridiculous, he didn't want another person to see his distorted and discolored face.

Glancy called out, "Conklin, you've got a visitor."

There was little Casey could do. He couldn't hide in the personal room. He held his foam-gloved hand in front of his mouth and bent his head forward when he entered the main cubicle. It was Lisa Bouviet, of all people.

She was wearing a forest-green scarf, which lifted her hair off her shoulders, fully exposing her naked neck. Despite his self-discipline, Casey was aroused to see the smooth whiteness of her brazenly exposed flesh. It seemed indecent for her not to be wearing a collar. In his experience, about the only time a person took off their collar was when they made love. His face flushed and he averted his eyes.

"Casey," she said, "I heard what happened. I'm so sorry. Aleksandr and I left when the commotion started. Did you get hurt badly?"

"No," Casey mumbled through his hand. "I'm okay."

"That's good," she said. "If you're feeling okay, then maybe you could help me out with a small favor, if you have the time."

Casey was amazed at the unabashed gall of the woman. How could she possibly even use those words with him?

Glancy interrupted Casey's as yet unexpressed outrage. "I can see you two have a lot to talk about, so I'll be going now." He saluted Casey and bowed deeply to Lisa.

She rewarded him with an appreciative giggle, and then he departed. Casey sighed as he soaked in her beauty and his anger ebbed.

"That's a pretty scarf," he said. "Did you bring it as part of your personal allotment?"

She smiled. "No, it's a gift, just a gift. Aleksandr gave it to me. I'll sure be glad when the mech-techs finish their repairs on the manufacturing units so we can get some decent clothes, and furniture, and all those other things that make life worth living. Don't you agree?"

Casey didn't respond, but Lisa continued as if he had. "We would have those things already if it hadn't been for the comp-wipe." She stopped, realizing what she had said, the pause plainly placing the blame on Casey.

Instead of trying to defend himself, he changed the subject.

"So, Lisa, what can I do for you?"

"Well, you see, I brought an antique camera from Earth and it seems to work just fine inside the domes, but when I take pictures outside they turn out dark and hazy. I tried to take a picture of our beautiful mountains and the picture came out black. It was the oddest thing. When I first saw the pictures of Aleksandr and me inside the dome, we looked like a couple of ragamuffins. It was hilarious. But, when I looked closer, we looked like I expected us to. The outside pictures were just black. I didn't even try to make out anything."

Casey stood a little straighter, his curiosity pricked. "Do you have the same problems with the electronic videos?"

"No, of course not, silly, but I think the old-fashioned camera somehow allows a better expression of a person's inner feelings. I find it a more creative medium. At any rate, the comp-techs are so busy trying to restructure the computer memories and assisting the other guilds in maintaining their hardware, that well...I know you have a great deal of experience with instrumentation and I thought maybe, in your spare time, you might take a look at my camera."

That seemed like a safe enough favor. "Sure, I'd be happy to, but are you sure it isn't just a problem with the film block?"

"I'm sure. I had them transported in my preservation locker and besides, if it works indoors, there is no reason it shouldn't work outdoors. It's got to be the camera."

She handed the small rectangular box to Casey, black on all sides except for a gray front. She showed him how to load the film blocks. When she leaned close to him, he could smell the sweetness of her. He stole a glance at her exposed neck and, in his distraction, his hand drifted away from in front of his mouth. A crease appeared between her eyebrows and she drew back. He immediately covered his swollen lips and tried to draw her attention away from himself.

"You sure look full of health and energy today," he said, when he really wanted to tell her how incredibly beautiful she was.

Her smile returned and the crease vanished. Her cheeks flushed a light pink, making her even more appealing.

"I haven't told anyone yet, except of course Aleksandr, but I'm pregnant."

Casey sat heavily onto his console chair and his hand fell into his lap. This time he let it lay there. "Pregnant? Do you want me to confirm it?"

"No, that's not necessary. I'm sure. Isn't it wonderful?"

Casey's voice was devoid of emotion. "Yes, wonderful," and then he added, "Congratulations." Inside he felt a secret, impossible fantasy die. The door of time was shut and could not be opened.

"Thank you. I'm so excited! Well, I still have much to do to get the next issue of the 'Gazette' ready. I must be off." She turned to leave.

"Lisa."

She turned back to face him.

"I have a favor to ask of you," he said.

"Oh?"

"I've discovered important information about ship's failure. I have definite proof that over two thousand years have passed since we left Earth."

"Amazing," she said lightly.

"I'm serious. I had the skull of Grace N'duforchu, you know the guardian found dead on the bridge, dated by the geo-techs and I studied micrograph slides of the stasis crystals. There was a molecular drift consistent with great age."

"Have you told Commander Slater?" she asked.

"I can't get him to listen to me."

"I see." She paused. "Sounds like an interesting story. Believe me, I truly would like to help, but I really think you should discuss this with Commander Slater first."

"Lisa, please listen to me. This is vitally important information for the welfare of the colony. Vital! Something really bad has happened."

She looked uncomfortably at Casey's com-collar. It was so much a part of him, he had forgotten all about it.

"We'll talk about it again," she said softly, with perhaps the first genuine sympathy she had shown, and then turned away and passed through the portal.

Casey sat without moving, until Marta pushed her nose against his hand to get his attention. He picked up the puppy, feeling her fat, warm tummy, and held her in his lap. He scratched her behind her ears and she looked up with big, brown eyes, filled with affection.

Gradually, Casey managed to attain a state of bearable depression and examined Lisa's photographs. One showed Protonov smiling and leaning back in his console chair, and another showed Protonov with his arms around Lisa's waist as they stared into each other's eyes with mutual adoration. *So this is art.* Casey smiled. It looked more like a family album.

Next he picked up one of the outside photos. It showed a grayish haze with barely discernible figures in the foreground, probably Protonov and Lisa, and behind the figures a blank blackness. Strange. A device that works indoors, but not outdoors. His mind wandered as he thought about the enigma.

He stood and walked over to lean against the work counter. Old memories came unbidden to his mind. The love he'd left behind. Like Lisa, but so different. He could only remember tantalizing morsels, the shape of her face, her smile, her laugh. Why had he ever left her? If only he could've seen the future, how empty and lonely it'd be. His heart sagged with grief. Another impossibility. Gone forever. He thought for a moment. She was twenty-six the last time he'd seen her, plus the hundred years of the voyage, would make her one-hundred and twenty-six. A new wave of sadness passed through him. She was dead of old age. Then his thinking took an unexpected leap. Two thousand years. Two thousand years had passed. She had turned to dust and he was the only one in the universe who knew she had ever existed. His legs felt weak. He managed to make it to his pallet and collapsed onto it. He held his face in his good hand and tears dripped from between his fingers.

He sat throughout the rest of the afternoon, finally rousing himself to meet his responsibilities to Klampor. The following day he would begin rescue from the regeneration tank. It would require all of his attention and expertise. He was looking forward to it, a useful task, a valuable service. After seeing to his puppy's needs and cleaning up her messes, he curled up on the pallet in the lab and, with the analgesic disks disguising his pain, found sleep, with his puppy at his side.

CHAPTER 23

Casey awakened early. He felt improved. His lips were considerably less swollen and his body less sore in general. He evaporated the firm-foam cast and worked some of the stiffness out of his hand. He would need both his hands today. When Glancy arrived he was ready.

"Good morning, Doctor Liver-Lips," Glancy said and laughed, always appreciative of himself.

Casey ignored his disrespect. "Contact Slater. For the next week I want all of your time. I want you to be in constant attendance while I perform the rescue of Klampor from the regenerator."

Glancy slowly shook his head. "I don't know. Commander Slater usually—"

"Perhaps I didn't make myself clear. It's not a request. It's an order."

Glancy shrugged and punched in Slater's code. After a brief, whispered exchange, he turned back to Casey. "You've got it. I'm fully at your disposal, Chief Medical Officer Conklin."

"Good. Your first duty is to clean up Marta's mess over there in the corner," Casey said with a satisfied smile.

"Now just a minute!" Glancy began, but then managed to find the humor in it and chuckled along with Casey. "You are the chief of shit and those of us who serve, salute you."

After Glancy had carried out his lesser duty, the two of them adjourned to the treatment room. For the next week Tabor Klampor was never alone. Gradually the metabolic boosters, circulatory assist, and extracorporeal respirator, were withdrawn. Meanwhile, in a controlled, step-by-step process, Klampor's metabolism was returned to the control of his intrinsic autonomic and endocrine systems. It required finesse, but went smoothly. By the end of the week the rescue had been accomplished and Tabor Klampor was once again an individually functioning organism, merely sedated.

The following day, the sedation was reversed. Tabor awakened disoriented and Casey had to restrain him while he screamed and tried to escape the burning current that was his last coherent memory. As his awareness returned to the present, he recognized that he was in a medical unit. The fear began to subside when he recognized the white jumpsuits of the two doctors who were bending over him. He gained a modicum of trust and listened to their words, which began to take on meaning.

"Tabor," Casey had been repeating, "you're all right. You're safe. You're with friends."

Tabor's eyes became focused. He was beginning to understand.

"Tabor," Casey continued, "you've had a serious accident, but now you've fully recovered. You're on the new planet, Eden."

"How is Erik?" Tabor asked as he raised himself up on his elbows.

"I'm sorry," Casey replied, "we weren't able to save Erik."

Tabor slumped back onto the recovery table as he digested the shock of his friend's death. It was some time before he spoke again. "What happened, Doctor?"

"We're not really sure," Casey answered. "I know it's painful for you but, if you're able, I'd like you to tell us what you remember."

Tabor closed his eyes and clenched his teeth as he relived those moments of terror. Although he kept his eyes shut he began to speak. "Erik and I had just completed the final inspection of the transformer and we were walking back toward the crowd that was watching. I remember I was excited, in a hurry to witness the first dome solidify, and was ahead of Erik when I heard a sputtering and crackling. I turned and saw Erik was already running back toward the transformer, to shut it down. I started running after him."

Tabor stopped and swallowed. When he began again, his voice was shaky. "Erik was probably twenty meters ahead of me when suddenly he jerked upward, as if he'd run into something, and then fell to the grass. I could smell ozone and singed hair. I ran...and then, I don't know. It was as if my legs were being pierced by red hot wires." He shook his head. "I can't remember anything more." After a few minutes his breathing quieted.

"Did you see an arc?" Casey asked.

Tabor reflected for a moment before answering. "No...there was no arc. It was as if Erik and I had run into a conducting pool, filled with energy leaking out of the transformer, but that's impossible. We were wearing insulator sandals." He paused. "It's as if we were ankle deep, but I distinctly remember the ground was dry." He looked, questioning and confused at Casey.

Casey just shook his head. "That's enough, Tabor. I've contacted Mika Ishida and informed her that you would be rejoining them today. He handed Tabor the red suit of a power-tech. "Why don't you put this on. Mister Glancy and I will try to bring you up to date. You've had quite a sleep."

While Casey spoke, his little dog dutifully sat in Tabor's lap and allowed herself to be petted and pampered. When Casey judged Tabor had stabilized mentally as well as physically, he asked Tabor if he thought he was ready to rejoin his section.

"Yes," Tabor answered, hesitantly, "I think so. Will you be coming with me?"

"I think it is better if Mister Glancy accompanies you," Casey said.

There was a sudden look of recognition on Tabor's face. "Aren't you the doctor who murdered Mitch Klaus?"

Although Casey still couldn't remember the events of that day clearly, he was convinced that he had indeed killed an innocent man. He bent his head in shame and in a nearly inaudible voice said, "Yes, that was me." Then he looked up, straight into Tabor's eyes, and rushed on, "but you have to understand. I didn't know what I was doing." Casey's gaze drifted back to the deck. Marta jumped down from Tabor's lap and put her paws on Casey's legs, looking upward at his downturned face.

Glancy assisted Tabor to his feet. When Casey heard the "swish" of the portal, he sat down on a stool. Tabor had not thanked Casey for saving his life, but Casey hadn't really expected gratitude. He had merely been fulfilling his function; it was what others expected of him and what he expected of himself.

He slowly straightened out his stiff knees and sore back in order to stand. Holding onto the recovery table edge, he scooped up his little dog and left the medical suite. He went down to his favorite place, the top of the storage bay ramp. While he stood there, Marta jumped at his motionless feet and played with him, even though his attention was directed elsewhere.

It wasn't long before he spotted Glancy's white jumpsuit as he walked across the grassy yard toward the ship. There should be dogs running around out there, he thought. But, there were only colonists. The grass was as pristine as the first day he'd seen it. There were no trampled areas or paths between the domes. From appearances, it looked like the domes had sprouted straight from the ground and humanity had yet to arrive and leave the inevitable trail of their daily activities.

When Glancy arrived at the top of the ramp, he turned with Casey to survey the colony. Then he looked upward, toward the mid-afternoon sun, set in a blue sky with its usual clumps of cumuli. Casey looked closely at his handsome protégé's face and noted that his pupils were large and black. Strange, thought Casey, but nearly before the thought was fully formed, Glancy's pupils were small. It wasn't as if they had constricted, first they were big, and then they weren't.

"Padrig, why do you think the grass stays so green when there is never any rain?"

Glancy gave Casey a double take before he responded. "What do I look like? Like I'm wearing agri-green or something? I'm a medical man, if you haven't noticed."

"Not yet, you aren't," Casey responded, and then walked back into the ship.

Glancy scowled as he watched the older man hobble stiff-legged toward the up-tube and flipped an obscene hand gesture at his retreating back.

CHAPTER 24

The next morning Glancy failed to appear at his usual time, which suited Casey just fine. It was the first day he could recall since awakening that he felt reasonably well and had no pressing responsibilities. He decided to make a holiday out of it.

He packed a lunch and put his puppy in his waist pouch. He was going to see the ocean and explore the seashore. When he walked out of the camp of clustered domes, he was excited and energetic. He felt younger.

He had covered no more than a kilometer, when he saw the unmistakable bulk of Yamaguchi standing ahead of him, waiting. The nearer Casey got, the more obvious were the changes in the normally stoic figure; his head was bowed slightly and he looked out of the top of his eyes at Casey, like a bull about to charge. Yamaguchi's hands were not still; he was rubbing them constantly on his thighs.

Casey stopped well out of reach, not trusting to the man's history of equanimity. Yamaguchi frightened him as much as any man he had ever seen. It seemed at any moment Yamaguchi was going to lose control and not be able to regain it again. The two men stood facing one another.

"Good morning, Yamaguchi. I was just on my way to visit the seashore. Would you care to join me?"

Yamaguchi's eyes flicked shut for a moment and then back open. It looked to Casey like he hadn't even heard him, almost as if he were barely aware that Casey was there at all. Then he spoke, causing Casey to jump.

"Go back."

Against Casey's better judgment, he decided to object. "This is ridiculous. Let's reason this out. We've been on this planet for months and no one has been more than five kilometers from the ship. You said your primary duty was to observe and question. How can you expect to do that if you keep your back turned to the world around you?"

Yamaguchi's dark eyes came to bear on him and, when the giant stepped forward, his face seemed to bulge with insipient violence. Casey backed up, but Yamaguchi continued to advance and started to reach out.

Casey bolted. Panic pulsed unchecked. His arms and legs moved of their own accord, carrying him as fast as possible toward the safety of the ship. He didn't stop to look back until he slumped breathless, at the base of the ramp that led to the storage bay. He huffed through a raw and dry throat until it seemed he would never recover. His eyes, blurry with sweat, searched the camp yard. It was a relief that he did not see Yamaguchi.

Gradually, he became aware of the puppy, squirming around in the pouch, and then heard her "yelp", complaining about the rough treatment. He reached in and gently placed the dog on the ground, but she just stood there stiff legged. She looked dolefully up at Casey, ears drooping. After a moment Casey reached down and picked her up. The puppy was shivering. He held her against his chest until, with fits and stops, the shaking subsided. He peered into the puppy's fuzzy, little face and spoke to the dog.

"Things are not as they appear, are they, Marta? You know it and I know it. What is the key?"

Marta looked back at Casey, as if she was trying her best to understand and quizzically tipped her head to the side.

Casey was frustrated and angry. He glanced across the yard at the Main Dome. Instead of going up the ramp and into the ship, he turned and walked with determination in his gait, directly toward the Main Dome, a place he hadn't the nerve to visit since his beating, until now.

Not this time, Casey thought, not this time.

Although not fully recovered from his hard run into camp, he jogged up the slight incline of the ramp and into the dome. After his eyes adjusted to the relative dimness, he searched the expansive room for Wheeler. The dome was nearly empty, a few browns and grays and a red were clustered about a single table in the center of room, but Wheeler was not in sight.

Casey walked over to the reconstitution area. "Hey, you!" he called out.

One of the two nutri-techs turned toward Casey. Casey recognized him. It was Joe Ng.

"What do you want?' Joe asked, not really interested. He turned back to cleaning up the grill.

"I want to talk with Wheeler," Casey said.

"So?" Ng said casually.

The insolence rekindled Casey's determination. He'd been frustrated at every turn, but not today.

"Joe, you can act like an asshole if you want to, but I am going to speak with Wheeler, with or without your help. If I need to contact Commander Slater and request back-up, I will." He reached for his com-collar.

Joe straightened and turned to face Casey, holding a sharp scrapper in his hand, bouncing it up and down in his palm. He returned to cleaning the grill, and then said, "All right. Why not? He's back in the storage area," indicating the direction with a nod of his head.

Casey walked past the shiny ovens and saw an old-fashioned door in the rear wall. He approached it and noticed it was open a crack, but the room beyond it was dark. He pushed against the foam-steel door and it swung open without a sound. While he stood on the threshold, searching the darkness, his puppy stuck her head out of his pouch and began a deep-throated growl unlike any Casey had ever heard from his little dog. The skin on his arms and legs grew tight and erupted with goose bumps.

He touched the light plate; light-lines immediately came to life. Wheeler was standing no more than three meters in front of him. He was facing Casey, rubbing his elbows, and seemed even stranger close-up than he had at a distance. His face was fixed with a frightening smile, like a mask, revealing both the upper and lower rows of teeth. His unblinking gaze was unnatural. It was a horrifying apparition, a caricature of a face, near enough to look human, yet far enough away to be grotesque.

Now that Casey had Wheeler before him, all he wanted was to escape, but he was mesmerized. Wheeler didn't speak, but did take a step toward Casey; the movement broke Casey's fearful paralysis. With his heart beating wildly, Casey stumbled backward, tripping on his own feet. He turned and ran for the second time within an hour, afraid to even look back over his shoulder. As he dashed heedlessly for the dome exit, he heard laughter from the counter area, but didn't care. All he wanted was to get out of there.

This time Casey didn't stop running until he'd raced up

the ramp and reached the up-tube. Old and out of condition, with an aching in his chest, he bent at the waist, his breath wheezing in and out of his mouth. He watched the Storage Deck entrance, but saw no sign of Wheeler. As soon as the ache in his chest subsided, he entered the up-tube and exited on Deck One. He had to talk with Slater.

Sten Olson was standing guard at Slater's portal.

Casey, his body still pulsating from the adrenaline rush, hardly had the breath to speak. "Sten," he gasped, "I've got to see Slater! It's vital!"

Olson rolled his pale-blue eyes upward, not even looking at Casey as he spoke. "Commander Slater is busy."

Casey could not stay still; he punched in Veck's code as he walked in a tight circle around the bridge. Sten's eyes followed him with mild curiosity.

"Speak," Jane said.

"Jane, this is Casey. I need to talk with Commander Slater. This is an emergency!"

There was a pause before Jane answered. "Not today, Casey. Maybe later in the week."

"Jane, please! I have to talk with Slater." The connection clicked closed. Casey's shoulders slumped, but then he pulled his shoulders back and walked over to Olson. "I'm not going to leave here until Slater comes out, or he agrees to see me."

"Suit yourself," Olson said without concern.

Casey walked over to the bulkhead with the still blank screens, and was about to sit in the control chair, but then remembered Grace N'duforchu. Instead, he squatted down and leaned back against the bulkhead. His puppy was struggling in his waist pouch and he lifted her out.

The puppy immediately ran around the bridge, exploring, her tail wagging at a ferocious rate. After a while she ran over to greet Olson and sniff his feet. Without warning, Olson kicked out and sent the puppy sliding across the floor, yelping and crying in surprise and pain. She watched Olson as she walked over to Casey, her tail tight between her legs, and crawled onto his lap.

"You're really a mean bastard. Did you know that, Sten?"

"Keep the mutt away. Animals shouldn't be allowed in the ship. They stink," Olson said without emotion.

"I imagine that means you'll soon have to leave the ship yourself, wouldn't you say?"

Olson ignored the remark. "If that foul little beast comes near me again, I guarantee you I will kill it, with pleasure."

Casey scratched his puppy's ears and the little dog licked his hand. It didn't appear that she'd been injured by Olson's kick.

The evening wore on. Casey sat resolutely in his spot and Olson lounged near Slater's portal. Then Casey heard Slater's door open and looked up; it was Jane Veck. She glared at Casey and then turned to walk toward the down-tube.

"Jane, wait!" Casey called. He struggled to his feet, keeping his dog in his arms, and hurried as best he could.

She stopped and turned toward him. Although still thin and sharp featured, she looked healthy and had an attractive flush to her cheeks. Casey had never seen her look quite so attractive, despite the slight bulge of her abdomen.

"What do you want?" Her voice hadn't changed; it still had that shrill edge.

"Jane, I need your help...please."

"Is that so? You, the important doctor, coming to little Jane Veck and begging for help. Isn't that a twist? When we were at Copper Mountain, you were so conceited, so filled with self-importance that you wouldn't even look at a woman, unless she had breasts the size of melons and was dressed in an important color. I would've done anything for you then, probably even if you had only said 'hello', or even once waved to me in a friendly way. Now look at you, old, despised...hated. It serves you right," she said, anger pushing her voice another hair-raising notch higher. "No, Casey, you had your chance. Now it's my turn to show you what it feels like to be rejected. I don't need or want you anymore. I have a real man. A man who notices me and appreciates me. I could care less about you and what you want."

"Jane, I never knew...." said a subdued Casey as he reached out to touch her shoulder.

"You have a bad habit of touching people. I find it offensive. Get your hand off me. Sten," she called, but Casey had already let his hand fall away.

Jane stepped forward and disappeared into the down-tube.

Olson laughed. "You really have a way with the women. Now I can see why you have a dog for a friend. Who else would have you?" He snorted in delight at his witticism.

Casey stood there for a moment, keeping his back to Olson.

His sense of urgency had faded. He was hungry and tired. He dropped into the tube and exited on Deck Two to find what little comfort he could in the emptiness of the medical suite.

When he entered the lab he saw a message on his temporary screen. It said: "Casey, I'll be by tomorrow to pick up my camera. I hope you've had a chance to fix it. Lisa B."

After feeding his puppy, he sat down and, without much enthusiasm, took out his tools to examine the camera. He checked the integrity of the circuits and components, without needing to know their specific functions. He could find no evidence of malfunction. He leaned back in his chair and idly glanced through Lisa's photos. What could cause the camera to function well indoors, but poorly outdoors? Nothing came to mind. Casey let the problem rest and fell asleep in the chair.

CHAPTER 25

The following morning found Casey waiting, impatiently. Glancy had failed to show again and this time Casey was definitely not pleased. He'd been looking forward to sharing more knowledge and discussing it with a quick mind but, as the morning wasted away, it was plain that this was not to be. He briefly considered contacting Jane Veck, but after last night's truth session with her, he didn't want to risk being rejected again. He thought about what she had said and was honestly astounded. He had no idea anyone would consider him a snob. It certainly didn't fit with his self-image.

He picked up Lisa's camera and the photos, which were still lying on the work counter from the night before, and slid them into his waist pouch. He decided he would return them himself. He should be safe enough as long as he avoided crowds. Besides, he could hardly imagine the self-righteous comp-techs soiling their hands with a physical confrontation, icy stares, turned up noses, yes, but fists? Extremely unlikely.

He took a last glance around the lab and stepped through the portal into the passageway. He was immediately struck a vicious blow on the back of his head, causing him to collapse in a motionless heap with bright red blood seeping from a gash in his scalp. He didn't hear Marta's barking and growling, or the "yelps" of pain when she was kicked aside. He was unaware of being lifted and carried down the passage toward the hall of sleep.

When he regained consciousness, he heard a moan, not immediately realizing it was his own. His head beat with a steady tempo of pain. He was on his knees and retched, but his stomach was empty. When he opened his eyes, he saw only the dim whiteness of opalescent light. Although sluggish, his mind began to process information. He touched the glassy surface. He knew then that he was inside a burnt out stasis-capsule. With effort, he reached up to activate the inside release, but in its place found a small area of roughness; someone had removed it. He sank down onto his buttocks and rested his arms on his knees, head bent forward.

He was at peace. Perhaps it was death he'd been longing for all along. He thought about his unknown assailant. There were certainly plenty of candidates. Whoever it was, they couldn't have found a better place to hide his body. The capsules were designed to transmit only one form of energy, light. His com-collar was useless. The capsules were opaque to all other wavelengths of electromagnetic energy. They were solid. No amount of yelling or pounding would be detected, even if there were someone standing just on the other side of the opaque surface. Nonetheless, he felt obligated to make some kind of an effort at escape. He reached into his pouch and took out Lisa's camera. He tried scratching the surface of the capsule with the sharp corner of the camera, but the vaporized body that surrounded him was permanently fused with the ceramic surface. The edge of the camera didn't even leave a scratch.

When he replaced the camera in his pouch, some photos spilled onto the capsule floor. He glanced at them and then looked closer. They looked different. He picked them up to get a better look. He rubbed his eyes and looked again; even in the dim light of the capsule he could see they were different.

He brought the picture of Protonov, embracing Lisa, close to his eyes and studied the detail. They looked filthy. Their uniforms were splotchy and tattered, with long tears reaching up the pant legs. Lisa's immaculate hair wasn't; it was stringy and gnarled. They both appeared gaunt, as if they hadn't eaten a nutritious meal in months. This was the picture of two degenerate bums, not meticulous professionals. But, they were both smiling like imbeciles, unaware and uncaring about their condition.

Was he hallucinating? He glanced down at his own torn and muddy uniform. Was the oxygen already becoming depleted? His sense of serene acceptance deserted him. He yelled and pounded with his fists on the capsule's hard surface, until his knuckles were raw and bleeding. Exhausted, he collapsed into the base of the capsule. The air was becoming thin. His breathing didn't satisfy his hunger for air. Gradually, imperceptibly, he became sleepy. He tried desperately to keep his eyes open, to stay awake, but slipped inevitably into unconsciousness. His body was still striving for oxygen, but the sleep of carbon dioxide and hypoxemia was the victor.

When he awakened he was on his pallet in the medical

lab. His head felt like it was being pounded by a brick. When he opened his eyes, the light was sharp and penetrating. He tried to sit up, but his arms were too weak to support his weight. He closed his eyes tightly and temporarily gave up the effort to move. It was unreal. He was trapped in a nightmare, knowing it was a nightmare, but unable to awaken.

After an interminable passage of time, Casey was aware again. He heard a voice. It was Glancy.

"Doctor Conklin, how nice of you to rejoin us. I've got to tip my hat to you. In all my days of brawling, I've never met anyone who managed to get himself beat up as often as you. Congratulations."

Casey opened one eye no wider than a slit. Glancy was leaning against the bulkhead and holding Marta, scratching her behind her ears.

"Get the synthesizer," Casey moaned.

"Yeah, yeah, I know the routine. It's right next to you, old man. Don't you wish you had taught me how to use it?" Glancy chuckled a cheery, little laugh.

Slowly, with repeated efforts, Casey managed to position his fingers and code in the proper sequence. In a moment, the analgesic disk was ejected from the cube. Casey lay back on the pallet, breathing heavily. When he caught his breath he spoke. "Would you mind applying the disk, or is that beneath your dignity?"

"Why you let yourself get like this I'll never understand."

Glancy picked up the disk and pressed it onto the skin of Casey's chest, next to the blue disk he always wore. Glancy continued, "I have a theory about you. You never attend to your appearance, nor do you treat your degenerative arthritis and other ills. You could give yourself a stem cell infusion if you don't think you can trust anyone to monitor you for full regeneration in the chamber. I think you want to suffer. I think you feel guilty about killing Mitch Klaus. Shit happens. The goal in life is to make certain that when shit happens, it happens to someone else. The first time you kill someone it feels like a big deal. At least that's the way it was for me, but you get over it."

The pain easing chemicals diffused into Casey's body. He was still aware that his head ached, but it was a distant sensation. He studied the smiling young man before he spoke.

"Shit happens," Casey said.

Glancy nodded.

"And the next time I kill someone it won't be such a big deal."

"You got it, doc."

"Good God. I'm training a sociopathic killer to be a physician."

"That's kind of harsh. You should be more careful or you might hurt my feelings. I didn't say I liked to kill people."

"That is so reassuring." Casey massaged his temples and began muttering. "My God, I'm living in a nightmare."

"Didn't catch that. What'd you say?"

"Nothing. What happened?"

"You tell me," Glancy said. "I stopped by and you were gone. If that little dog of yours hadn't been creating such a ruckus in the hall of sleep, you would no longer be with us, as they say. It took an effort, but when I finally managed to pop open the capsule, wouldn't you know it, there you were, curled up in the bottom and looking rather grim. I'll grant you this; you do have a certain resiliency. I guess if someone really wanted to do away with you, he'd have to be a bit more direct. Who did it?"

Casey considered for a moment before he answered. "I don't know." It was a soft whisper.

Glancy continued. "I guess you don't have any shortage of suspects, do you?" And then laughed heartily.

Casey drifted back to sleep. This time it was a more peaceful slumber.

Glancy took up a position outside Casey's portal.

Later that day, Lisa came by for her camera. Glancy peeked in at Casey and saw he was still asleep, so sent her away, despite her indignant protestations. Lisa had become more secure about her position in the colony hierarchy and, as a result, was openly assertive, even threatening, but Glancy wasn't impressed. He knew where the real power in the community resided.

When Casey reawakened, he was unsure if it was morning or evening. His little dog, which had been curled at his side, jumped up when Casey first stirred. By the time Casey's eyes were open, the dog was wagging its tail with abandon, nose to nose with him. He found he could move without much pain, but his joints were always stiff. Although momentarily light-headed, he was able to gain his feet by the time his portal swished open. He expected to see Glancy's smiling face, but was disappointed to see the bland and rigid Sten Olson.

"Get clean. Slater wants to see you," Olson ordered.

"Good morning to you too, Sten, if it is morning."

Olson didn't respond.

Casey took his puppy with him while he attended to his needs in the personal room. He thought about Olson and Yamaguchi, both were so reserved, yet so different. He imagined that if he looked closely enough, he would probably see a seam along Olson's side, like those antique, vacuum-formed dolls he had seen in a museum, completely empty on the inside. The thought brought a smile to Casey's face. He exited the personal room and turned to face Olson, statuesque in more ways than one.

"Hey, Sten, I need to clean up after my puppy before we go. If you help it wouldn't take nearly as long," Casey said, still smiling.

"If you choose to live with shit, that's up to you, but you're coming with me, now. And, if that scurvy beast jumps up on my legs, you won't have to worry about cleaning up after it ever again," Olson added with a snarl.

Casey bent and gave the dog a quick little scratch behind her ears before straightening. "Stay, Marta." The dog crawled forward. "Stay!" Marta's tail stopped wagging and she sank to the deck.

Casey judged that he had probably pushed Olson's patience to the limit, so he walked toward the portal. As he neared Olson, Olson reached out and grabbed Casey's arm, squeezing much tighter than he needed to, and jerked Casey through the portal with him. Despite the analgesic patch, Casey felt a dull thudding in his head while he was pulled roughly along the corridor and literally tossed into the up-tube.

When Casey bobbed out of the tube and onto Deck One, he saw Yamaguchi standing in front of Slater's portal. He stepped aside to let Casey pass, but when he moved, it was a blocky movement. His gracefulness had deserted him. Casey looked up at the man's face as he walked past. Yamaguchi's lips were compressed and he had a deep crease at the base of his nose. He didn't speak to Casey, but it was obvious that Yamaguchi was suffering terribly. He needed help. It couldn't have been more obvious than if Yamaguchi had fallen on his knees in tears.

Casey refocused his attention when he entered Slater's cubicle. He was relieved to see that Sabine was not present. Jane Veck was standing at the array of screens along the rear bulkhead, but she had her back to Casey. Glancy was leaning on the bulkhead to Casey's left, his ever present smile gracing his face, but Slater was the one to whom Casey's gaze came to rest. Slater was sitting at his console, his hands held with fingertips touching, as if deep in contemplation. It was nearly a minute before he spoke.

"For a person who always espoused the virtue of non-violence back on Earth, you certainly bring violence out in others."

Casey was about to respond, but Slater held up his hand. "Please, don't interrupt. You have caused me great inconvenience and a huge waste of resources. I have had to assign my staff to constantly look after you. I ease up on your protection, just a little, and look what happens. Do you still think my people are only around to spy on you?"

That brought a one-sided smile to Casey's face. He sheepishly scratched under his collar before answering. "No." He could have elaborated, but didn't want to give Slater the satisfaction.

"I understand you've been wanting to talk with me. I agreed to see you today, despite the fact that you characterize me as a self-serving tyrant, because I wanted you to know how pleased I am with the progress you're making with Glancy, and because, inexplicably I might add, Jane asked me to."

The unexpected support deeply moved Casey. He looked over at Glancy, who nodded in recognition, and then turned his gaze to Jane, but she kept her back toward him so he couldn't see her face.

"Thank you," Casey said quietly, "but, to be honest, it's not just my efforts. Padrig has proven himself to be a worthy student. I have every confidence he'll become a first class physician." He didn't look back to Glancy, but if he had, he would've seen Glancy's typical smile grow, until it involved his entire face.

"I'm glad to hear that," Slater said. "Not surprised, but glad that you've been able to recognize Padrig's true intent and potential. In fact, he told me you went so far as to suffer a cut on your scalp, just so he could get some practice with the skin-fuser."

Casey smiled wryly and again looked to Glancy, who responded by pantomiming a tip of an invisible hat. When he returned his gaze to Slater, Slater appeared serious.

"As our Chief Medical Officer, you should be made aware that a high percentage of our females are pregnant," Slater said as a matter of fact.

"A high percentage?" Casey asked.

"Well, actually, all the females are pregnant. Isn't that incredible?" Slater said rhetorically.

Casey glanced sharply over at Jane, but she refused to turn and made as if busy at the screens.

"Incredible isn't the word for it," Casey said. "Impossible is more like it. How—"

"Now, Casey, don't start," Slater said sternly.

"What if—" Casey began.

"What if?" Slater again interrupted. "That's all you ever say. Your 'what if's' are like a swarm of hornets, making you jump this way and that. It's part of the reason you're so ineffective. I deal with 'what is', not 'what if'. It's a fact. Deal with it."

"All right, Commander. There is much to be done. I'll get started today."

"That's the rub, Casey. There is a strong sentiment among the crew that you're not worthy of trust. They are reluctant to place their well-being in the hands of a psychotic killer." Slater chuckled as if it were a joke. "No, this is not an appropriate task for you. Your job will be to emphasize Glancy's training, so that he'll be competent to handle this particular aspect of health care."

All the warmth and goodwill that Casey had been savoring was gone in a flash. "I attend to my special needs. I've demonstrated nothing but tolerance and a desire to help since planet-fall."

"Give them time," counseled Slater.

"Time? How much time do I need to give? I've given nearly my entire life already, to all the colonists, including you, Slater."

"When are you ever going to come down out of orbit? Try to see things as they are. Be more accepting. You cannot simply wish the colonist's suspicions and ill will away. Try to be a little less eccentric. They'll come around."

"You mean try to ignore the fact that this whole colony is based on a fallacious reality? Ignore the fact that the entire colony has been transformed from vigorous, questioning humans into docile animals?" Casey leaned forward, shouting the last sentence.

Slater took a deep breath and leaned lazily back in his chair. "You are so excitable. You should increase the dosage of your medication. Calm down."

"Calm down? The hell I will! Have you seen Wheeler up close?" Casey asked.

"Is that what you wanted to talk to me about?"

"Yes, among other things. Have you seen him, up close?"

"Of course I've seen him. Wheeler is the chief nutri-tech and, as such, he does attend our weekly executive meetings in the Main Dome. Other than the fact that he has a bad back and stands during the meeting—"

"A bad back?"

"Oh, come on, Casey. Now you're suspicious of colonists who have back pain? Give me a break. Wheeler is doing a very solid job. For instance, he's already provided supplemental nutrition for the women. Now what do you have to say? Has it occurred to you that your paranoia has only been partially treated, that you're still sick in the mind?"

Casey sagged back in his chair. He couldn't help but doubt himself. Was he still insane like everyone seemed to believe? He thought about the photographs and stole a glance at the legs of his suit, crisp, bright, white. Was this a hallucination, or was his vision inside the capsule a hallucination? They could not both be reality. He felt heavy with fatigue, but wasn't ready to surrender just yet, a spark of resistance still remained. He looked up; Slater was smiling smugly, his elbow on the desk, resting his chin in the palm of his hand.

"What have the geo-techs discovered?" Casey asked.

"After an extensive and careful evaluation of the data, all of their expectations have been verified. This is a virgin planet with extensive untapped mineral resources."

"Why does it never rain, yet the grass remains green and abundant?" Casey asked.

Slater snorted and pounced on the question as if he had been waiting for it. "Gao Min asked herself that very question. She theorized that there was an underground water flow and her instrumentation verified that theory. Furthermore, every one of their speculations on the local flora has been confirmed. Eden has fully met our expectations."

"Truly amazing," said Casey without emotion. "A new planet, with alien life, and no surprises." It was beginning to make sense. Casey was beginning to see the outline of a pattern.

"Anything else, Casey?"

"Yes, as a matter of fact. I have hard evidence that we left Earth over two thousand years ago. What do you make of that?"

"Yeah, you already told me that. I asked Jarmo to take a look at his instruments. I told him there was probably something wrong with them and, as it turned out, it was exactly as I predicted—an instrument malfunction. That skull fragment is no more two thousand years old than I am. Now you, on the other hand, look like you could be two thousand years old." Slater laughed.

"Don't make a joke out of this, Geoff."

Slater let the familiarity pass.

Casey continued. "The stasis crystals show deterioration. Believe me, please, there is something terribly wrong."

Slater ignored Casey's comment and turned toward Jane. "Are you satisfied now, Jane?"

Jane smiled at Slater with immoderate affection. "Thank you, Geoff."

He redirected his attention to Casey. "You have a lot of work to do, Doctor Conklin. Think about my suggestion concerning your medication. This interview is over."

"I have a request," Casey said.

"Why am I not surprised?"

Casey ignored the comment and continued. "If you decide to continue my protection, I would like to have Mister Yamaguchi assigned to me." Casey paused, and then added, "I think he needs help."

Slater frowned. "You'll get whoever I can spare and I'll decide if Mister Yamaguchi needs help, not you. Now get out of here."

Casey stared at Slater for a moment, and then got stiffly to his feet. He turned his back on Slater and shuffled through the portal. As he passed Yamaguchi, he whispered, "I think I can help you. See me when you can." He walked on by and then glanced back. He could not tell if Yamaguchi had heard or not.

CHAPTER 26

Glancy pushed away from the bulkhead after Casey had left. "I'll be going."

"Wait." Slater swiveled around toward Jane. "Sweetheart, would you leave Padrig and me alone for a few minutes?"

She smiled her thin smile and nodded her head. "Of course, dear." She followed after Casey and walked through the portal, onto the bridge.

After the portal closed, Slater focused his gaze on Glancy. "I want you to push that old man. I want you to squeeze every last drop of information out of him, but I want it done quickly. There's something repulsive about him. He's not like us. He's not one of us. Haven't you sensed that?"

Glancy answered slowly, thoughtfully. "Yes, I know what you mean, but you do have to give him credit. He's cranky and there is something about him that grates on me, but he seems to be a real master of his profession and has been freely sharing his expertise with me. I may not like being around him, but I've come to respect the old guy."

Slater's voice was cold. "Get this straight, Glancy. As soon as he's given you all he has, kill him! I don't care if you make it look like an accident or not. I want that man dead."

Glancy said nothing.

"What's the matter? Is that white suit making you soft? You forget, I know your real history. You've killed many a man and at least one woman for far less reason than this. Do you have a problem with my orders?"

Glancy stood still. He had never experienced even a minor reservation before. It was simple to kill another human.

"Well do you!" Slater shouted.

"I understand and, no, I don't have a problem."

"Good. I want you to escort that creep back down to Deck Two and begin the next phase of your training, today. I'll send relief by later."

Glancy didn't move.

Slater stood. "Get going!"

Glancy turned away and headed out the portal.

The Pinnacle

"And send Jane back in," Slater called after him.

When Glancy walked past Yamaguchi, he saw that Casey and Jane were talking.

"I want you to know, Jane," Casey was saying, "I'm very happy for you. The joy of your pregnancy actually makes you radiant."

Jane grinned and rested her hand on the small bulge of her abdomen.

"I also wanted to thank—"

"Come on, Conklin. We don't have all day." Glancy's voice was unusually harsh.

"Thank you, Jane," Casey finished, and then walked across the bridge to join Glancy at the down-tube. He took one last look back, and Jane smiled at him just before she re-entered Slater's office. Yamaguchi remained as he was.

CHAPTER 27

Casey began to feel the thud of a headache breaking through the masking of the analgesic disk. Six solid hours of intensive review of maternal physiology was about as much as he could take.

"Padraig, that's about as much as I can handle for today. So if you have other duties, why don't you go? Tomorrow we can pick up from where we've left off. I'm sure I'll be all right as long as I stay in the lab."

Glancy touched his com-collar. "I'm ready," he announced and, after listening for a moment, added, "I'll wait until he arrives." He leaned against the counter. "Casey, you could do me a favor."

"I could, could I?" Casey said as he reached down and picked up his puppy.

"This place smells like dog shit and wet hair. Do you think you could increase the circulation and deodorize the place a bit?"

Casey chuckled. He'd become accustomed to the odor. "Of course, Padraig, I'll be happy to. By the way," he added, "do you know who my companion will be tonight?"

Glancy nodded. "Sabine."

Casey stopped stroking Marta and became still.

"Don't worry. He won't hurt you without Slater's approval and right now you seem to be in his good graces, wouldn't you say?"

Casey looked up, searching for confirmation in Glancy's eyes, but Glancy was studying the deck at his feet.

"Padraig, I don't trust him."

"You mean Commander Slater?"

"I don't trust either of them," Casey replied, self-consciously fingering his collar.

Glancy said nothing. A moment later the portal swished open. Sabine entered and Glancy left.

"Doctor, how are you? Well, I hope," Sabine said with a mocking sneer. He withdrew a stiletto from his pouch and began playing with it. Occasionally he would eye Casey, whose attention was fixed on the blade.

"You know," Sabine said, "if you think a few broken fingers evens the score between us, you are sadly mistaken. And that boated Yamaguchi will get his, when the time is right." He made a quick move and Casey flinched. He withdrew and laughed. "Kind of a scaredy-cat aren't you. I hate to waste my time protecting trash like you." Casey didn't respond, so he continued. "This joint smells like a place a man like you would live. It would be a public service if I slit that little beast's throat." For emphasis he slashed the blade through the air and laughed again when he saw Casey wrap his arms more securely around the little dog.

"You touch this dog and I promise you, she'll be the last being you ever harm."

Sabine leaned forward. "You make my knees shake."

Casey touched his com-collar. "Jane, this is Casey. I need to speak with Commander Slater." He paused while he listened, and then answered, "Yes, this is an emergency!" There was another pause. "No, he's here. That's the problem." Pause. "No, I'm not injured." Pause. "All right, Jane." The connection went dead.

"Tsk, tsk, tattling isn't nice. Don't look at me like that or I may be forced to come sit next to you. You'd probably piss in your suit and it already stinks enough in here."

The portal swished open and Sabine turned, his eyes opening wide. "You—"

It was the only word he managed before one of Yamaguchi's hands found his neck and pressed firmly on his carotids, while the other slammed Sabine's arm against the wall with such force that the stiletto flew out of his hand and clattered to the deck. A few moments later Yamaguchi released his grip. Sabine slid down the bulkhead and slumped over, with his head dangling on his neck.

Casey arose and checked to make certain Yamaguchi hadn't killed him. Satisfied Sabine was basically okay, he went over to the synthesizer to produce a sedative disk, which he applied to Sabine's forehead. He gave it a pat for good measure and Sabine's head flopped back against the bulkhead with an audible "crack". He stared at Sabine for a moment and then focused on the swastika. On impulse, he jerked the gold chain from around Sabine's neck.

After Casey stood, he reluctantly released the catch on

his com-collar. If Slater finds out, Casey thought, he'll consider this an act of treason. He held out his hand and Yamaguchi placed his com-collar in it as well. Casey put both collars on the work counter and exited the room for the corridor.

He looked down the curve of the passage. They were alone. At first, he thought it would be best to go to the hall of sleep, but was afraid they'd be observed. Instead, he led Yamaguchi down to the Storage Deck. On his way he dumped Sabine's gold chain into a hopper that emptied into ship recycling.

He led Yamaguchi to the land-shaper and quickly climbed the ladder with Yamaguchi close behind. He entered through the hatch and descended the short interior ladder, jumping down from the last step. When his feet hit the deck, the sound was muffled by a thick layer of debris, which puffed into the air as a nose-itching cloud. Old memories lapped at his mind, like waves against a shore, touching and then receding before they could be captured.

When Casey closed the hatch, the cabin became black. From memory, he switched on the lights. He stared at the clear crystal of his cryo-capsule, arising from the deck as if it had sprouted out of the powdery dust. There was one set of footprints leading across the fine dust to where he stood. Lying against the base of the control console was a head. His breath caught in his throat, but on closer inspection it was clearly the head of a mannequin. It appeared to be partially melted and one glass eye was missing, possibly hidden within the thick dust. There was purpose here, but the memories eluded him.

He abandoned these reflections and studied Yamaguchi. There was a dark sparkle in the giant's eyes and he swung his arm back and forth in a tight arc. Casey was more than a little frightened. It was like being caged with a wild beast.

"Yamaguchi, this is my cryo-capsule." His voice was weak. He cleared his throat and tried to speak with more authority. "It is my belief that our perceptions are being influenced by some form of electromagnetic wave that is part of a feedback system based on our expectations. The cryo-capsule is able to insulate our brain from the wavefront."

Before Casey was through talking, Yamaguchi was already moving forward. The door opened without resistance and Yamaguchi turned his face back toward Casey. His look promised more than pain if Casey was wrong. He stepped into the capsule and pulled the door shut.

Casey found himself holding each breath, but as the minutes passed and Yamaguchi remained inside the capsule, he felt exhilaration. He'd been right! He wasn't insane. His reality was more accurate than that of the majority.

Casey watched Yamaguchi, clearly visible within the glass-like tube. The name "Unsmiling Buddha" came strongly to mind and he was instantly transported to the past, to a time when he was guardian of the sleeping dead. The moment passed. While he watched, he noticed that the capsule was still connected to power. He bent and undid the coupling; the last thing he needed was to have his bodyguard go into stasis.

Casey continued his vigil, feeling oddly nostalgic, until a worry began to insinuate itself into his new found confidence. The passage of time began to taint his sense of triumph with anxiety. He forced himself to wait until he could wait no longer, and then lunged for the capsule and swung open the door.

Yamaguchi moved only his head as he turned to fix his eyes on Casey, as if awakening from a trance.

Casey spoke first. "Sorry. I didn't mean to disturb you, but there is only a limited air supply in there and...you didn't appear to be breathing."

"Do you judge me to be incompetent," the giant rumbled.

"No, I—"

"Do you offer a man, dying of thirst, just one drop of water?"

"But Slater is going to find out I took my collar off and it'll look like I attacked Sabine. I need your protection." Casey glanced anxiously toward the hatch of the land-shaper. "The risk grows with each passing moment. Help me."

Yamaguchi pulled the capsule door shut and activated the inner latch, effectively ending any further discussion.

Casey stood around, indecisive. He shivered. If he believed in ghosts, he could imagine this place was haunted. Fragmentary memories chilled him. He seemed to recall a flight of terror that ended in this hiding place. From what? He wondered. The memory escaped him, becoming distant within himself, until it seemed to disappear altogether, but he couldn't shake the sense that an unknown horror lurked nearby.

Finally, he could tolerate it no longer. He activated the hatch and hurriedly climbed down the land-shaper's ladder with total disregard for anyone watching. He slipped and rapped his kneecap painfully against a rung, but ignored the pain and jumped the last meter to land on the deck. He crouched as he turned, expecting to see Meat-Man and Barracuda bearing down on him, not even aware that he was using the old names. He didn't look back at the land-shaper as he ran the short distance to the up-tube and dived into its mouth.

He exited on Deck Two and walked as fast as his aching joints would allow toward the medical suite. When he reached the lab, he paused, afraid he would find Sabine and afraid he wouldn't. He could imagine Sabine waiting, just on the other side of the portal, wolfish grin, stiletto in hand.

With a spasm of will Casey pushed himself through the portal and quickly glanced to the left. Sabine was gone. He scanned the rest of the room, ignoring his puppy that barked a friendly greeting and jumped to put her paws on his leg. The room was empty, but his scalp crawled as if he was being watched. He glanced toward the work counter; the collars were gone. He became sick with dread and tremulous with fear.

He sat down on the pallet and held his head in his hands. How would he explain this to Slater? What would he say? He felt nauseated with remembered pain. He wanted to run, but there was no place to hide.

He was afraid to sleep, aware that with each passing moment some dreadful retribution was coming inevitably closer. He rehearsed arguments in his mind, about how it was his duty as a physician to attend to those in need, but his only real hope for rescue rested with Yamaguchi. Surely Yamaguchi wouldn't stay in the capsule. Surely he would come to his defense. Fear swirled through his mind. Eventually, he collapsed into a fitful doze and then, just before an unseen dawn, he lapsed into a deep sleep.

CHAPTER 28

Casey didn't even stir when his portal opened. It was not until Glancy shook him that he awoke, with a start. It was a moment before he remembered where he was. He had been dreaming of distant Earth.

"Why did you do it?" Glancy asked with genuine regret.

Casey's tongue felt thick and dry. He pushed himself to a sitting position and Marta jumped, trying to get into his lap, but he ignored the puppy.

"You know why I'm here, don't you?" Glancy asked.

"Yes," Casey mumbled, "I suppose so."

When he tried to stand, Glancy took hold of his arm and helped him to his feet.

"Thank you, Padraig," Casey said, and stumbled his way into the personal room.

After attending to his needs, he re-entered the lab and stood there, swaying and squinting. "Do you know where Yamaguchi is? Have you seen him?" Casey asked.

"As a matter of fact, no. Do you know where he is? Slater wants to have chat with him."

Casey said nothing.

"If you know something, this would be good time to start singing."

Casey opened his mouth, as if he were about to speak, but then shut it.

"For such a smart guy, you sure are stupid. But then, Slater says you're the most stubborn man he's ever met. Well, actually, he calls you a bull-headed son of a bitch, but I guess it's about the same. Come on. It's time." He held out his hand and made a crook out of his index finger.

"All right," Casey answered, but it was more mouthed than voiced. Marta wanted to play and, as he walked toward the portal, she ran around his feet. Somehow he avoided stepping on her and followed Glancy into the passageway, managing to shut the portal with the puppy still inside the lab.

Once in the passage he turned to Glancy. "What's going to happen?" he asked. "He's not going to hurt me again is he?"

"No clue, but I doubt it. You still have value."

"Then you think I'll be okay?" Casey said with naked hope in his voice.

"Come on old man."

He took hold of Casey's arm but Casey pulled away from his grip and Glancy allowed it. They walked to the up-tube and exited on Deck One. Olson was standing outside Slater's suite and touched his collar to whisper a brief message. He stepped aside so Casey could enter, followed by Glancy.

Slater had his back to Casey with his hands clasped behind, but Casey's attention was fixed on the two com-collars lying on Slater's console. Jane wasn't there. The room was quiet.

Casey shifted his eyes, without turning his head, and saw Sabine standing against the bulkhead. Something caught his eye. He turned his head fully and his gaze froze on the pink plastic of a burn-gun, nestled in a holster strapped to Sabine's waistband. Its oversized barrel and pastel color seemed to declare it was nothing more than a toy but, in fact, it was an outlawed weapon. Now that he saw it, he wasn't surprised Sabine possessed one. Despite his predicament, he was outraged that Slater would allow such a weapon in the colony. Perhaps it was the hopelessness of his situation rather than courage that gave him the power to speak.

"Slater!" he yelled. "You're a perverted bastard to allow an animal like Sabine loose in the colony, and now a burn-gun. You are sick!"

Slater slowly turned to reveal a face that was tight with restrained rage. His cheeks were flushed, his nose a pale beak, but when he spoke his voice was deceptively mild.

"And you are a disappointment. I give, give, give, and you take, take, take. I generously give of my time to discuss your idiotic theories and fears. I tell you how much I appreciate the job you're doing and how do you repay me? You use your skills as a physician to overcome one of my trusted men, while he was risking his life to protect you, and you subvert another."

Casey opened his mouth to respond, but Slater cut him short. "Shut up! I'll tell you when to speak and what to say. We have a colony of five hundred souls working desperately to establish a viable colony and one man who feels he's above the rest. Who feels his needs come first. He is a traitor, morally bankrupt, self-serving. Do you know who that is Casey?"

Casey couldn't help himself. "Yes, I do. It's you."

Slater picked up one of the com-collars and dangled it from his fingers. Suddenly, he leaned forward and whipped it violently in an arc; it struck Casey in the mouth, causing a trickle of blood to drip down his chin.

"Where is Mister Yamaguchi?" Slater asked.

Casey didn't want to tell, but the fear of pain reached into him and he began shaking. He shifted his eyes to Sabine and saw him smiling as he caressed the butt of the burn-gun.

Casey wanted Slater to ask him again. He couldn't tolerate more pain. He just couldn't. He would tell. He would say or do anything but, before he could give Slater whatever he wanted, the portal opened.

Slater's eyebrows rose in surprise. Casey crouched slightly to turn in his chair, so he could see who had entered. It was Yamaguchi! Casey felt warm, melting relief, and a revival of his determination not to bow to Slater's intimidation.

"Mister Yamaguchi," Slater said, "how thoughtful of you to join us."

Sabine grasped the butt of his gun and backed a little farther away.

"Where, might I ask, have you been?" Slater asked.

"Doctor Conklin has shown me a place of peace, a place where I can regain my strength."

"How nice. And what about your duty? Tell me, Mister Yamaguchi, what is your primary duty?" Slater asked with confidence.

"To question and to observe," Yamaguchi answered.

Slater shifted uncomfortably in his chair and Casey looked down to hide a small smile.

"All right then," Slater continued, "what is your second duty?"

"To maintain order and serve the leader."

It was Slater's turn to smile. He sat down in his chair and leaned back. "And who is the leader?"

"You," Yamaguchi said.

Casey shifted farther into his seat and glanced up at Yamaguchi, with a terrible cold creeping into his bones. Yamaguchi looked more like he used to, aloof, controlled, and distant.

Slater continued. "Your behavior last night would seem to indicate that you've forgotten your duty. Is that the case?"

"No," Yamaguchi said without hesitation.

Slater paused. His eyes returned to his console. He appeared pleased. When he looked back up, he stared directly into Casey's eyes, even though he spoke to Yamaguchi. "I need proof that you have not forgotten who the leader is. Are you willing to prove it?"

"Yes," Yamaguchi answered.

Casey slumped in his chair. Despite the sensation of freezing cold, a trickle of perspiration slowly wormed its way down his back.

"Very well then," Slater said. "Doctor Conklin seems to have difficulty hearing my orders, so it seems he has no real use for his ears. Cut them off."

Casey's breath caught. When he spoke his voice quaked with fear. "Please, Geoff. I didn't mean to do anything wrong. All I did was try to help Yamaguchi, one of your men. Please, give me another chance. Have mercy on me!"

When Casey began to rise out of his chair, Slater nodded to Sabine who pulled Casey roughly back into it and held him in place.

"Mister Glancy," Slater said in his pleasant baritone, "will you assist Mister Sabine and Mister Yamaguchi?"

Glancy stepped forward.

Sabine leaned down until his mouth was next to Casey's ear. "You stole my gold chain, you asshole. What'd you do with it?"

Casey struggled to escape but was held in place by two men, one dressed in white, the other in black. They took hold of his arms and pinned him to the chair.

"Where'd you hide it?" Sabine yelled.

"So, now we must add larceny to your growing list of crimes," Slater said and shook his head as if disappointed.

Casey's eyes were fixed on Slater. "Commander, please! I beg you. Please—" His voice choked off and he began crying, tears flowing down his cheeks.

"Do it," Slater ordered.

Casey's head was grasped in a rigid grip. His body was shaking, but his head was held still. He felt the first sharp, slicing pain. It was a burning. The blood warmed the side of his face. His vision began to gray and he lost consciousness.

Yamaguchi met Slater's eyes.

"What are you waiting for? Both ears. And when you get

done put that collar back around his neck."

Yamaguchi proceeded to slice off the other ear of the now limp and bloody figure.

CHAPTER 29

When Casey awakened he was on his pallet in the medical lab. There was searing pain on both sides of his head. The skin of his face and neck was stiff and tight with dried blood, but he was afraid to touch the sides of his head to confirm what he already knew. He was curled up in the fetal position, alone except for his puppy. He sobbed with pain and the fear of disfigurement. He cried without pride, without dignity, until he found temporary solace in sleep.

He did not awaken until someone gently shook him. He opened his eyes. It was Yamaguchi.

"Get away from me." Casey said it like a curse.

Yamaguchi did not leave.

"I said get out of here!" Casey yelled, nearly hysterical.

Still Yamaguchi remained, kneeling next to Casey's pallet.

"I thought you were my friend," Casey whispered.

"Can you have a friend without respect? Can you respect a man who fails in his duty?" Yamaguchi asked.

Casey forced himself into a sitting position. "What complete bullshit. What duty? Where does your duty to your friends fit into your hierarchy of duties? Just after the duty of wiping your ass after you shit? I put myself on the line for you and you thank me by torturing me. You call that friendship? I don't call you a friend. I call you a monster."

"Didn't you lead me to the cryo-capsule to confirm a theory?" Yamaguchi asked.

"Hell no. I took you there to help your sorry ass. And this is how you repay me."

"You did not want to know what I observed?"

"I could give a shit about what you observed. Get the hell out of here."

"You have paid the price. You may have my observations. There is a constant distortion of our perceptions but, even in the peace of the capsule, there are questions I cannot ask. There is a fundamental change in me."

Yamaguchi stood and walked over to the personal room. He returned with a moist cloth and was about to cleanse

Casey's wounds when Casey pushed his hand away.

"Why?" Casey asked plaintively. "Why did you do it? I needed you. I—" His voice broke.

"It was only pain."

"Only pain?" His head drooped forward and he felt the stiffness of dried blood. "You are a monster. You are all monsters."

"Can't you apply your craft to heal your wounds?" Yamaguchi asked.

"You mean regeneration? Who would manage the life support? Glancy? Who would I trust my sedated body to, you? I don't need you! I don't need any of you! Did you hear that, Jane!" he yelled. "I loved you. I loved you all, but no longer." He jerked his collar off and threw it onto the deck. "Get out of here," he commanded with gritty determination.

Yamaguchi stood, paused for a moment, and finally left the room. Casey was alone, except for his puppy. He lifted the dog into his lap and began stroking her fur.

He was not visited again until later in the afternoon, when Glancy entered the cubicle. Glancy's face was unusually sober, but Casey didn't believe or appreciate his solemnity and didn't choose to recognize his presence until he spoke.

"I didn't have a choice," Glancy said.

"The hell you didn't."

The silence returned. Glancy walked around the lab, looking at various pieces of equipment, then he turned back to Casey.

"Do you plan to continue my instruction?" he asked.

Casey directed his gaze to Glancy, considering, weighing the possibilities before he spoke. "I will continue. It'll give me something to do and the colony will need it, but I don't want to suffer the offense of your presence. I'll leave instruction cubes for you in the passageway, but understand this; I don't want you to contaminate this room with your person again. If you do, I swear you'll not get one more damn thing from me. Is that understood? Slater, are you listening? I hope so, you psychopath. I never fully appreciated the depth of your depravity. You are evil incarnate. If you have a problem with what I'm saying then kill me. I don't care anymore. Do you hear me Slater!"

After a moment Glancy spoke. "You can't make it alone. No one can."

"Can't I? Isn't that what I have been doing, despite my fantasies to the contrary?"

"You underestimate yourself. Despite recent events, you do have allies."

Casey laughed; it was a coarse, unpleasant sound. "Get out of here. You turn my stomach."

Glancy remained as he searched for the right thing to say.

"I'm warning you, Glancy. Get out of here before I change my mind."

Glancy pursed his lips, but after a minute of silence, he turned and disappeared through the portal.

CHAPTER 30

During the following weeks Casey's depression remained undiminished, until it finally began to bloom into the black flower of self-neglect and self-destruction. He no longer ran painstaking diagnostics on himself and no longer replaced the blue disk that had provided a chemical lifeline to sanity. As the level of chemical support dwindled, Casey withdrew further into himself. His only source of information about the colony came from issues of the "Eden Gazette" that were left in the passage outside the lab. Each morning he would trade an instructional cube for the paper, like a pack rat gathering nuts.

His lucidity waxed and waned like a slowly flickering candle. The isolation imposed upon him by the colony was reinforced by Casey's own desire to shield himself from his own emotions and unmet needs.

From time to time, Yamaguchi would attempt to communicate with him, but he never responded, never even seemed to recognize his presence. Yamaguchi would find Casey sitting cross-legged on his pallet, amidst the excrement-strewn deck, wearing his increasingly filthy turban and underwear, but nothing else.

As the fabric of Casey's mind unraveled and became increasingly threadbare, the instructional cube's contents became ever more filled with exacting detail. He hadn't spoken to Glancy since the day of the mutilation. It had become a one-way relationship, with Casey producing his cubes as part of his daily ritual, without concern or thought about their fate once he placed them in the passage.

Yamaguchi began spending increasing periods of time in Casey's cubicle, apparently impervious to the sensual assault. He would feed Casey's puppy and set out food for Casey, some of which Casey would occasionally nibble. Slater did not interfere; his needs were being met. Casey had become productive and quiet. While in the room, Yamaguchi would stand silently alert, observing, but not questioning. At night, he would retreat to Casey's cryo-capsule.

After Yamaguchi had left for the night, Casey would venture out of the ship to wander like a shadow in the dark. Rumors began circulating in the colony about an apparition, but it was only Casey, head wrapped in a turban of white bandage, wearing a black raincoat and black rain boots. He took Lisa's camera with him, which he had rigged with a powerful strobe. On those occasions when a colonist was out at that time, there would be a sudden flash of bright light out of the dark and the colonist would scurry for the security of a dome.

In the morning, Casey would inspect the pictures, produced by a photochemical rather than an electromagnetic process. He looked at them without a preconceived notion of what he would see and viewed sights that would have terrified a more rational being, but he didn't speak of it. He was alone by force, and now, by choice as well.

At times Yamaguchi would clean up the worst of the mess. Casey didn't voice objection or approval. It was becoming rare for Slater to call on Yamaguchi for a task and Yamaguchi too began traveling along a private trajectory.

There came a day when Protonov and two trusted aids stopped by to claim Lisa's camera. They were filled with themselves to overflowing, but they were met at the portal by Yamaguchi's intimidating bulk. Protonov and his band peered around him. Casey shifted his attention and stared at them with eyes that flashed with a feverish fire set deep in an increasingly bony face. They retreated without even voicing their demand.

And the days passed by.

When a copy of the "Gazette" arrived, Casey would read it carefully, silently mouthing each word. He read about expectations met. All expectations were met, without exception. He read about Swine Day and Chicken Day, and then one day he read the special bulletin, the only issue not edited by Lisa Bouviet. It told of the miracle of the Day of Delivery; within a twenty-four hour period, all the women gave birth. None needed a physician's assistance. All the babies were healthy.

Casey searched his memory. How long had it been since the Awakening? Five or six months at most, and no one wondered, except Casey during his momentary bouts of clarity. Plausible explanations were exchanged among the colonists, until an acceptable rationale prevailed. Everyone said the planet was fertile, that it encouraged reproduction. That was why the births were early.

The babies grew and none needed the attention of a physician. The world was perfect, just as the colonists expected it to be. Casey knew otherwise, but there was no one to share his private perceptions with, except Yamaguchi, and Casey judged that Yamaguchi had not earned the right to share in his observations.

Casey sat on his pallet day after day, smiling benignly and petting his dog, as expectation after expectation was fulfilled. Only he asked questions and found answers.

He began using the "Gazette" to cover the deck of the lab, eager for the next issue, so another rectangle of the deck could be covered. He was careful never to disturb them, as was Yamaguchi when he stood his silent vigil, only Marta treated the sheets of paper without regard. It was during one of these days, numberless in their similarity, that Casey's solitude was interrupted.

CHAPTER 31

Glancy entered the lab to find Casey sitting with his puppy and staring without focus at the instrument-packed bulkhead. Glancy stood uncomfortably just inside the portal, reluctant to step forward and walk on the "Gazettes" spread across the deck, many stained with the waste products of Casey's dog. He studied Casey.

It had been a long while since the last time Glancy had seen Casey and Casey had undergone a metamorphosis; he looked ancient, head wrapped in a filthy turban, stained black with old blood and other unidentifiable substances. He was naked now, except for black rain boots that reached to his knees. His spindly legs appeared as if they would rattle around in the boots when he walked in them. The frozen ripple of his ribs was plainly visible and was topped by the prominent ridges of his collarbones.

A feeling for others was something new for Glancy, but mainly, he felt revulsion. Compassion was there also, but he was ill prepared to cope with it. He could not or would not identify with this man as someone he'd known. He debated with himself, whether to proceed or not. Ultimately he spoke, in a soft voice, as if afraid to crack the silence.

"Casey," he whispered.

There was no response.

"Casey, I need your help. It's not for me. Simon Weiss needs your help."

There was no sign that Casey heard him.

"Casey," Glancy said, raising his voice, "I don't know what to do."

He had never before been placed in a position of responsibility without a clue how to proceed. He was baffled. Although he had studied Casey's instructional cubes with determination, he could find no answers.

Two days before, Li Quon had brought Simon to the ship. He was unconscious. Then, yesterday, Brita Baldus had brought in Jon Brent and Tran Nugyen, both completely unresponsive. He had laid them out on treatment tables in the adjoining cubicles, but could find no evidence of illness; yet, they continued to sleep on, unarousable.

"Casey, listen to me, please! I need your help. It's not for me. It's for the colony."

Casey stared forward. He appeared awake, but could just as easily have been in an open-eyed coma.

Glancy continued, daring to step closer. "It's your duty as a physician. Remember your oath. You swore to provide care for others." He crept even closer, with Casey's puppy watching the approaching man with mild interest. Finally, he was within reach and rested his hand on Casey's bony shoulder.

"Casey," he said as he touched him, but still there was no response. He took hold of Casey's shoulders and twisted Casey's body so they were face to face. The foul odor of putrefaction was on Casey's breath and hung like a cloud around his face.

Impatience and frustration caused Glancy to squeeze harder and to shake the old man with increasing violence while he shouted his name.

Then, with breath-taking surprise, Glancy's arms were pinned to his sides and, in the same moment, he was jerked to his feet and propelled toward the portal with such force that he was unable to maintain his balance. He tripped and fell prone onto the passageway deck.

With instincts more basic to him than any other, he rolled and came up in a crotch as he turned to face his attacker. Yamaguchi was unimpressed and stood with his arms at his sides. Glancy straightened warily, keeping his balance for flight or attack.

"Yamaguchi, old friend," Glancy said and attempted to laugh. "I wasn't trying to hurt him. I was just trying to talk with him. We...the colony needs him." While he spoke he began to relax. It appeared Yamaguchi wasn't going to follow through on his initial attack, but Glancy continued to hold his hands ready, as if they were weapons, which indeed they were.

"I mean it, Yamaguchi. I'm asking for your help. Will you help us?"

Yamaguchi turned and re-entered the lab. He gave no indication of his intentions so Glancy waited in the passage, at first hopeful, then doubtful, and finally angry. He struck the bulkhead with his fist, overcome with the need to discharge his frustration.

Glancy walked the passageway and re-entered the treatment room where Li Quon awaited word. She was standing over Simon, her eyes on his face and the fingers of one hand on his pulse. She looked up and saw the anger that still flared as ruddy patches on Glancy's cheeks. He didn't need to tell Li he had failed. Li dropped her gaze back to Simon's flaccid hand, which she was holding in her own. They had tried, both of them, but Simon's problem was beyond their ability to understand or treat. Li had also examined the other two unconscious colonists with no success.

Glancy spoke. "I'm out of ideas." After a moment of silence he added, "I'm sorry." He said the words automatically, as he had in the past when they were expected, but surprised himself by feeling real regret. Perhaps, he thought, training as a physician hadn't been such a good idea after all. He felt vulnerable and didn't like it. Then he remembered that Li had successfully treated Casey's mental illness once before.

"Li, do you think you could prepare a therapeutic disk for Casey like you did while we were in orbit?"

She looked up. The glimmer of hope in her eyes faded rapidly. "Those days were so chaotic. I don't know. I was so tired and when I recall those days, which I try not to, all I can think about was when Casey attacked me." She shook her head. "I don't know."

"It's worth a try, don't you think?"

"Without diagnostics it could be no better than an approximation, but maybe it's just possible...." Her voice faded away as she dropped into thought.

Glancy smiled and said, with more confidence than he felt, "We can do this." But then, after a moment, he added, "I think you should know, Yamaguchi is usually with him. It would probably be best if we wait until evening. At night Yamaguchi goes down to the land-shaper in the Storage Deck."

Li had no desire to confront Yamaguchi. She nodded agreement.

"What does he do down there?" she asked.

"I have no idea and I'm not about to try to find out."

After a few minutes, the feeling of helplessness returned.

Glancy was restless. "I'm going to go down the passage and wait in the hall of sleep to watch for Yamaguchi. When I see him enter the down-tube, I'll come for you."

Li nodded and then looked back down at Simon.

Glancy paused at the portal. It was perfectly quiet except for the barely audible "hiss" of respirations passing in and out of Simon's lax mouth. He stepped into the passageway and the portal shut.

CHAPTER 32

Li didn't hear the portal open when Glancy returned. She was sitting in a chair, leaning against the treatment table, overcome by sleep. He touched her shoulder and she awakened. She rubbed her eyes and face to try to restore alertness. Grabbing hold of Glancy's outstretched hand, she pulled herself to her feet.

"Is he gone?" she whispered, as if she was afraid Yamaguchi could hear through walls.

In an equally quiet voice Glancy answered. "Yes, I followed him down to storage. He went into the land-shaper and closed the hatch. He shouldn't return for hours. Li...I have to warn you. Expect the worst. Casey isn't the same man he was a few months ago." Glancy paused. "He's changed."

"Changed?" It was uncanny. So much like that time in space. She shivered with remembrance.

Glancy continued. "He looks ancient, but it's more than that. He seems absent. He has retreated so far into himself that he may no longer be reachable. It's as if his body is on automatic and his mind burnt out. And the room! It's a foul pit, thick with the stench of animal waste from that damn dog."

Li said nothing.

"Are you ready?" Glancy asked.

"I guess so."

"Then let's get to it before Yamaguchi returns."

When they entered the passage Li could feel her heart thudding in her chest, fear and fatigue. She recalled the last time she had been in the lab with an insane Casey; her left hand began to tingle and her throat felt like it was closing. She slowed further, letting Glancy enter the room first, and then forced herself to follow after him.

The light-lines had been dimmed, but as their eyes adjusted they saw the beads of bone that marked the curvature of Casey's spine while he leaned forward, hunched over the computer console. The puppy wagged its tail and ran over to play. Glancy picked the dog up and began scratching behind her ears to keep her quiet. They remained where they were for a moment longer and heard Casey mumbling to himself as he produced yet another instructional cube for no apparent reason.

Glancy spotted the molecular synthesizer, partially buried in pile of soiled and crumpled papers. He touched Li on the arm and pointed it out to her. She took a couple of steps to the side, her eyes not leaving the bony form of Casey, whose slovenly-wrapped turban glowed in the light from the computer screen. She squatted and picked up the synthesizer, wanting to wipe off its grimy surface, but afraid to make any unnecessary movement. She glanced down and punched in the code. The corners of the cube glowed green, indicating that it was still functional and, shortly, a blue disk slid out of a slot on the top. She held the disk in her hand and squatted slowly to replace the synthesizer on the deck.

She looked up and Glancy motioned her forward. Though reluctant, she stood and began to tiptoe toward Casey. When she was within two steps of him, he began a gradual stretching and arose to his feet. Li froze. Glancy quickly moved to her side, to attack or protect.

After standing, Casey made a slow, deliberate turn. His eyes, deeply shadowed within their bony orbits, came to rest on Li. A small cry of terror escaped her lips. She began backing away and Glancy stepped between them. Casey walked forward.

Glancy tossed the dog to the deck, causing Marta to "yip" in surprise. He flattened his hands and prepared to strike a blow, but Casey kept his arms at his sides and walked directly into Glancy, bounced back a step, and then walked forward again. Glancy took hold of Casey's shoulders and held him in place while he continued to make walking movements.

"Li, help me out here a little for God's sake!"

She opened her eyes and lowered her hand from where she had been holding it, tight against her mouth.

"Give me the damn disk," Glancy demanded gruffly.

Li remained standing in the same place. She held her hand out, blue disk on her palm, but she would not come closer. Glancy planted his forearm firmly against Casey's chest and reached back to pluck the disk from her palm. He pressed the disk firmly onto Casey's chest and then stepped aside, at the same time pulling Li out of Casey's intended path. Li felt herself trembling in his grasp.

Casey completed his short walk to the pallet as if it had been uninterrupted. He sat on the pallet, pulled up his legs, and raised his head to stare off into the distance.

"Come on," Glancy hissed, but had to physically drag Li out of the room and into the passage.

Glancy caught her as she began a slow collapse to the deck and carried her into the adjacent treatment room. He laid her out on the deck where her color gradually returned and her skin dried.

"How long will it take?" he asked.

Her voice was so weak it was nearly inaudible. "We should know by tomorrow."

"Assuming Yamaguchi doesn't remove it," Glancy added.

He placed a pad under her head and she soon fell asleep.

CHAPTER 33

Glancy watched her for a while. When he was convinced she would be all right, he exited the suite. He walked the curve of the passage and entered the up-tube to arrive on Deck One.

Glancy walked toward Olson, who was standing in front of Slater's portal.

"Is he in?" Glancy asked.

Olson nodded. "He's expecting you." He stepped aside to let Glancy pass.

Slater was standing next to the monitoring screens that were usually attended by Jane Veck. When Glancy entered, Slater turned to face him.

"Well, Chief Medical Officer Glancy, what do you have to report?"

Glancy took a moment to study Sabine, who was leaning against the bulkhead, causally tossing a stiletto from one hand to the other and back again.

"Your report?" Slater urged.

Glancy returned his attention to Slater. "I've successfully applied a therapeutic disk to Casey. I should know the results by tomorrow. As for the unconscious colonists, their condition remains unchanged."

Slater stood motionless for a moment, clicking the tip of his index fingernail against a tooth, and then lowered his hand to refocus his attention on Glancy.

"I made you Chief Medical Officer, as you requested—"

"I didn't request it. You ordered me to—"

"Quiet!" After a moment to confirm obedience, Slater continued. "This was your assignment. When I give one of my staff an order, I expect results. I demand it!"

Glancy's eyes narrowed. "It was you who isolated our only fully-qualified physician and then pushed and intimidated him into a mental break. Intimidated isn't the right word. Tortured is the word."

Slater raised his head slightly, emphasizing the height advantage he had on Glancy, and looked down his nose with disdain. His voice was cool and sharp. "You don't know diddly-squat about Conklin. At Copper Mountain, he was such a sanctimonious bastard. As Chief of Medicine, he took part in our training scenarios and always insisted that we do the 'right thing', whatever the hell that means, even if it led to mission failure. What a complete idiot. Thank God he wasn't put in charge. We'd all be dead by now. I had to take strong measures to break him, anything less wouldn't have worked."

"You broke him all right."

"Shut up, Glancy. I had to take expedient measures for the good of the colony. He was already a wreck, beyond salvage. You do realize what we're really talking about here, don't you?"

Glancy didn't respond.

"Apparently not. It's not just the lives of a few rather inconsequential colonists. With the birth of over two hundred babies, the gene pool is in good condition. The point is, all the swine and foul are dying. I am sick and tired of eating nutrient slime from the vats. In the long run, we cannot possibly become a viable colony without a replenishable supply of real food. Those idiot bio-techs believe that Casey inserted a lethal gene into their stock. Hell, I think the guy's capable of a lot, but it's a little difficult to believe that he was able to alter every single gamete. There's got to be another answer and that's where you come in. You will find that answer and you will fix it."

"If that's the most important issue, perhaps I should try to treat the chickens and pigs and let the humans go to hell."

Slater thought for a moment, as if this had been a legitimate suggestion, but then shook his head. "No, I think we should focus on the colonists and then apply what we learn to the animals. Neither Timmins nor Merryman survived. We have no veterinarian, but we do have a physician, well advanced in his training. Don't we, Glancy?"

"I have a lot more to learn. It's only been a few months."

"Long enough."

"It's going to take me years."

"You've had enough time."

"If you say so," Glancy said.

"I do say so."

"Geoff, think about it. Casey was always talking about there being something wrong on this planet."

"Don't you dare start on me with that crazy shit. We have to deal with reality."

Glancy said nothing.

After a moment, Slater continued. "I'm not responsible for the weaknesses in others...or their failures. Each person is responsible for his own fate. A commander has to make difficult decisions, even painful decisions, for the overall good, and in return he expects and deserves the loyalty and support of his people. Don't you agree, Chief Glancy?" His face became like stone as he pinned Glancy with a hard stare.

Glancy felt trapped. If he agreed, he was in essence agreeing that he would succeed or else. If he disagreed, it was plain that Slater would interpret it as a sign of rebellion. His hands began automatically to flatten into their weapon shape. He bent slightly at the knees, but even while the desire to attack filled his mind, he remained aware of Sabine.

Slater merely stood there. "Don't you agree?" he repeated.

This was neither the time, nor the place. Glancy relaxed his hands and smiled the chameleon smile that had served him so well in the past.

"Yes, Commander Slater, I hear your message loud and clear and, as usual, you can count on me."

Slater also smiled, but it was a dead smile that was matched by the hard glint in his eyes. It was a smile of self-assurance, without the least distraction of doubt. It was a smile of uncontested dominance.

"Good, very good," Slater said. "I think you should return to your duties, don't you?"

Glancy nodded, but, as he turned to leave, Slater spoke again. "Chief Glancy, I will expect a report of your success tomorrow."

Glancy's smile deserted him. "Yes, Commander."

He retreated through the portal to the bridge and walked past Olson without speaking, but then heard footsteps behind him. It had to be Sabine. He would not give Sabine the satisfaction of seeing him turn around to face the implied threat. As he walked toward the down-tube, he heard the unmistakable "whine" of a burn-gun being charged. He continued with a steady pace toward the tube, refusing to be intimidated, but feeling uneasy vulnerability between his shoulder blades. He heard Sabine laugh as, with relief, he dropped into the mouth of the tube.

While he floated down to Deck Two he decided, if it came to it, he'd have to kill Sabine first and then go after Slater. As he gave it more thought, the heat of humiliation cooled. The more he thought about it, the lighter his step became while he walked the passage.

CHAPTER 34

Padraig Glancy waited the slow minutes of morning, but by mid-afternoon he could wait no longer. He looked to Li and noticed dark crescents under her eyes. Throughout the morning they had spoken very little, each desperate in their own way for an answer.

"I can't wait any longer," Glancy said. "Are you ready?"

Li stood and reluctantly let go of Simon's hand. She took slow, measured steps until she was standing next to Glancy. He looked down at the diminutive woman and she raised her face to meet his gaze.

"You do realize Yamaguchi will be with him," Glancy said. Li nodded.

"You don't need to come with me," he added.

"Yes, I do." There was no doubt in her voice.

Glancy turned and walked into the passage with Li behind him. He didn't hesitate at Casey's portal and walked in with a rehearsed confidence. He glanced momentarily at Casey, but then directed his attention to Yamaguchi. Yamaguchi did not move or speak. There were no greetings exchanged. There was no permission to be asked.

With Li standing close against his side, Glancy turned his attention to Casey. There was no obvious change. The blue disk stood out starkly against Casey's chalky-white skin while he sat motionless on his pallet. The dog nestled in his lap and watched the visitors as they studied Casey.

Glancy turned to Li. Her shoulders slumped. He drew her toward him and she buried her face against is chest.

"Do you think he's any better?" she whispered.

"No," he said softly. He paused, took a deep breath, and then spoke again in the same quiet voice, but with force nonetheless. "Damn Slater." He ignored his collar, reckless with anger and frustration. "My whole life I've thought that the path to sure success lay in following the orders of the person with the most power, regardless of what those orders might be."

Li pulled back from him. "What are you saying?"

"I took part," Glancy confessed, his eyes downcast on the paper strewn deck. "I was at that last meeting Casey had with Slater. Meeting. That's a laugh. It was torture session." Glancy nodded toward Yamaguchi. "So was he. It was a mistake, just an automatic response. Hell, I'd come to like the old guy. Well...maybe not like, but at least respect him, as strange as he was."

Li nodded as she watched the motionless figure sitting cross-legged on the pallet. "I guess we all bear responsibility for this atrocity."

Glancy saw a flicker of light in Casey's eyes; he appeared to be looking at them. Without turning back to Li, he whispered, "Do you think he can hear us?"

A quiet voice spoke. It wasn't weak, just so gentle and peaceful it didn't even demand a listener. Casey's lips barely moved.

"I hear you. I've had much to consider. I don't hold a grudge against you, or you either my friend, Yamaguchi, or any of the colonists. Except...to be truthful, Slater. He always was a sociopath. And Sabine is his perfect tool. Did you know that originally there were twelve of you?"

"Twelve of what?" Glancy asked.

"Blanks. Only four of you survived. I wonder what the other eight were like. Probably more of the same."

"What the hell do you mean by that?" responded Glancy.

Li put a restraining hand on Glancy's arm. "Don't," she said in a demanding tone.

Casey continued. "Never mind. I know you can't help yourselves. None of you. You don't have free will. And I know you all sense a difference in me, of not belonging. You feel a compulsion to push me away. You cannot help yourselves and I cannot help you. Yamaguchi was the first to notice it, even before I did, but he couldn't ask the right question and, if I had asked it for him, he wouldn't have been able to remember it. Your rejection of me does not come from within you. It comes from without. While I don't hold you responsible, I do question your decision to bring me back when you really want to be rid of me."

Glancy and Li looked to one another. What was he rambling on about? And more important, was he sane enough to be of any help?

"I know," Casey said. "You think I'm crazy. Unfortunately,

I'm the only sane one here. What do you want of me?"

Glancy returned his gaze to Casey. He clasped his hands in front and lowered his eyes, becoming as humble as he was able.

"We need your help," Glancy began. "There is some kind of illness attacking the livestock and now the colonists themselves. We can't figure out what it is. We desperately need your help and, although you may not believe it, I'm truly sorry for the pain I've caused you."

Li nodded her head in agreement with each of Glancy's statements.

"You're sorry all right," Casey answered. "Sorry I'm not at your disposal, to be used as needed. You're sorry like Slater is sorry, but I can expect nothing more."

"Please," Li begged.

"This may surprise you, but I don't want either of you to suffer. I know, on a more honest level, your feelings haven't changed. They can't. If I agree to do what I can, will you make a solemn pledge never to medicate me again? Promise never again to bring me back to where I'm unloved and unwanted. That would be unpardonable cruelty."

"Casey," said Glancy with apparent earnestness, "we do want you. We respect—"

Casey held up a bony hand to interrupt. "Don't jeopardize your integrity further. Just answer my question. Do you promise?"

"You have my word," Glancy said, while Li simultaneously said, "I promise."

"It's a senseless task," Casey said. "It'll change nothing, but I'll do what I can. However, you must do as I say, no matter how strange it may seem, without question."

"I swear it," Glancy said.

"I think you swear too easily," Casey replied, but then he untangled his legs and stood on the deck.

Glancy stared at his nakedness and Li averted her eyes.

"It appears my lack of clothing offends you, or perhaps it's my age. Get me something to wear."

Glancy rushed to the preservation chest and returned with a new white jumpsuit.

"Do you need help?" Glancy asked.

"I can manage." After he was clothed, he focused on Glancy. "Take me to them."

Glancy led Casey into the passage, followed by Li, with Yamaguchi bringing up the rear. When the small procession entered the passage, they were immediately confronted by two agri-techs, waiting for news about their ill friends. As soon as they saw Casey, one of the men stepped forward, his face congested with instant rage.

"I will not allow this monster near our brothers!" he yelled, pointing his finger at Casey as if it were a weapon. "How dare you!" As he spoke, he lost the last thread of control and lunged forward, swinging his fist at Casey's face, but Glancy effortlessly deflected the blow and sent the man tumbling to the deck. Although the second agri-tech's facial features were squeezed together by hate and unexpressed accusations, he did not attempt to interfere as the group walked past and entered the treatment room.

CHAPTER 35

Casey examined Simon, and then went to the next room and examined the other two men, surprised to discover that one of them was Jon Brent. When he had completed his cursory examination, he turned to Glancy and spoke.

"I don't know what is causing this state."

Glancy responded with heat. "You don't know? You haven't even used any of the diagnostic equipment! You—"

Casey brought his bony finger up to his lips and Glancy fell silent. Casey lowered his hand and said, "The instruments are useless when used here. Take the men and the large diagnostic unit, and meet me in the Deck Two hall of sleep. They need to be completely naked. And clear the passages. I will not tolerate any further violent confrontations." Then he sank to the floor and sat cross-legged in the middle of the room.

"Are you serious?" Glancy challenged.

But Casey just stared straight ahead.

Li edged over to Glancy. "Let's do what he says."

Glancy shrugged his shoulders, as if to say, "What the hell", and began making preparations. He spoke into his com-collar and, while he was conversing in an inaudible whisper, Casey spoke again.

"When I say I want the passageways cleared, I mean everybody. That includes Geoff Slater, Sten Olson and Jack Sabine."

Glancy paused for only a moment and then whispered into his collar again. He refocused on Casey. "All right. It'll be as you say. I'll have it arranged within the hour."

Casey nodded and seemed to retreat into himself.

When the time arrived, Casey and Yamaguchi walked the curve of the passage and entered the hall of sleep. It was vacant, except for Li Quon, Padraig Glancy, and the three still bodies resting on stretchers. The diagnostic unit, a white, ceramic trough with computer screens at either end, was farther down the passage.

Casey walked past the group and on down the passage

until he found a clear capsule. He motioned for them to follow. Glancy gave Li a disgruntled look, but complied, and with Yamaguchi's assistance moved the unconscious men farther down the hallway.

While they carried out his instructions, Casey remembered a time long ago, when the capsules were all like glass and each contained a sleeping youth. He was stroking the smooth, cool surface of the capsule when Li touched his arm. He turned to her.

"Casey, we've done what you asked. What should we do next?"

"I'm going to enter this capsule and seal it. When I do, I want you to bring each patient before me for a visual inspection." He turned from Li to focus on Glancy.

Frank doubt was present on Glancy's face, but he indicated he understood. Casey stepped into the capsule and activated the closing mechanism. Simon Weiss was the first to be inspected, lying motionless on the stretcher.

When the capsule closed Simon's appearance, as well as the appearance of the others, underwent a dramatic transformation. Simon's left arm was bloated and purple. It was covered with festering sores and an angry redness spread over his shoulder and upper chest. His breathing was rapid and deep. He had little subcutaneous tissue. He appeared to be starving.

Glancy was standing behind the figure on the stretcher. His white jump suit was torn and ragged, with crusted mud covering the lower one-third of his pant legs. Meticulous Glancy looked filthy, his hair hung in stringy clumps and spots of dried mud speckled his face and arms.

Beside him stood Li Quon. Most of the front of her jump suit was torn away, leaving her small, peaked breasts and chest fully exposed. Her chest, breasts, neck and arms were covered with coin-like crusts. Her suit also was caked with mud and her hair and complexion were dull, reflecting malnutrition and the exposure to harsh weather, and her lips were pale, indicating a severe anemia.

When Casey turned his attention to Yamaguchi, he was pleased. Yamaguchi wore a crisp, new suit and was free of filth and mud. His appearance had changed very little, possibly slightly more gaunt, but otherwise he was the Yamaguchi Casey was used to seeing. He had obviously been able to take some information away with him from the time he spent in Casey's cryo-capsule.

Casey motioned with his hands and Jon Brent was placed before him. He could detect no sign of injury. Other than for the ubiquitous malnutrition, he appeared to be simply asleep. The same was true for the other agri-tech, Ravi Ved.

Casey popped open the capsule and stepped back into the passage. As if by magic, everyone looked normal again. Even Simon's gangrenous arm appeared normal. He turned to Glancy. "Padraig, I want you to put each of these men into the diagnostic tub. When I motion, move the focus. When I raise my hand increase the magnification. I want the screens on simple visual output. Do you understand?"

Glancy nodded that he did and Casey re-entered the capsule. When Simon was placed in the tub, it was as Casey knew it would be, septic shock from a devitalized and infected left arm, but when each of the other two were placed in the unit, the overall picture was one of metabolic balance. Casey opened the capsule a crack and instructed Glancy and Li to repeat the process, but to focus on various parts of the men's bodies and at various depths. When his new instructions were carried out, Casey saw a fine patchiness. This fine, mottled appearance was present in Ravi Ved and Jon Brent's legs and in their heads, even though they appeared to be sleeping.

Casey directed them to focus on Jon's legs at increasing depth and magnification. At first it looked like light reflecting off a shimmering surface but, as the magnification was increased, the reason for the patchy appearance became apparent. There were multitudes of fine, silvery worms slithering slowly through the tissues. Despite Casey's experiences and training, he found the sight of the worms overwhelmingly disgusting. He refocused the machine on Jon's head and found the brain stem free of infestation. Either through instinct or outer control, the parasites were leaving the basic vegetative functions intact. Next he examined Jon's cerebral areas. The sight was intensely revolting. More than half of Jon's frontal lobes consisted of writhing worms. Ravi's examination was much the same, with only slightly less central nervous system involvement.

He motioned for them to replace Simon in the tub and searched him as he had the other two men. Simon too had evidence of infestation, but it was limited to his left foot.

Casey cracked open the capsule and stepped into the passage. He was moist with perspiration and pasty white. He eased down onto the deck and searched for professional detachment.

Glancy and Li immediately stepped forward, alarmed by Casey's ill appearance. Li took his pulse, temporarily forgetting her fear of the old guardian. After a couple of minutes, Casey's color returned to a more acceptable shade of white and his lips became pink again. He raised his eyes to Glancy and Li, who were standing over him.

"Well?" Glancy asked.

Casey met their intense gazes with equanimity and then spoke. "I know the cause of their condition. Jon and Ravi have the same problem, but Simon's is different." Casey looked into Li's black eyes, underlined with a light purple from stress and fatigue. "Li, if you are to save Simon, you must amputate his left arm and treat him vigorously with antimicrobials while maintaining cardiovascular support. He is in septic shock and will not live long without aggressive intervention. I would also strongly urge you to amputate his left foot."

Li was stunned. "You are crazy! Why should I amputate perfectly healthy tissue? There's nothing wrong with his arm or his leg. You don't have to be a physician to tell that." Hope was gone from her voice. "This is ridiculous. You are insane," she said, purposefully malicious. "Do you hear me? Insane!"

"Li, did Simon hurt his left arm a few weeks ago? Did he stop using his arm?" Casey asked in an even voice.

"This is utter bullshit," she scoffed and was about to turn away when an unexpected memory surfaced.

"Do you remember something?" Glancy asked.

After another moment, Li spoke. "Simon told me about a fall. He told me that at first the pain was terrible and he'd been afraid to look at his arm. He said it felt like it was broken, but hoped it wasn't. Then the pain just melted away. He said at that point he knew his arm was going to be all right and, when he looked, it looked normal. He thought it was funny and had laughed at himself when he told me about it." She shook her head. "No, not possible. Look at it, Casey. His arm is fine. Ridiculous!"

Casey answered her with a peaceful equanimity. "I'm not here to argue with you. You've asked for my help and I've given it. If you choose to ignore my advice, that is your affair entirely."

Glancy spoke from Casey's other side. "Now just a minute—"

"No." Casey replied. "I will now return to my room. Jon and Ravi have an extensive parasitic infestation. They are beyond salvage."

Glancy ran his fingers through his red hair. Both Glancy and Li looked at Casey with open disbelieve.

Casey ignored their obvious opinion and continued. "The parasites are somehow able to maintain a metabolic balance in the victim's body, so that the overall picture is one of health. It probably allows the parasites a maximum amount of time to live off their host's tissues. I don't know what therapy to recommend, but I suggest you begin with mast cell stimulation and be prepared for total respiratory and cardiovascular support. There is little doubt that Ravi and Jon are terminal, but by treating them you may learn something that will be useful when the next victims begin to arrive."

Casey directed his attention to Li. "Simon also has an early infestation. That is why you must amputate his foot to save him. I would also suggest that you have Glancy examine you for infestation. It appears the agri-techs are at greatest risk, but it also seems there is a predilection for male victims. So, with luck, you'll be found to be free of the parasite."

Li was shaking her head while he spoke.

"I'm sorry, Li."

Casey eased his stiff body up. When he had completed the slow process, he looked directly into Glancy's blue eyes. "Padraig, I don't ask or expect you to believe me. I suspect all our efforts are futile, but you and Li are the medical team now and the responsibility is yours. I give you only two other recommendations: incinerate Jon and Ravi's bodies when they die, and spend a few minutes in the cryo-capsule to examine them yourselves. What do you have to lose?"

Casey turned away and shuffled off down the passage with Yamaguchi following closely behind him. Casey heard Li and Glancy become involved in a quiet, yet intense argument, but he did not turn back. He had done all he could.

When Casey was about to disappear around the curve, Glancy called out, "Casey, wait!"

Casey half turned. "Padraig, you don't need me. I'll be available for a few days if you have questions about the instrumentation, but you'll soon become proficient. I'm afraid you'll have plenty of opportunity to gain experience."

CHAPTER 35

When Casey returned to the medical lab, he was greeted joyously by his little dog, its tail whipping back and forth with eye-blurring speed. Casey walked over to his pallet and sat down, pulling his legs up. Marta jumped into his lap, even before he had completely settled in place. He began scratching behind her ears and she pushed her head back against his hand with uninhibited pleasure.

Yamaguchi resumed his position across the room and then spoke. "What is reality?"

That question was one that had been central to Casey's life since the Awakening. He remembered when Yamaguchi had first asked him that question, during their pleasant stroll in the countryside. This time the question did not seem either esoteric or irrelevant. His focus returned to the present and to Yamaguchi who was patiently waiting, but expecting an answer.

"Before I tell you what I believe about reality, I have a couple of questions for you."

Yamaguchi remained silent.

"I will take that as a 'yes'. Is it possible for the Pinnacle to return to space and be reconnected to the star engine? Can we escape this planet?"

Yamaguchi did not speak.

"I have earned the right to know."

After a moment more, Yamaguchi nodded. "It is possible for the Pinnacle to return to space and reattach to the star engine."

"Could we return to Earth?"

"No. You have told me we have been in stasis for two thousand years. We do not know where we are or where Earth is and it is not possible for us to locate another suitable planet."

"Wouldn't it be better, even if we died trying?"

"The reality of the colony is that they have found paradise. They would not come."

Casey reluctantly nodded. "You're right, of course. There is no hope. I have one more question. I told you there were twelve blanks included in the crew. The truth is, there were eleven, and then there is you. You are different. Why were you included?"

This time Yamaguchi's silence was so long, Casey was beginning to think he would not answer but then he did.

"I am the mission fail-safe. The WSA did not want us to return to Earth. There is nothing to be gained if we were to return. We were to succeed or perish."

"How would you have prevented it?"

"I know how to destroy the star engine."

Casey thought for a minute. "Then, you would not allow us to return to Earth even if we could locate it."

"It is too dangerous for those we left behind."

Casey sighed. "You are right."

"Now, answer my question. What is reality?"

Casey gathered his thoughts before answering. "Reality is what we believe about ourselves and the universe around us. It corresponds, more or less, with the ultimate and unknowable reality of the universe. The more accurately our beliefs and perceptions correspond to the unknowable reality, the more successful we are as organisms. We are waves on a bottomless sea without shores, knowing only that small peak of water that is ourselves and possibly a little of the surrounding sea, but never knowing the breadth or the depth of the sea, never knowing the unknowable that is ultimate reality. To know ultimate reality is to know the universe in all its detail. To know the universe is to be the universe."

Casey shifted his position to get more comfortable and smiled. "Sounds kind of mystical, doesn't it?" Yamaguchi didn't reply, so he continued. "We all see and interpret our existence in terms of our expectations but, on this little Eden of ours, that trait has been pathologically exaggerated. Specifically, our window on reality has been narrowed to the point that, what our senses and minds tell us is real is nothing more than a reflection of our expectations and desires, and as our perception of reality falls further and further away from that great and unknowable reality, we come ever closer to extinction. I see no hope for this colony's survival."

Yamaguchi was listening, desperately trying to hold onto the meaning of the words even as they fled, leaving nothing more than the faint afterglow of an unremembered dream. "How do I know what is real if you do not tell me?" he asked.

Casey focused his attention on little Marta and patted her fat belly. He didn't feel frustrated or superior. He was resigned to the fact that the rest of the colony could not remember, or understand, what he knew to be their true state of being.

He reached under his pallet and withdrew a stack of rectangular cards. "Come here, Yamaguchi. I have a gift for you."

The big man obediently stepped forward and dropped to his knees in front of Casey, so their faces were approximately at the same height.

"Yamaguchi, my friend, I'm going to show you some pictures I've taken. When you look at these pictures do not expect at all, let your eyes see, not your mind, and then remember what your eyes have seen."

Yamaguchi viewed each of the pictures without expression and Casey was certain this reflected his inner state as well. When he had finished, he handed the pictures back to Casey.

"Now I am going to explain to you what you've just seen. You saw a green, globular structure that rises directly out of the mud in the center of our camp, rising upward until its peak is lost to sight in a haze of gray clouds. It looks like a free form structure, but it is not. It changes in each picture. It is, in my opinion, alive. It's also my observation that it is always drizzling or raining, whether it's apparent day, or apparent night. The ground is not covered by grass, but rather, by a mucky goo of mud and puddles of water. That is the answer to the transformer malfunction. It was sitting in water. In some of the photographs there are white streaks that look like the roots of a tree. At first I thought they were artifacts, but after my recent observation of our unfortunate fellow colonists, I believe they represent some kind of worm life. If that is the case, some of these worms must be over a meter in diameter and a hundred meters long."

Casey met Yamaguchi's eyes and the intensity of Yamaguchi's gaze would have frightened him, if he really cared about such things anymore.

Though Casey had no reason to believe that Yamaguchi could understand or remember, he continued. "I've stood in front of this green tower and tried to visualize it, but I can't see it. I've tried to touch it, but I can't feel it. I believe the expectations of the rest of the colonists are too great for my meager expectations to overcome. I also believe something has happened to the colonists, that they, and you, have been tampered with, but I escaped this manipulation, possibly because of the unconventional location of my cryo-capsule. I can almost remember... something... something happened near the end of my term as guardian. I was terrorized by...." Casey's forehead wrinkled in concentration, but the memory slipped away once again.

Casey looked down into the big, brown eyes of his adoring puppy. When he looked up he was amazed to see Yamaguchi's cheeks moist with tears, but the big man's eyes shown with the brightness of undisguised joy.

"I can remember the pictures," Yamaguchi said, his voice choking with emotion. "You are the teacher of reality." He bowed his head until his forehead was touching the filthy deck next to Casey's pallet.

Casey was embarrassed for himself and for Yamaguchi. "Please," he said, while gently trying to pull Yamaguchi's head up, but it would not budge.

Yamaguchi continued. "I am but a pebble and you are a mountain. You are the One," he declared fervently, his face pressed against the deck.

"Yamaguchi," Casey said firmly, "get up. I'm only a man, spared by luck, if you can call this luck."

"Ask me to do. Be the will that directs me. Honor me, Teacher. I live to serve," the giant rumbled into the deck.

"Would you please get up? Here, get up, and I'll give you another gift."

"I do as you command." The big man sat up and rocked back on his heels, clasping his hands in front of him in a reverent salute.

"This will never do," Casey muttered. He released a long, exasperated breath and then thought, what difference does it really make? He looked on the deck between his pallet and the bulkhead and found the small, gray box that Lisa had left with him to repair. He held it out to Yamaguchi. "Here, Yamaguchi. Here," he urged, "take this."

The man took the camera in his hands, but had eyes only for Casey. Casey tried to ignore the look, but had to stifle a laugh when he thought how much Yamaguchi resembled his little puppy when he scratched her tummy.

"This is a camera," Casey said. "I don't have any photographic blocks left, but I'm sure Lisa Bouviet has some, if you can persuade her to part with them." He showed Yamaguchi how the camera worked and then got up to find the strobe he had rigged to work in conjunction with the camera's flash. "Now, if you do manage to get hold of some photo blocks, you'll be able to observe, even if you're not free to question."

Yamaguchi's wide smile revealed teeth that were like little, white rocks spaced along a ridge. "I will do as you instruct, Teacher."

"Good, fine," Casey said with a note of resignation. "I do have one more question."

"Yes, Teacher."

"Why did you stop me from going to the ocean that day?"

Yamaguchi's brow wrinkled in concentration as he thought. "It's hard to remember."

"I understand. Don't worry about it."

"No, I must answer." He spoke slowly, as if each word caused pain. "The ocean is bad. It would've killed you...and then...then I knew I had to kill you. Wheeler was inside my head. I—"

"Wheeler? What do you mean?"

Yamaguchi let out a long breath and shook his head. "What did you ask me?"

"Nothing, my friend, nothing at all."

The strain left Yamaguchi's face. He stood, bowed, and then strode purposefully from the room, leaving Casey alone with his only other friend, little Marta.

CHAPTER 37

The following days passed quickly for Casey as he produced cube after cube of instructions and information. He had temporarily managed to suppress his thoughts about the future and was enthusiastic when he interacted with his two students. It was pleasurable and satisfying for him to discuss the science and art of healing.

He made occasional inspections of the cardio-respiratory devices and the regeneration tank, which now contained the floating body of Simon Weiss, making adjustments and explaining while he worked. Both Glancy and Quon were bright, learned their lessons quickly, and began developing the seeds of good judgment. Li Quon was particularly motivated, spending much of her time monitoring the regeneration tank, which bubbled around the father of her child, a child that was being cared for by guild members in the Agri-Dome. She had given up all pretense of returning to her idyllic life as an agri-tech and had begun wearing guardian white.

Casey noticed, the last time he had visited the treatment room, that there was a pile of discarded uniforms in the rear corner and surmised Li and Padraig had not only seen their patients, but had also seen themselves. Although he still considered it impossible, he made repeated efforts to get them to generalize from their observations of the victims to the planet as a whole, but they inevitably ended up looking at him blankly. The change that had been inflicted on them, and the grip the planet had on them, was too strong to overcome.

However, Casey could claim one other small victory; he had managed to convince Li and Padraig to insist that the new fowl and swine be sequestered inside the Bio-Dome. That small success had been enough to satisfy Slater, at least for the time being. Gradually, Casey relinquished his efforts and began to spend less time in the treatment rooms and more time sitting on his pallet in the lab.

As Casey had predicted, Jon and Ravi had died in a matter of days, and also as predicted, there were others to take their place. He received the information with calm acceptance. He could feel the hold of the therapeutic disk weakening and he resisted the temptation of replacing it. He consciously chose to allow himself to drift away from the terrifying reality he knew to exist, choosing instead a more palatable reality that corresponded less accurately with that of the great unknowable.

On one such day, while Casey sat cross-legged, his mind clear of thoughts, Yamaguchi entered and bowed before him. Casey had given up asking Yamaguchi to halt his inappropriate obsequiousness. He knew that regardless of what they each chose to do, it would have little impact on their ultimate destiny.

"Teacher, I have an offering. Will you accept?" Yamaguchi waited for Casey's response with a face that anyone other than Casey would have considered empty, but Casey had learned to detect the subtle signs of controlled emotion. He noticed a minuscule narrowing of Yamaguchi's eyelids; he was concerned, and a small lip pressure; he was hopeful.

"Sure, my friend," Casey said, "any gift from you is more than acceptable."

Yamaguchi bent at the waist and extended a hand, holding out a photograph.

"I see you had success with Lisa. Must have been your gift for gab." Casey smiled as he took the photograph and began to study it. It showed a woman in the tattered remains of a yellow uniform, holding a white, tapering object in her arms. He instructed Yamaguchi to increase the intensity of the light-lines and held the picture close to his face so he could see the details better. There was a red strand extending from the object to the woman, touching her chest. He looked back up at Yamaguchi without the slightest idea of what he was being shown.

Yamaguchi smiled his pebbly smile and with satisfaction answered Casey's unspoken question. "It's a baby."

Casey first experienced denial, and then acceptance and repugnance in rapid succession. He felt sick with yet another confirmation of the hopeless situation of his fellow humans. And such a fate! It was better that they remained ignorant and had at least a taste of happiness, even if it was based on fantasy.

"I wonder what they are." Casey mused. It was only a spoken thought, a question that he didn't expect to answer. He reached down and lifted his dog onto his lap. The dog nudged her cool nose against Casey's hand, urging him to pet her, but he only sat there, retreating and withdrawing. Then his hands began their mindless stroking of the little dog. He was not even aware that Yamaguchi had left.

The next Casey was aware, he was trying to force his eyes to focus, as if struggling to the surface after a deep dive in cold water. Finally, he saw a face and then recognized the face as belonging to Yamaguchi.

"I have returned," Yamaguchi said.

It was late in the evening, but to Casey it seemed like no time had passed, or else ages had passed, he couldn't quite decide.

"What is it, my friend?" Casey asked, his speech thick and indistinct.

"I live to serve," Yamaguchi replied.

"A fine sentiment. What can I do for you?"

"No, Teacher, that time has passed. Now I do for you."

Yamaguchi brought a small bundle into view. It was squirming with concealed movement. He pulled the covering open and shocked Casey back to full alertness. It was a baby with chubby, dimpled cheeks and long, dark lashes. The baby reached out to Casey, its pudgy fingers widely spread in appealing supplication. Marta jumped off Casey's lap and stood straight-legged with her teeth barred, growling and barking.

"Where did you get this?" Casey demanded.

Yamaguchi bowed his head and lowered his eyes to the deck, which was still partially covered with stained copies of the "Gazette".

"Our duty is to question and observe," Yamaguchi said in a quiet voice, including Casey in his rigid ethical framework. "Did you not wonder what the babies really were? Did you not ask? Is it not our duty to find the answer after we have asked the question?" Yamaguchi's tone turned accusatory and he seemed confused by his teacher's response.

Casey looked again at the pink-cheeked babe, smiling and flapping its arms with apparent joy. He tried to see beyond the appealing facade, but the mother's expectations were too strong for him to overcome. He wondered what this world would have been like if the colonists hadn't been young and optimistic.

"It must be observed. It is our duty," Yamaguchi declared.

Casey thought about the mother, somewhere out there in

the colony, frantically searching for her missing baby. Well, the harm had been done. There would be a price to pay now whether the baby was inspected or not. He was reluctant, but he was still susceptible to the expectations others placed on him, despite his protestations to the contrary. He arose and Marta stood near his feet, continuing her deep-throated growl. He didn't rebuke the dog, but did command her to stay, before leading the way to the adjacent treatment room.

When he entered, he saw there was a body on each of the two tables. Both of the supine figures were partially hidden from view by cardio-support devices. Casey couldn't resist walking over to get a closer look. He recognized them both, of course, and both were male agri-techs.

He wondered how long it would be before members from other guilds become hosts for the parasites.

He picked up a portable surgical kit from the work counter, mentally scolding his students for sloppiness, and walked over to the cryo-capsule they had moved into the room. He was glad that neither of his protégés was present. He doubted they would've been able to comprehend that the baby was not real.

He stood for a moment with his back to Yamaguchi. He didn't really want to hold the baby. Thoughts continued to tumble through his mind. He could always escape back to his lab and blame it all on Yamaguchi. The thought was there. He didn't pay any serious attention to it, but was ashamed that such an idea should even occur to him and glad for the privacy of thoughts, at least among humans.

He clicked open the capsule door and stepped in with the kit in his hand. Yamaguchi stood nearby, holding the covered cherub in his arms. Casey felt inexplicably depraved as he reached out to collect the little bundle. It was warm and full of movement, definitely alive and vigorous. He leaned back into the capsule and nodded for Yamaguchi to close the door. Then Yamaguchi walked out of the room to stand guard in the passageway.

Casey remained still for a minute, hesitant to look upon the life form he held in his arms, knowing what he would probably see, but reluctant to witness the fact that the charming little baby had been transformed into a pale, fat worm. His stomach churned as he delicately took hold of a corner of the blanket and pulled it back. When he saw the contents, he went rigid.

The sickly paleness and the waves of movement up its segmented body said "putrefaction and rot" to Casey's mind. The general appearance of the beast was that of a giant maggot. He would surely have dropped the undulating ugliness if he hadn't felt, at the same time, a horrifying curiosity about the creature.

He could see no mouth or eyes. As he unwrapped the abomination further, a thin appendage slithered toward him. He quickly held it away and pushed back against the smooth, hard surface of the capsule, but it wasn't far enough. He turned his head to the side and felt with disgust the cool touch of a small suction pad being attached to the skin of his chest. A thin, pulsating line of red blood traveled down the translucent appendage and into the creature's body. Frantic, he looked through the clear crystal of the capsule into the room, but Yamaguchi was still in the corridor.

He jerked open his kit and withdrew a laser-scalpel, spilling the rest of the kit's contents onto the floor of the capsule. He flicked the blade on and stabbed at the body of the creature, but the blade didn't even leave a mark. He slashed the blade across the tentacle attached to his chest and, when he severed it, instantly perceived a high-pitched cry, at the upper limits of human hearing. Perhaps it wasn't even hearing at all. It pierced his skull like a sharp pick, causing him to wince and grind his teeth.

The severed appendage writhed its way back into a hole in the worm's side, but the portion still attached to Casey chest continued to pump out his blood, so that it was spurting onto the floor of capsule, making it red and slick. With the skill of a surgeon, Casey next used the scalpel on himself, neatly excising the suction cup from his chest wall. The wound continued to ooze and coated his chest with blood.

He was overcome by rage. He stared at the creature squirming around the floor of the capsule, screeching its painful cry. He reached down with determination and pinned the beast to the floor. It wriggled and slithered, but he managed to stick the blade into the orifice through which the tentacle had disappeared. The blade entered without resistance, causing the worm to curl around the wound. Four new tentacles sprouted and searched for Casey's hand, but he held tight. He felt the edge of the blade enter a crevice that encircled that segment of the worm and pulled the blade into the crack, enlarging it as he made a circumferential cut around the struggling beast, which was becoming increasing slippery as a thick brown substance oozed from the line of the incision. When the cut was complete, the worm split along the seam with a distinct "snap" and then lay still. The piercing screams of the creature ceased.

Casey retched from the sight of the severed worm. He reached up with a shaky hand and opened the latch, falling out the door and onto the deck.

While he lay there, Yamaguchi re-entered the room. He quickly rushed over to Casey, who was covered with blood, and knelt at his side, but his eyes were drawn to the contents of the capsule.

Casey shifted his weight and looked over his shoulder; he too was stunned by the gruesome sight of a decapitated baby. It was a revolting sight. Please, he begged to himself, let the truth be as I saw it in the capsule, not as I see it now. The warmth and wetness drew his attention to the wound on his own chest. His rocking sanity began to stabilize, although his body continued to react with uncontrollable shuddering.

He shifted his eyes to Yamaguchi, who remained as he was, his gaze fixed on the horrendous sight on the floor of the capsule. Casey knew without a doubt that what he'd just done would result in his own death, but he didn't want his death to be at the hands of his friend.

Yamaguchi's muscles were visibly tensing. He appeared as if he was about to lash out.

"Yamaguchi," Casey gasped, "it's not a baby. It's a worm."

Yamaguchi's face appeared stern and unforgiving but, instead of releasing himself to reach out and crush Casey, he maintained his tenuous control and stiffly reached into his pouch. He pulled out a photograph and studied it for a moment. As Casey watched with held breath, the enormous tension in Yamaguchi's musculature eased.

"It is as you say, Teacher," Yamaguchi said in a flat voice.

Exhausted by his ordeal, Casey slumped onto the deck, thankful for the discipline that allowed the giant to resist the pressure of the combined expectation of an entire colony. After resting for a moment, he pushed himself up to a squat.

"Go away, Yamaguchi. There'll be hell to pay. Go down to my cryo-capsule."

"No." It was a response that did not invite discussion. He stood and pulled Casey to his feet. He practically carried Casey back to the lab, where he released him to collapse onto his pallet. Marta smelled the blood and stood back from Casey, barking and running back and forth in a half circle. Yamaguchi immediately turned to the portal and passed through to reenter the corridor.

After a short while, Casey stumbled his way to the personal room and cleansed the blood from his chest, carefully leaving the blue, dermal disk in place. The coin-like wound continued to ooze. He returned to the lab and applied a coagulant gel. His gaze fell on the molecular synthesizer. He thought for a moment and then picked it up. This would be the last time he would ever use it. With a sigh, he entered a special code and a black disk was produced.

He was suddenly so exhausted, he could barely walk. He staggered over to his pallet and collapsed onto it. After a few minutes, he gathered his strength and sat up. He lifted the edge of the bedding, put the black disk under it, and let the bedding fall into place. With one more effort, he pulled his legs up and sat cross-legged, back against the bulkhead, eyes closed, but not asleep.

The portal "swished" open and Casey looked up. It was Yamaguchi.

Yamaguchi first filled Marta's food and water bowels, as was his custom, and then walked over and knelt in front of Casey, head bowed. "Teacher, I'm ashamed of my weakness, but I must return to the cryo-capsule. I'm losing the thread of true reality. I've hidden the worm and will return when I'm able."

Casey nodded. "Go, my friend. It's your duty."

When the big man arose, Casey was barely aware of the movement. He had withdrawn to his private place, a place of peace. Marta jumped onto his lap and snuggled until comfortable.

CHAPTER 38

Casey awakened from his trance after an hour of mindless meditation, refreshed and at peace with his fate. It shouldn't be long now, Casey thought, and smoothed the fur on his little puppy's back and scratched her behind her ears. Marta settled deeper into Casey's lap with contentment.

The portal opened. Casey didn't have to look. When the visitor spoke, it was the voice he expected to hear.

"Conklin, I'm surprised to find you here. I would've expected you to run and hide like a yellow-belly coward."

"Hello, Jack," Casey said in a calm voice. "That's kind of redundant, isn't it?"

Sabine walked over and jerked Casey's head around, so that Casey's face was only a few centimeters from his own. "You think you're so smart, smarter than the rest of us, but you're stupid. Stupid!" he yelled, and then smiled and pushed Casey roughly against the bulkhead. He backed up a couple of steps and studied Casey, looking for a reaction, looking for fear and then his gaze drifted to the wall above Casey's pallet.

Casey had cut out individual letters from the "Gazette" and had permanently attached them to the wall with surgical glue. The letters varied in size, like an old-fashioned ransom note. It read: "WiThouT rEaliTy ThErE is no fuTurE. Joy bEcomEs sorrow. SuccEss bEcomEs fAilurE. LifE bEcomEs dEATh."

"Would you like me to read it for you?" Casey asked.

"I know how to read."

"Will wonders never cease?"

"Shut up, you moron. There's a missing baby."

Casey said nothing.

Sabine hardly noticed. "Don't deny it. I know you took the baby. I know you caused the death aboard the Pinnacle, the computer memory wipe, all of it."

Casey remained as he was.

"So, you don't deny it," Sabine declared with satisfaction.

The warmth of Casey's serenity cooled. A chill spread out from his stomach and traveled down his arms and legs. He had no doubt that this was the end of his life. His memory cut loose and began to wander, back to Earth, to his time as a youth at the Stanford-San Jose Bubble and of his mentor, Doctor Marta, and then on to Copper Mountain and Britty, especially Britty. The memories clutched at his heart; of his entire life, these memories were what he valued most.

Sabine continued to drone on in the background of Casey's consciousness. "You have no idea how I've longed for this moment. You've been a poison in our midst. I'm going to cleanse us and there will be no reprisal, only praise. You will not get a last minute reprieve. Commander Slater knows I'm here. In fact, I'm sure he's listening at this very minute." Sabine barked out a coarse, unpleasant sound that for him was a laugh.

Marta had been snarling softly since Sabine's appearance. When he laughed, Marta jumped off Casey lap and began growling loudly, teeth barred. Sabine smiled. He withdrew the pink gun with the over-sized barrel from his holster and activated it; a soft "whine" could be heard.

"No!" Casey yelled.

"You stole my gold chain, you thieving bastard. If you tell me where you hid it, I might be persuaded to spare your mangy dog."

"I can't. I threw it into ship recycling."

"You must think I'm the stupid one. Who would throw a gold chain into recycling? Last chance."

"Honest! I'm telling the truth. Please, don't hurt—"

There was an innocent sounding "pop", followed by the squealing cry of intolerable pain. The little dog's fur was smoking as it writhed on the deck, crying piteously as she tried to crawl back to her friend and protector but, once started, the fire burned with a relentless consumption. The puppy stopped its hopeless struggle and became quiet and still in death, but the fire burned on until Marta had been reduced to a small pile of ash. The room filled with the odor of burnt fur and flesh.

Casey's heart was torn. He could withhold tears for himself, but not for his little puppy, faithful and innocent. It was a grief too intense for sound. With blurred vision, he turned his gaze to Sabine. When he spoke his voice was a feral growl of pain and anger.

"I'm not afraid of you, Sabine. I'm not afraid of death. There is nothing for me here, nothing for any of us really, but

I have one last duty to perform, so that what remains of this colony's existence will not be fouled further by the existence of an evil creature like you."

While Casey spoke he slipped his hand under the edge of the bedding and then secretly brought it out again. "It's not a metabolic problem with you, an imbalance that could be treated with proper molecular therapy. It's functional. It is you. The pleasure you take in other's suffering, the total lack of regard you have for others, is so much a part of you, that to remove it, would be to remove you and that is what I intend to do."

Sabine smiled his predatory smile, pleased to see the pain he had caused. He had scored. He swaggered over to Casey and spoke. "You are a weak, old man." For emphasis he slapped Casey's face with the back of his hand. "You make me sick with your whining talk and empty threats." He brought the burn-gun up to Casey's forehead. "Makes you sweat, doesn't it? But it's not going to be that easy for you. That would be too quick. I want you to know what I'm going to do, so you can think about it. I'm going to place the burn pellet in your foot. Do you know how long it will take for the fire to reach up and kill you?" He grabbed Casey's neck. "Do you know, Conklin?"

Casey said nothing.

"I'll tell you. It'll be four or possibly five minutes of the most excruciating pain it's possible for a human to feel. It'll seem like a lifetime. You'll beg me to kill you before you die. And after I've finished with you, I'll treat that bloated Yamaguchi to the same and watch with pleasure as he withers away to nothing." Sabine kept a tight hold on Casey's neck as he spoke, but he pulled the barrel of the gun away from Casey's forehead.

With a barely noticeable gesture, Casey reached up and touched the hand that squeezed his throat. Where Casey's fingers touched Sabine, there was now a black disk. The smile fled from Sabine's face. Casey could see him struggling to raise the burn gun, but he could not. His hand fell away from Casey's neck and he collapsed into a limp heap on the deck, eyelids partially open.

Casey spoke in a quiet voice to the motionless body crumpled next to his pallet. "Only you could force me to do something as repugnant as this. Only you could hurt me so deeply, when I thought I was safely beyond such feelings. I know you're awake. It must be terrible to be awake, but unable to breath, unable to move. I will keep you company until you die. I'm sorry to be so barbaric about your eradication but, as you say, I'm only a weak, old man."

Casey took a moment to stare at the ash that had been his little dog and then returned his attention to the crumpled and motionless man lying on the deck. He knew that Sabine was not yet dead.

"It's based on an ancient chemical," Casey said, "from Earth itself, called curare. I altered it to make it ultra-fast acting. I was hoping I would never have to use it, but you have forced my last act to be one of violence. You are probably unconscious by now, but I'll sit with you for the next few minutes to ensure that you'll never return to haunt this colony after I'm gone."

When the minutes had passed, Casey felt empty and incredibly sad. He felt alone and defiled. He reached up and ripped the blue disk off his chest, and then tossed it onto the deck, searching for oblivion.

Before Slater could organize a response, Yamaguchi entered the room. He quickly deduced the events that had transpired, from the pink gun, to the small mound of ashes, to the lifeless form of Sabine with the black disk showing plainly on the back of his hand, to the blank stare and bare chest of Casey, who sat cross-legged on his pallet.

He did not hesitate. He scooped up Casey and re-entered the passage. Running swiftly down the curve of the corridor, he dropped into the down-tube and exited on the Storage Deck. With no wasted motion, he climbed the land-shaper ladder and lowered Casey through the hatch. He laid Casey out on the powdery deck of the cabin and activated the closing mechanism. Then he sat down next to him to wait.

CHAPTER 39

Slater stood looking up at the control cabin of the land-shaper. Black-suited Olson stood to his left and white-suited Glancy to his right. Lisa Bouviet had come rushing over when she heard the rumors and a short time later Aleksandr Protonov arrived.

"They're in there all right," Slater said, and then turned to the power-tech who was standing behind him. "Tabor, make sure the energy conduits are interrupted. I don't want them to power up and break out of here. I want their heads."

Tabor nodded and trotted over to the oversized machine where he removed a panel. After inspecting it, he used insulated tongs to remove a blue, crystalline cylinder and then returned to stand near Slater.

"The storage cells have a minimal charge," Tabor reported. "They'll still have limited back-up power in the cabin, but not enough to activate the land-shaper. With this transducer out of the circuit, they won't be able to access ship's power," he added with pride.

Glancy stared at the man, but said nothing about the fact that Casey had saved his life.

"Good! Good," Slater rubbed his hands together. "I want you to go up to the bridge and monitor energy use so you can take action if they've set up a backup system."

"Yes, Commander." Tabor hurried away and disappeared into the up-tube.

Next, Slater turned to Glancy. "How long will it take you to prepare a lethal toxin that can be pumped into the land-shaper?"

Glancy stared at the hawk-faced man before he answered. "Don't you think we should try to find out what happened? Find out if they did it and if so why?"

Slater turned to face him fully. "I saw the blood around that cryo-capsule and Sabine's corpse. He was a good man. You saw it too."

"A good man? Sabine?"

"You're one to talk."

"I never took pleasure—"

"Shut the hell up. There's no explanation that would make one iota of difference. They are baby killers."

"Geoff, please. I've seen some strange things lately. We should at least hear their side of what happened."

"Glancy, you may be the current receptacle of medical knowledge, but I have the information cubes that Casey so thoughtfully prepared and I have Li Quon. You are dispensable. Am I making myself clear?"

Glancy looked down at the gray deck.

"I asked you how long it'd take to make a poison. I think a gas would suit our purposes."

"About an hour," Glancy mumbled.

"Then what are you waiting for!" Slater screamed.

Glancy turned away and slowly walked toward the stairs that led to the up-tube.

After he had disappeared into the tube, Slater leaned close to Olson. "Glancy's not the same man he was. Somehow Conklin has subverted him, just like he subverted Yamaguchi. I don't trust him anymore. When I give the word, I want you to kill him. Do you think you can take him?"

"Not a problem. It'll be my pleasure. You do realize with Yamaguchi, Sabine and Glancy no longer with us, I'll be your last man."

"Aren't you up to it?"

"I am and I can recruit a few solid men from the guilds. I know who they are."

"Excellent. You'll be Captain of the Guard and…you'll be compensated appropriately."

Slater patted Olson on his back and walked over to where Lisa and Protonov were standing.

"Good afternoon, Aleksandr. We have the baby kidnappers trapped in the land-shaper."

"Who are they?" Protonov asked.

"Casey Conklin and Yamaguchi. They also killed Jack Sabine."

"I wouldn't exactly call that a loss." Protonov scratched his beard as he thought. "Conklin is no surprise, but Yamaguchi?"

"Conklin did something medical to him. Gave him some sort of mind altering drug."

"And the baby?" Protonov asked.

"Still missing. I think we should prepare ourselves for the

worst. How's Brita doing?"

"Badly, of course. When I think about her missing baby all I can think about is our little Luka. You plan to kill the bastards, I assume."

"Of course." Slater turned his attention to Lisa. "What do you think? Will this make the 'Gazette'?"

Lisa smiled brightly. "Great story."

"I'll want to see the copy before you print it."

"Not a problem."

Slater took to a deep, satisfying breath. Things were finally coming together. All the loose ends were tied up, except one.

"Would you excuse me for a moment?" he asked with a slight bow at the waist.

"Of course, Commander," Lisa answered with a curtsey.

He took a few steps away and waved Olson over.

"Sten, you said you knew of a few colonists who could be enlisted in the...we'll call it the Public Safety Service."

"Yes."

"Does that also mean that you know of some who don't support my leadership, other than the obvious, like Li Quon?"

"Yes, I do."

Slater nodded while he thought and then refocused on Sten. "Did you know Mitchell Mason?"

"Not really. I only met him once. He was the one who recruited me."

"Well, he taught me once a leader has a person or group under control to never let up, to never give even a sliver of an opportunity for them to resist. What would happen if a dissident group gained control of the Pinnacle and lifted off to land elsewhere on the planet to start a competing colony? We need the technology of the Pinnacle and the instrumentation and machinery. Ultimately, they'd win."

"But, Commander, how could that possibly happen?"

"I admit, it's not likely. Still, it's not impossible." Slater tapped a tooth with his index finger as he thought and then suddenly stopped. He touched his collar. "Jane, connect me with Mika Ishida."

A few seconds later, Mika's soft voice came through. "Commander, what can I do for you?"

"Mika, can the Pinnacle's engines lift it off Eden?"

There was a pause and then, "Yes, but why would you ask that? This is a perfect planet and a perfect location on the planet."

"I'm not suggesting that we move the Pinnacle, exactly the opposite. I want to make certain it stays where it is. Can you permanently disable the engines while keeping the power and other functions intact?"

There was another pause and then Mika answered. "Yes, we could do that but it would never lift off again. You do realize that, right?"

"That's exactly what I want."

"Very well. I'll be over with a crew. Shouldn't take long. May I ask a question?"

"Certainly."

"I heard you caught the person who stole Brita's baby. I bet it's Casey Conklin."

"Bingo. But he did have an accomplice...Yamaguchi."

"No kidding. That's really something. I guess you never know. We'll be over shortly. When we get done, I'll be able to guarantee you that the Pinnacle will never be a spaceship again."

"Excellent. See you soon." Such joy and satisfaction.

Slater walked with Olson back toward Lisa and Protonov and noticed another person had joined them.

Slater paused. "Wheeler? Why are you here?"

"We cannot allow you to disable the ship. We have need of it," Wheeler said.

"Excuse me. Who the hell do you think you are? Get the fuck out of here! You have no say in this matter and who the hell is 'we'?" Slater asked.

The question was never answered. Darkness descended upon all the humans of Eden. All sensory in-put ceased, external and internal. There was no feedback to even verify existence. It was a disembodiment, like a mind floating in the deepest void of a starless space. It could easily have been the feeling of death.

CHAPTER 40

Casey was floating in a warm sea. Years led to decades and decades led to centuries and centuries led to millennia. He was safe and content, but then there came a cooling change. He was irritated at being disturbed. His consciousness began to coalesce, returning from a place of comfort and softness to a place of hard edges and pain. He was angry. Rage began pumping through him. It was an unwelcome intrusion, an interruption of serenity, and then there was light. He opened his eyes more and saw an indistinct glow. He was aware of his body. It felt young and powerful. He could feel the position of his arms and legs and against his skin a warm, moist surface, hugging every square centimeter, except for the crack of light and the light was growing. As it grew, he shut his eyes again. He wanted to return to where he'd been, but the comfortable warmth continued to retreat.

He was being pushed out. His place of security and love was disappearing. He fell forward and found himself lying on a resilient surface. He opened his eyes and saw mint-green. He moaned and rolled onto his side. Moment by moment he became an individual again.

He looked across the pastel green surface and saw other bodies. He pushed his torso off the surface and swung around to sit cross-legged, feeling vaguely at home in that position.

The others were moving. He heard groans and then a soft sobbing from one of them. They looked strange, like babies, yet they were adults. They looked like animated mannequins, smooth, hairless. Their heads were bald and round; they had no ears. One of them turned toward Casey. There was something familiar. He felt he should know this person. The person sat up and stared back at Casey with an answering look of confusion. The person had no breasts, no nipples, and no genitals.

Casey turned his attention to himself, hardly recognizing his own body: no penis, no scrotum, no pubic hair or umbilicus. He touched his chest, no nipples. It felt like he was touching himself, yet, it was not himself. The others were also touching and examining their bodies, as if they had never seen themselves before.

One of the strange bodies stood. It was not a man and not a woman, but there could be no mistaking that physique.

"Yamaguchi?" Casey whispered.

The giant turned toward Casey. His head, without his small ears, was more like a ball than ever.

Casey stood and glanced down at himself, embarrassed by his lack of genitals, but Yamaguchi seemed unconcerned. The others remained sitting, looking at themselves and each other. Besides Yamaguchi, there were four others. They all looked familiar, yet so different.

"What's happened?" Casey asked, his voice hoarse and tight.

"It is not time to ask questions, Teacher. It is time to observe," Yamaguchi responded with his steady rumble.

Casey found comfort in its sameness.

"Who are you?" a person began squealing, and then scooted on hands and knees like a crab, until he-she-it was up against the resilient green wall, pressing into it, as if to escape. "Who are you?" the person screamed.

Casey's memories began to gather back into a linear continuity. There had to be a relationship between that beastly planet and their current predicament.

"Who are you?" the voice cried out.

It was a reasonable question. "I am Casey Conklin. I suggest we all introduce ourselves. I think I know who most of you are, but let's firm up our perceptions." Casey nodded toward a person who was sitting quietly and watching.

"I am Commander Geoffrey Slater."

Just as arrogant and presumptuous as ever, thought Casey. That hadn't changed.

"And you?" Casey said, pointing to a person who was staring straight ahead, motionless.

The person didn't respond. His physique suggested he was a man, or at least had been. Casey walked over to him and gently pushed on his shoulder, causing him to sway slightly, but then he returned to his prior position.

"And you?" Casey repeated softly. "Who are you?"

There was no response, no indication of sentience in his gray eyes.

Slater spoke. "Looks like Protonov to me."

Casey studied the man again. His sharp, authoritarian beard had been covering a weak, receding chin but, otherwise, with the addition of hair and ears, the person would look like Protonov. Protonov, a man who took great pains to establish control and order, a man who preferred to exist in the realm of exacting mathematics, was unable to break through into their current reality.

When Slater had identified the man as Protonov, the person sitting next to him began scooting away. She was still beautiful, hair or no hair. Her green eyes looked to Casey, beseeching, but then she bent forward, trying to cover her chest when she no longer had breasts. It was a contradiction to see her now modest when there was nothing to hide.

"Casey," she said. "Help me."

Casey knelt next to her, but she pulled away from his touch.

"I'll help you, Lisa," Casey said, "when I can, but for now you need to be strong. Don't drift away. We'll find a way out of this."

Slater laughed.

Casey ignored Slater and looked over at the person crab walking along the curve of the oval chamber, stopping only after he had gained the farthest distance possible from the rest of the group, about fifteen meters. He was big and fair skinned. His ice-blue eyes darted wildly about. It could only be Sten Olson.

Casey walked slowly toward the cringing figure. "Sten?"

The man shivered with fear and brought his arms up to ward off Casey's approach. "Stay away!" he screamed. He renewed his efforts to escape, pushing with his legs, seemingly unaware that the pumping of his legs resulted in no further movement.

Casey stopped and returned to the group at the other end of the oval room.

"Sit down, Conklin," Slater ordered. "I'm in charge here."

Casey glared at Slater for a moment before replying. "No one is in charge here, least of all you."

Casey was no longer a feeble old man; he was taller and stronger than Slater. Slater made a motion as if he was going to stand up and physically confront Casey, but then settled back into place and smiled.

"All right, Casey," Slater said easily, "tell us what to do, if you think you're capable of making command decisions."

"What decisions? We don't know where we are, or why our bodies have been subjected to these weird changes, or even who did this to us. It's time for us to pool our thoughts and work as a team. Did you do something that triggered this...change?"

Slater grunted derisively. "Did you? That seems more likely. You are such a simpleton. All teams need a leader and I'm the only one trained to lead. I'm the only one capable of assuming—" He stopped in mid-sentence and stared past Casey.

Casey followed the direction of Slater's gaze. He was as speechless as the rest.

The being had arrived soundlessly. Its skin was a rich indigo and its large, black eyes seemed to stare, with the occasional flickering of a transparent membrane. The creature's mouth was shark-like with a jack-o-lantern smile filled with sharp triangular teeth. Its arms appeared to end in stubs but, when the creature spoke, it flipped the lower part of its arms forward. It had triple-jointed arms that ended in two delicate fingers and a thumb and, when the lower arm was extended, a sharp blade projected backward from its lower elbow. Its legs were bent at the knees and seemed to consist of two parts, like that of a human. There was something about the creature that touched a memory in Casey's mind.

"I am CkCkCk," the creature said. It was a guttural sound, from deep in the creature's throat. When it spoke, the wide shark-like smile did not change. It was as if the words were being projected out of a monstrous marionette. "I serve the Masters and the Mother. They are pleased with you. The new generation of Masters was well nurtured. All but one survived and were strong and healthy when they were harvested from your care."

The voice issuing from the creature's mouth paused. When no one said anything, it continued. "You are confused and frightened. Rebirth can be stressful. I am here to introduce you to your new lives, as the fortunate chosen. You are currently being cradled within the Space-Mother. I am going to transport your perceptions into space. Do not be afraid."

The green, seamless walls, floor and ceiling dissolved, along with body perception, until Casey existed as only a point of consciousness, hanging in the vacuum of space. He saw innumerable, sharp points of light, stars as he had never seen them before, but the focus of his attention was an object that appeared to be suspended in space, with the stars as a backdrop.

It was a green, globular structure, with a large cylinder projecting from one end. It was not difficult to identify the cylinder as the star-engine and a portion of the Pinnacle, but the amorphous, green substance engulfed the forward end of the Pinnacle.

With only a thought, Casey's orientation changed. He was now looking toward a yellow star. When he focused on it, his consciousness shot toward it. He passed three colorful gas giants and came to a stop above an Earth-sized planet. His vision was god-like. He saw human beings inside enclosed cities and some on the surface of the planet. He could almost smell the ongoing transformation of the atmosphere and the sweetness of oxygen.

Casey's attention returned to the defiled starship Pinnacle and he plunged forward to enter the green mass directly adjacent to the starship. The view faded and Casey stumbled to maintain his balance as the room reappeared around them. It had been a stunning sight, an awesome view of the galaxy and a horrifying view of the degraded starship...and then there was that planet, inhabited by humans.

Casey turned to Yamaguchi. "Did you see them? It wasn't Earth, but there were people."

"Yes," Yamaguchi replied, "we traveled with you and saw what you saw."

The creature spoke again. "You now know your place. Your function will be to serve the Masters and the Mother and you will be rewarded, just as I serve and am rewarded."

The association in Casey's mind clicked into place. "You're Wheeler!" he blurted.

The creature rotated as if its back and neck were inflexible. Its large, black eyes were directed at Casey. "I serve the Masters and the Space-Mother, but when I was on the Birth-World and served the Land-Mother, you perceived me as Wheeler. I am not Wheeler. I am CkCkCk."

The creature returned its unblinking gaze to the group as a whole. "Your species is particularly suited to nurture the birth of new Masters and, although your artifacts are crude, they are worth preserving. Under the direction of the Masters you will refine them. Your spacecraft has already been upgraded. You have been chosen to join in the Glorious Symbiosis. Your lives will be extended into the distant future. You will be the hands of Masters and Mothers. You will be the bridge through which the Masters and Mother work their magic. You will be the channel that allows the power of the Mother to work the will of the Masters. You will enable the recruitment of other fortunate members of your species, who will be granted the opportunity to feed and care for new Masters. It is a noble fate and you will be rewarded."

"If these so called Masters and Mothers think our species is so wonderful, why did they mutilate our bodies?" Casey asked.

"You are not lessened. You are improved. The Masters know smoothness and simplicity are the basic beauties of the universe," the creature said to the group as a whole.

Casey objected. "Improved? You've destroyed the delicate balance in our bodies. Among other things, we won't be able to rid ourselves of waste. We'll die."

The creature turned to Casey. "There will be no waste. You have been raised to a higher plane. You will feed on the love of the Mother and want nothing more. You will find more joy and contentment that you could ever have imagined."

"Where is the rest of your kind?" Casey asked.

"They are gone. They have served the Masters and Mothers and now they are gone. I am the last."

"What happened to—" Casey began.

"I don't give a shit about that," Slater declared. "Where are my people? I demand that you return them to me."

"You have no further need of them. They are in their stasis capsules, awaiting their turn to be uplifted and to serve," the creature said.

"They'll die!" Casey shouted.

"If you are referring to the impurities in your stasis system, that was an unfortunate oversight. It has been purified."

"An unfortunate oversight," Casey repeated with disbelief. "You call the death of a thousand men and women 'an unfortunate oversight'?"

"The Masters have reaped the knowledge of a hundred species. The Masters know all there is to know," the creature replied.

"And what happened to those hundred species?" Casey

yelled.

"After sharing their knowledge with the Masters, most have been allowed to nurture the Birth-World with their bodies, but few can nurture the Masters."

"What the hell are you talking about?"

This time the creature ignored Casey's outburst.

Yamaguchi spoke. "Where have we been and where are we going?"

"You have been to the Birth-World of the Masters and the Mothers. Our destination is your destination. Thousands of your years ago, you set out to visit a planet. Soon, you will complete that journey. Others of your kind followed after you and found a hostile world, barely capable of supporting your species. They endured hardship. They did not have the benefit of a Land-Mother and the Masters to shape their perceptions. They suffered. It has taken them millennia to tame and transform the planet, and now they have finally reached the stage of producing deep space traveling artifacts of their own. The Space-Mother and the Masters will accept the gift of their starship. They are ripe."

"What if they don't want to give it to you? They'll never give it to you." Casey declared.

Suddenly, the mint green room was gone. A balmy wind caressed Casey's skin. The sea was a bright turquoise and the beach, a fine white sand. High overhead, the tops of tall palm trees swayed in the breeze. He leaned his head back against the pillowed chaise.

"I've missed you."

Casey turned his head. "Britty?"

She smiled and reached toward him. He grasped her hand and felt her again, after so many years.

"Britty, I've missed you so terribly."

"Me too. Do you remember that night before the starship crew went into seclusion in preparation for the journey?"

He sighed. "Yes."

"You came to my room and you slept with me in my bed. Why didn't you make love with me?"

"I don't know. Maybe I was afraid. Maybe out of respect for you."

"I wanted you to. I wanted to make love with you. I've dreamed about it."

"If I had, I would never have left you. I would've stayed at

Copper Mountain."

She leaned across and he met her halfway. Her lips were soft and the kiss delicious. Her kisses were special; each time it was like it was the first time she had ever kissed anyone.

When they parted he noticed three people walking up the beach. They were holding hands and the woman was gorgeous, with her blond hair blowing in the sea breeze. Her breasts were barely contained by her minimal bikini. Her waist narrowed and then flared to a womanly pelvis with her genitals covered by a tiny triangle of cloth. Her buttocks were bare. On her left was a tall, well-muscled man with blond hair, and on her right was a man with a black beard, pointed at the chin, but it was to the woman that his gaze returned.

"Do you know her?" Britty asked.

Casey chuckled and returned his attention to Britty, to her round face and serious expression. "Yeah, I know her, but you're the most beautiful woman I've ever seen."

She smiled and then laughed; her laugh made his heart ring.

"I love you, Britty."

"I love you, too. I have a room, we could finally make love or, if you want to, we could make love right here on the beach, right now. She reached up and undid the top of her bikini, throwing it aside and exposing her breasts, her nipples erect with excitement.

Casey's breath caught and he could feel the response in his groin. He swung around to sit up and was about to join her, to smother her with kisses and hugs and to find ultimate pleasure, ultimate intimacy, at long last, when his gaze momentarily strayed. He noticed a giant samurai warrior, wearing black leather armor and a helmet with horns. There was a katana hanging at his side in its sheath. He was standing perfectly still in the shade of a palm tree, observing.

He paused. Britty scooted over to make room for him, but he continued to stare at the giant. And then he noticed another man, lounging on a nearby chaise and watching them, with a lascivious smile. His nose was narrow, his lips thin and his jaw blocky.

A tuxedo dressed waiter approached. "Can I get you a drink, perhaps a mojito?" The waiter's mouth was stretched with a plastered smile and he stared without blinking.

Casey moaned. He glanced toward Lisa who was cavorting

in the surf with Olson and Protonov. What were they doing here? Where was here? His expectation of fulfillment collapsed. It was a sharp-edged, brittle crumbling.

"What's wrong?" Britty asked.

The softness of her hand warmed his thigh.

He returned his gaze to her. "This is not reality."

"How can you even say that? You can feel me and see me and hear me." She took his hand in hers and pressed it against the soft fullness of her breast.

"Britty...."

"Are you crying?" she asked. "After so many years, we're finally together. Come to me." She opened her arms. "Make love to me."

"Yamaguchi, help me!" he yelled.

The samurai warrior stepped from the shade of the palm tree into light.

"I can't overcome my desire by myself. Help me," Casey begged.

The warrior drew his katana from its sheath and held it two-handed. Sunlight sparkled off the edge of the long, curved blade.

The green room reappeared.

"Why did you bring us back?" Lisa yelled. "I don't want to be here. I want to be back there. Take us back, right now! I demand it!"

"Yeah, Casey," Slater said. "I would've enjoyed watching you fuck that babe. You are such a loser."

The tears were gone. His new body could not cry. He had no means to express the devastation of his loss. He wanted to go back, real or not. His gaze met Yamaguchi's.

Yamaguchi answered Casey's look. "You taught me that without reality there is no future. Joy will become sorrow. Success will become failure. Life will become death."

"Yes," Casey whispered.

The blue alien turned its attention away from the two men to address the group as a whole. "The dreams and desires of the humans on the planet will be fulfilled. They will give us their starship, just as you did. They will want to."

"How did you find this planet?" Yamaguchi asked.

"Your ship told the Masters much before we cleansed it of useless data. This is your original destination. We brought you here and waited."

"That's stupid," Slater said. "You aren't so smart."

"Shut the hell up, Slater!" Casey ordered and walked toward him.

The alien turned its large eyes toward the two men as Casey stood ready, his hands balled into fists.

"So, now you're a tough guy," Slater said with a sneer. "Don't take it out on me. I wasn't the one who turned down that bitch who offered to fuck you. She was hot."

"Shut up, Slater!"

"You never would've satisfied her. She needed a real man. I bet she would've fucked me next. Too bad."

"I could kill you," Casey snarled.

Yamaguchi joined them and stood at Casey's side.

The alien seemed to be listening to something and then refocused on the group. "The Masters thank you, human Slater. Your recommendation that we first offer the gift to your birth world is well received. While you slept, we visited the star you call the Sun and discovered a Slan starship on the fourth planet from the star. The Masters and Mothers have learned that it is best not to enter a system that has been claimed by the Slan."

Slater smiled. "Oh, really?"

Yamaguchi wrapped a giant hand around Slater's throat. "You speak again, you die."

"Remember your duty, Mister. I'm your leader."

Yamaguchi began squeezing. Slater clawed desperately at the hand around his neck. His face became ruddy and then took on a purple tinge.

Casey touched Yamaguchi's arm. "Let him live, for now."

Yamaguchi loosened his grip but kept his hand around Slater's neck. Slater sucked in some deep breaths, the only sound in the room until the alien spoke.

"When the Masters determined the inhabitants of this world were ready to receive the gift of the Glorious Symbiosis, you were awakened."

Casey pivoted to face the alien. "This isn't a symbiosis," he growled. "This is slavery. It's xenocide. This is an abominable infestation by parasites. Your artificial manipulation of our perceptions does not lead us closer to the unknowable reality. It is destructive. I saw the parasitic invasion of the bodies of our friends. Was that a 'Glorious Symbiosis'?"

The creature's tone remained flat, words well-spaced. "You

are referring to the Little Ones. If you had not interfered, your fellow humans would have lived far beyond their expected life spans, but you took them into the sterile bowels of the ship, depriving them of the life-giving mud. The symbiosis was destroyed. Your ignorance killed them, but you cannot be held responsible. The Land-Mother is indulgent with the Little Ones and did not object when a few of the non-reproductive members of your species were visited and took an alternate path of service."

"Alternate path?" Casey's voice shook. "They were killed by the so-called Little Ones, little killers is more like it, little monsters!"

"Transformational adjustment can be difficult but you will witness the truth," the alien said. "You will give but you will receive more than you have given. You will join in a true symbiosis."

"The hell I will!" Casey declared. "You and your glorious infestation will destroy our species, just like it did to all the others. Just like it did to your kind."

"To the contrary," the creature replied, "as long as you survive, your species will survive. Humankind will survive far longer than its projected time of existence. You will be protected from the Slan."

"Wrong!" Casey yelled. "The survival of individuals does not equate with the survival of a species. Only reproduction insures survival. Look what happened to your species. They're dead. You said so yourself."

"I am uncountable thousands of your years old. When great reptiles roamed your birth world, I was alive. Adjustment to a higher plane is not easy, but you will come to understand."

Casey turned with frustration to his companions. "Don't any of you have anything to say?"

Yamaguchi's hand was still around Slater's neck. Slater glared at Casey with hard anger on his face, as if he blamed Casey for their current crisis, but said nothing.

Next Casey turned to Lisa; her gaze was directed at her feet and her shoulders were shaking in silent sobs. Near her, Protonov, remained motionless in his catatonic stare. Looking past the alien, he could see Olson, rolled into a tight ball, face against the wall.

"Who are the Masters?" Yamaguchi asked.

"A Master comes. After the Mother rewards you, I will

return. You will know much more. You will understand. The Master comes."

There was a wet, smacking sound, followed by the appearance of a pearly-white cone that protruded through the wall near the curled form of Olson. The cone grew in length until the slug-like creature slid completely through the wall and slithered onto the green floor. Casey stared at it with shocked fascination. It was about half the size of a human, but there was no doubt; it was a bigger version of the worm that he had killed inside the cryo-capsule. The tendrils were still present, but instead of ending in a cup, they terminated in fine filaments that waved and undulated endlessly. It was a Master.

Casey felt his revulsion slipping helplessly away and, in its place, radiant warmth flushed across his skin and penetrated his being, bringing peace and contentment. He experienced unadulterated, overwhelming love, but he wasn't drawn toward the object of his love; instead, his legs carried him toward the green wall. His face bent toward the wall and a mouth-like hole smacked open, wet and seductive, urging him to kiss it. His tongue began extending toward the moist mouth but, at the last second, his innate perversity arose. He raised his hand and, instead of his tongue, he jammed his thumb into the hole. The pain was an instantaneous burning. It was so intense that he screamed. His arm felt as if was being probed by a thousand red-hot needles, a thousand stings from a wasp, and then his arm went dead, without feeling or strength. He groaned and collapsed onto the green floor.

After a few minutes he was aware of other moans, but these were the sounds of immodest ecstasy, muted by fettered tongues. He opened his eyes. The Master had gone. He focused on Olson, Protonov and Lisa, who were writhing with sensual rapture while they kissed the Mother. The blue alien was also face first against the wall, its distal arms folded back over the blade-like projection of its lower elbows, gurgling its version of orgasmic satiation.

Casey pushed himself up with his good arm and anxiously looked to where Yamaguchi had been standing. Casey smiled. The giant was standing near Salter, but no longer had his hand around Slater's neck. Their eyes met. Yamaguchi's eyes were clear as he maintained a state of pure observation.

Surprisingly, Slater too had not moved. His mouth was

turned down in disgust as he watched the others. For the first time, Casey felt gratified by Slater's lack of humanity. Love was not what motivated the man, nor was it sensuality; it was power. He probably didn't even have the capacity for love.

Casey heard the "smack" of suction being broken and turned back to look at those who had been in communion with the alien Mother. Lisa turned, no longer concerned about her appearance. She had an idiotic smile on her face and eyes that were unfocused. She slid down to lean against the wall, followed by the languid movements of Olson and Protonov.

The blue alien lay supine on the floor. Its unblinking eyes dulled by a membrane, its breath whispering in and out of its carnivorous smile that wasn't a smile at all.

CHAPTER 41

Casey was pleased with himself for having resisted, but the sharp burr of hunger began to demand attention. He pushed the gnawing in his gut from his mind when the worm returned. He watched while the worm used its delicate appearing tentacles to grasp the head of the blue alien. Then it pushed its pointed rear into the floor, pulling the shark-faced alien along with it. They disappeared without a ripple.

Lisa began to stir, and then Olson and Protonov. They crawled the short distance to one another and wrapped their arms and legs around each other as if they would merge into one being, if it were at all possible. Then they became motionless, a tangled mass of entwined limbs and bodies, and seemed to be asleep or in a stupor.

The hunger became terrible. It peaked with a feeling of knife-like colic, combined with acidic burning. Casey began rhythmically pounding the resilient floor with his fist, but then the pain began to subside. It didn't disappear, but it did recede to a level that allowed him the freedom to think. With an intense prickly sensation, the strength returned to his paralyzed arm and he began flexing his fingers.

Yamaguchi walked over and sat down next to Casey, crossing his legs as he had seen Casey do so many times in the past. His face was blank, but his eyes were bright.

"You know, my friend," Casey said, "my mom always told me it was bad manners to turn down a gift."

No one laughed; no one smiled.

Casey looked back and forth at his two remaining companions, thankful that he wasn't the only one who had been able to resist. For all their mastery of biology, Casey thought, the aliens did not fully understand human behavior. But then he thought with dread about his next exposure to the mouths in the wall. The aching hunger was a constant reminder of unfulfilled needs. His body wouldn't allow him to forget. He thought about the master worm and it triggered a memory.

"Yamaguchi, do you remember that picture scratched into

the arm of the control chair on the bridge?"

"Yes."

Casey shook his head. "How stupid of me. It was a picture of a segmented worm with tentacles ending in filaments, not a ribbed canoe with flowers."

"You have answered your question."

"Yeah, I guess so. Poor Grace. She must have awakened from cryogenic sleep to find that worms had invaded the ship." Casey refocused on Yamaguchi. "What did you observe?"

It was as if he had been waiting for the question. "I observed that we are contained within a living organism, similar to the one that you showed me in the pictures taken on the planet's surface only far larger, and that this encompassing organism lives in symbiosis with the worm Masters, but it does seem to be a tripartite relationship, with the additional species acting as a link or key to the minds of other species. The Mothers furnish the power, the Masters the brain, and the enslaved species provides the means, the ability to project altered perceptions and the hands to manipulate tools. I observed that the reward of cooperation includes the direct administration of energy, which produces a powerful stimulation of the pleasure area of the brain as well as nutrition. I believe that once a person has been exposed to this stimulant, the need to experience it again becomes the primary purpose in life, supplanting all learned ethical codes, the instinct for self-preservation, and the instinct for species preservation."

Casey nodded. "Impressive." And then asked, "Are you hungry?"

"I am aware of the internal signals that would be consistent with hunger, if I were still fully human," Yamaguchi said.

"So, you're hungry, right?"

Yamaguchi did not elaborate further, or even nod.

Casey shrugged, and then asked, "Did you observe anything else?"

"Yes. I observed that the master worm provided the stimulus that caused the mother creature to allow passage."

Casey leaned forward so he could see Slater. "What about you, Slater?"

"I hate them." Slater said. "They stole my people. My people! They had no right. They've lumped me together with the rest of you," he said with disgust in his voice. "I am the leader."

Casey suppressed his first response and instead said, "If you hate them so much, then get with it. If you observed something helpful, share it. Maybe we can use it."

Slater stared morosely at Casey, but said nothing.

"Slater, don't you get it?"

He remained silent so Casey continued. "This abomination of Mother and Masters has destroyed at least a hundred species. It is likely that most of these species were technologically advanced far beyond us. They will consume the humans who inhabit that planet we saw and sooner or later they'll discover...well, enough said. We all know what Jack Nichols did."

Slater finally spoke. "Don't speak that name in my presence. He treated me like dirt. Mitchell Mason told me the real truth. It was Mitchell's plan all along. Nichols only carried it out and then took the credit. Nichols was no hero. He was only a tool."

"My God, you are—oh, what the hell. Is that all you have to say? Don't you have anything useful to add?" Casey asked.

Slater didn't reply.

They sat in silence until Casey spoke again. "Yamaguchi, I'm not sure I can resist another exposure to those mouths. If we don't find a solution soon, I'm afraid I'm going to lose my ability to question and observe. Do you understand?"

"I understand, but you are the Teacher. You must take the observations and ask the right question."

"I'm no teacher. I'm a doctor."

"No," Yamaguchi responded, "you are the Teacher."

Casey looked into himself and saw nothing special. *How has this responsibility fallen on me?* he wondered. *It's not fair. Fair, that's a laugh. Fair doesn't exist.* That triggered a memory from his time as a guardian. Something about everything being fair. It was an odd memory but he couldn't hold on to it. He reclined and let his full weight rest on the soft, warm skin of the Mother, vaguely afraid that a mouth would open under him, or a worm would poke its snout through.

He let his mind wander, trying to escape the hunger pain that demanded his attention. He couldn't let hunger become his primary focus or he'd become as useless as that bundle of bodies on the other side of the room. He remembered Earth and days of optimistic expectation. He remembered his joy at being selected for the role of guardian and remembered Dr. Marta and Britty, both long dead. Britty, the recent experience, real or not, had honed the edge of his longing for her until it was razor sharp. If only he had made love to her those many years ago. He would never have left her, never have left Earth.

"Yamaguchi, how did you break that spell and bring us back? I remember seeing you draw that big sword and then...I don't know. What did you do?"

"It was not real."

Casey suppressed his hideous imaginings. It was not real. His thoughts turned to Eden and the only comfort it had held for him, his little puppy, Marta. This pain also was fresh, not yet blurred by time. He thought about that fateful day when he had willfully killed Sabine and then focused on the memory of killing a worm.

His mind chewed on that memory. He had succeeded in killing a worm. If he could do it once, perhaps he could do it again. Would that be helpful? It was difficult to see how it could make things worse. But, back then he had a tool, a weapon, and now he had nothing. Not even Yamaguchi could penetrate that laser-resistant hide. Still, it is possible that the vulnerable spot persisted into maturity. He remembered the easy penetration of the tentacle hole and catching the blade in a crevice that allowed the beast to be bisected. Sentient, yes, but still a beast to Casey's way of thinking. He felt no pangs of guilt about that murder.

He remembered the suddenness of the transition from being trapped in the land-shaper to nothing. He had thought he was somehow immune to the planet but they had been able to reach into him, into everyone, and turn them off. That and his recent fantasy trip to the beach probably required Wheeler as the conduit to their brains. Wheeler, the shark-faced alien with its strange arms. He wondered what the alien had looked like before it had undergone "esthetic" reconstruction. Did it originally have knife-like blades sticking out all over it? Did it have purple feathers? Did it cover its elbows because of some ancient instinctive behavior? That last thought clung to his mind to the exclusion of all others.

CHAPTER 42

Casey's thoughts fell into place. He wanted to speak of it with Yamaguchi, but was worried the Mother would overhear them. He suspected it made little difference if he yelled or whispered, but felt an irresistible desire for secrecy, even if it was only cosmetic. He sat and mulled over his idea. It was fraught with unpredictables, but even death would be preferable to living only for a kiss from the Mother. At least it would be a cleansing act.

He sat up and motioned for Yamaguchi to come closer. Yamaguchi scooted over and bent his head near Casey. Casey cupped his hand to funnel his whispers into the man's exposed auditory canal. When he had finished, he pulled back and studied Yamaguchi's face for a reaction.

Yamaguchi's face remained blank for a moment and then it transformed as Casey had never seen it before. His tiny-toothed smile spread across his face and his eyes sparkled. Then he began to laugh, it was a high-pitched tittering, such a tiny sound coming from such a big body. The strangeness of seeing Yamaguchi laugh struck Casey as quite funny and he joined his friend in laughter. Hope brought cheer.

It only lasted for a moment, but it felt wonderful. Then Yamaguchi returned to his sober face, but not completely. Casey could see traces of a smile at the corners of his mouth.

"So," Yamaguchi said, "you believe the Mother is more of an instinctual creature than a critically thinking entity."

"I certainly hope so."

Yamaguchi bowed his head to Casey. "You are the One. Teacher, you have asked the right questions and then answered them. It is an honor." He placed his forehead on the soft, green floor at Casey's feet.

Casey immediately reached down and pulled Yamaguchi's head up. "Please, my friend, let's not tempt fate. All we need is an unexpected kiss from the Mother."

Yamaguchi rolled back and sat on his legs. His face looked truly inscrutable again, but Casey knew, beneath that bland exterior, the man was processing information, formulating details. He had great confidence in Yamaguchi.

"Teacher, it seems unjust that the least worthy will survive."

Casey motioned with his hand and Yamaguchi bent forward to hear his whispered answer. "You need have no concern on that topic. We are counting on his self-serving egocentrism. It's part of what'll make the plan work. He'll believe that his value will soar, that he'll have power, but he will not. He'll be ostracized and isolated and, ultimately, he'll starve to death. As a physician, I can assure you that the changes in our bodies are far more than cosmetic. He will suffer and then he will die."

Yamaguchi sat back and nodded. "Thank you, my teacher. I am ready."

"Do you know which direction to go?" Casey asked.

"Yes. I observed when we returned to the Mother from the outside."

Casey held out his hands and Yamaguchi gently engulfed them in his own giant hands and then leaned forward to kiss Casey's wrist. The heat of that kiss spread throughout Casey's body and mind. All the pain melted away, leaving a glowing core of fulfillment and love.

"Queers," Slater snarled.

Casey released Yamaguchi's hands to look in Slater's direction.

Slater deepened the scowl that hovered ever ready on his face. "What bullshit," he snapped. "Gossiping like two old women. I'm sure you're talking about me. If you think I'll stoop to ask you what you've been whispering and laughing about, you're mistaken. I could care less."

"Slater," Casey said, "the only thing I'm expecting from you is your pathologic narcissism, nothing more. Would you be interested in escape and survival?"

Slater's eyes narrowed. "What do you have in mind?"

"Come here and I'll tell you," Casey said.

"No, you come here."

Casey let out a long breath and slid over to sit next to him. He cupped his hand and whispered his plan into Slater's ear hole. When he had finished, Slater pushed him away, causing him to lose his balance and fall onto the floor. He quickly scrambled to his knees.

Slater laughed at Casey's discomfort, but his head was up. His face had more tone. The fantasy of control was resurrecting itself within him. He looked to Yamaguchi.

"What makes you think you have the ability to fulfill your part?" Slater asked.

Yamaguchi answered Slater's doubt with his usual blank stare, forcing Casey to respond in his stead.

"Slater, I was surprised when I found mercenaries among the colonists, but you evidently were not."

Slater did not deny the statement.

Casey continued. "What I've always found is that when a person stumbles onto a secret, there are probably others. Would you be surprised if I told you that within the secrets that you were privy to, there were yet other secrets?"

Slater shrugged, as if such a statement had no relevance to a man like him.

"Do you think the entire WSA Central Committee trusted you, and the rest of us, to the point that they wouldn't provide a failsafe to prevent our return to Earth?"

Slater still said nothing, but sat straighter and stared off across the room, not meeting Casey's eyes.

"Yamaguchi knows how to overload the star engine. With your help, it can be done."

Still Slater said nothing.

After a few moments, Casey spoke again. "Are you in?"

Slater's face was as unreadable as Yamaguchi's. "I'm in."

Casey didn't trust him and most likely they would fail. There was too much chance involved; yet, it was worth a try. As the thrill of formulating a plan faded, doubt worked its way through the meager confidence Casey had managed to muster. His hunger grew and came to the forefront of his consciousness. It was getting worse. He observed Yamaguchi, sitting motionless; and then Slater, who looked like a man scheming if ever a man did. Slater was tough and determined; Casey was willing to grant him that.

Time seemed to creep by. Casey turned his attention to Lisa and the others, who had slowly returned to a wakeful state. They appeared refreshed and happy, but they didn't speak, not among themselves or to those who had not partaken. They sat in a circle and held hands, not losing contact with one another for even a moment.

Casey was beginning to despair. He felt his plan was doomed to failure even before it had a chance to be tried. Slater was beginning to fidget, snapping his fingers and jiggling his legs.

Yamaguchi remained as he was. Casey would have preferred to talk, but there was nothing more to be said. Yamaguchi would be proud of me, Casey thought.

Then Casey saw the white cone that was the snout of a worm poke its way through the wall. As the worm slithered into the room, Casey saw the blue head and then the body of the alien being towed into the chamber. Once fully in the room, the alien stood and flipped his lower arms back over his elbows. The worm continued on its way; its snout penetrated the floor and it disappeared.

Casey stood and walked toward the blue alien. Meanwhile, Yamaguchi began easing along the wall of the oval chamber.

"I need to speak with a Master," Casey said.

The alien's big, black eyes centered on the human that stood before it. "You can speak with me. I am the Master's ears," the alien said.

Casey shook his head. "No. It's important. I want to speak with a Master present. I know something about humans that the Masters do not. I know how the immature Master was killed on the birth world and I know how to prevent it, but I demand that a Master be present."

The alien continued to look at Casey, his fixed, shark-like smile spread widely across his deep-blue face, a face that was totally unintelligible to Casey.

Slater remained where he was, sitting on the floor at the far end of the room. Yamaguchi had worked his way around until he was in back of the creature. The other humans stared at the alien with silly smiles and open adoration.

The alien remained still. Standing this close, Casey could detect a faint fragrance, like jasmine, on the creature's breath, and he could clearly see the nictitating membranes occasionally flash across the creature's over-sized eyes.

The alien spoke. "The Master will return."

Those were the words that Casey and Yamaguchi had been waiting for. Yamaguchi took a quick step forward and, as Casey grabbed the creature's smooth, lower arms, Yamaguchi grasped the creature's head and began forcing it back. Casey was nearly lifted off the floor by the alien's surprising strength. Then the alien whipped its leg up and back with an unbelievable range of motion in its hip and knee joints, striking Yamaguchi in the chest, but the force was inadequate to dislodge the giant man. The creature's strength seemed to waver for a moment and Yamaguchi jerked the creature's neck again. This time there was an audible "crack" and the creature collapsed to the floor.

The three possessed humans began to walk forward, still holding hands, eyes wide with shock. Yamaguchi swung a kick at them and sent them sprawling to the floor, still holding onto one another. Then he planted his foot on the creature's chest and pulled until the veins bulged on his forehead. Suddenly, the joint gave and Yamaguchi was left holding the creature's lower arm, topped by a nasty looking blade. The wound on the creature began to ooze a red liquid that looked like human blood.

Casey backed away, pivoting as he looked at the walls, ceiling and floor, searching for the first sign of an entering worm. Slater was standing by this time, also turning as he, too, searched the walls. Meanwhile the Lisa-Protonov-Olson abomination wailed an eerie cry and held each other closely.

"Behind you!" Casey said urgently.

Yamaguchi turned. The snout of a worm appeared and then took shape as it entered the room. As soon as it was fully through the wall, Yamaguchi swung the sickle-like elbow into the base of a tentacle; it pierced the creature with ease. The worm began to curl away, emitting a shrill cry that made it difficult to think and made Casey's teeth chatter with pain, but Yamaguchi caught the "blade" in the hole and pulled with all his weight. A gash appeared between two of the worm's segments and began to seep thick, brownish slurry. Yamaguchi kicked the creature over and continued to pull the "blade" circumferentially while the creature tried to squirm away. The worm reached toward Yamaguchi with its other tentacles, trying to grasp him, but he swayed first one-way and then another, avoiding their touch.

It was too late for the worm. Yamaguchi completed his cut and then jammed the blade-tipped arm deep into the creature's soft interior. He twisted it and raked it back and forth. The piercing scream stopped. The bisected worm lay still, brownish fluid dripping from both halves, filling the room with a musty odor.

There was not going to be much time. The "floor" began undulating with recognition as the worm's life fluid leaked onto it. Yamaguchi did not pause, but immediately began scooping out the soft interior of one-half of the worm, while

Casey and Slater worked on cleaning out the other half. As Casey reached in and pulled out tissue, he could not help but notice that about a third of the worm consisted of neural tissue, a fantastic amount for a creature this size. This was definitely the murder of an intellectually superior, sapient being, but Casey didn't pause to consider the implications. He continued to dig out the shell of the worm as quickly as his hands could move.

While his hands flashed in front of his face, his mind raced along the possibilities. He was hoping that the death of the blue alien would limit the Master and Mother's ability to intervene directly in a human's perception or turn them off altogether, but there was no proof to support that theory; it was more of a hope. Casey doubted that it would take long for the Masters to turn the Lisa-Protonov-Olson abomination into a much more effective mind tool than the indigo alien had been. However, for now, the transformed humans were hugging each other in a tangled mass on the floor. If they had been attuned to the Masters and Mother by that one exposure, then they would have to be killed as well, assuming of course that any alteration of perception proceeded at a leisurely rate. There were just too many "ifs". Casey focused on the messy job before him.

The inside of the worm's shell was moist and warm, and was covered by interlacing muscles that had provided movement. When Casey took a moment to glance toward the transformed humans, his heart missed a few beats. It felt like a series of "gulps" deep in his chest. Two new snouts were growing from the green surface of the floor.

"Worms!" Casey yelled and stepped back from the nearly empty shell. He managed to maintain his balance on a floor that was rippling beneath the muddy-brown gore.

Slater hesitated, eyes fixed on the worms, but Yamaguchi didn't pause. He picked up the lightweight cone-shaped shell and began pushing it against the far wall, snout first. The wall resisted for only a moment and then began to allow penetration by the worm shell.

"Get going, Slater!" Casey ordered as he dredged the alien's dismembered arm out of the muck. He stood near the worm snouts, ready for the first tentacle spot to appear. When the tendril passed the plane of the floor, Casey swung the grisly ax and penetrated the worm, causing it to screech its mental cry and partially withdraw. Then the worms' snouts became motionless, neither retreating, nor advancing. They were two innocent appearing white cones on the pale-green floor.

Casey risked a glance at Yamaguchi, who was nearly ready to make the final push to whatever lay beyond. Yamaguchi turned to meet Casey's eyes. He was smiling his pebbly smile, as his rumbling voice spoke. "Good-bye my Teacher, my friend."

"Good-bye, friend," Casey answered, and then reluctantly forced himself to return his attention to the worms and began searching the surfaces of the chamber for new penetrations.

Slater was also pushing his half of the worm shell through the wall, but he did not divert his attention to either Yamaguchi or Casey. When Casey next turned his attention to the wall, they were both gone, without a sign to mark their exit.

Casey was alone, standing with his weapon raised above the worms, with only the wailing of the perverted half-humans for company. He needed to be the parasite within the parasite. It was a grim but accurate portrayal. He needed to buy his partners some time.

It wasn't fair, Casey thought to himself. He would only know if they failed, not if they succeeded. If Yamaguchi guessed wrong and led Slater in the wrong direction, they would penetrate into the vacuum of space. They would boil and bloat. The thought touched a memory, but Casey didn't have time to follow it.

There were so many incalculables. If they failed to find an airlock that would allow them to enter the Pinnacle before they were discovered and neutralized, then all would be for nothing.

How much time? Casey wondered. Another unknown.

The worms remained as they had been, neither entering the chamber nor disappearing beneath its surface. At least I can still think and perceive, Casey thought, unless all this is an illusion. *Is this all simply a reflection of what I expect? Am I actually sitting on the floor and staring at nothing?* He glanced over at the alien; its vivid blue coloring had paled in death. Its face was still filled by the shark-smile, but its eyes were cloudy and dull. Its death marked the extinction of its species.

The minutes passed, each one longer than the one before. Casey surmised that this was a totally unexpected development, perhaps a unique event for the Masters and Mother. Perhaps they had never encountered a species still so violent, still so close to their primitive roots that the preservation of the species was a stronger motivation than self-preservation. Casey became giddy with the possibility of success, but he knew it wouldn't be much longer before the Masters formulated a solution. The floor began to soften under Casey's feet.

He quickly high-stepped over to the dead alien and stood on to its back. When he glanced back across the room he saw that the worm snouts had disappeared. The Lisa-Protonov-Olson complex was lying face down on the floor, motionless as they sank into it. To Casey they looked dead.

The brief burst of confidence deserted him. Please, he thought, Yamaguchi, at least you must succeed. Destroy us cleanly.

A strong ripple swept across the floor and a wave front passed along the ceiling and walls. It caused him to lose his balance and he slipped to his knees, but he quickly regained his feet.

"The Pinnacle has broken free!" Casey yelled, even though there was no one to hear him. It seemed right somehow to speak out loud. All was as it should be. The fail-safe had not failed. He had finally succeeded as guardian. Although he couldn't justify it, even to himself, he still truly loved them. They were his children and he had set them free. He was ready. For him, the circle was finally complete. There was nothing more he could do for the sleeping colonists; their fate was in Yamaguchi and Slater's hands now.

Casey glanced over at Lisa-Protonov-Olson, but all that remained of them was an oval island that marked each of their backs as the green floor continued to swallow them whole. Casey's grotesque perch was also nearly completely covered. Soon the Mother would begin to swallow Casey as well. He thought about Yamaguchi. He still had unlimited confidence in the man, in his friend.

He was alone as the floor eked upward. First, it covered his ankles, then his calves and, as the warmth of the resilient but inescapable grip of the Mother hugged his thighs, Casey began sinking faster. He continued to exist so he knew that Yamaguchi had not yet succeeded. The Mother began to crawl its way up Casey's abdomen and back and he raised his arms, trying to keep them free as long as possible, still holding the blade-tipped arm of the alien. *Please, my friend, do it!*

Then, his current reality ceased to exist.

CHAPTER 43

Aboard the starship Pinnacle, Slater sat in the control chair on the bridge with his left forearm resting on a scratched picture that could have been a canoe with flowers, but wasn't. The instruments he was monitoring recorded a brief, but very intense blast in deep space. It was a miniature nova. Yamaguchi had succeeded in bringing the star-engine to critical. Slater thought only briefly about Casey, Yamaguchi, and the other three, and then dismissed them from his mind. They weren't important.

The improvements the aliens had made in the Pinnacle's propulsion unit were remarkable. The starship was well on its way along the final leg of its long delayed journey. Its cargo of humans was oblivious and timeless in their sleep, a contingent of ancient humans who had time traveled to the distant future.

When the Pinnacle approached communication range of the planetary system, Slater heard a human voice come over his scanner. The scanner locked on the beam and he listened. It was definitely a human voice, although the language was unknown. He maneuvered the Pinnacle into an orbit that was near the planet's odd, egg-shaped moon. He would wait for them to come to him. He was not about to risk destruction. Even though a terrible, painful hunger demanded food, he was strong. He could wait.

He swiveled in the control chair and stared across the bridge, down the softly glowing hall of sleep. He was pleased. Although the hunger was agonizing, he smiled with satisfaction. He was certain that a planet full of technicians and scientists would be able to find a way to satisfy his appetite. He was important and would be the top priority of an entire planet. He had information that would translate into immediate power. These thoughts filled his mind and he felt better. He had no doubts about himself, or his place in the universe.

What Slater did not realize was that his reality did not correspond in the least to the ultimate and unknowable reality.

If he had the benefit of a teacher and had the capacity to learn, he would've understood that this failure would bring unendurable suffering and, ultimately, his death.

EPILOGUE

The tremendous flash of the miniature nova from beyond the distant gas giant had lit the night sky of the third planet from the yellow star. It was a burst of daylight in the dead of night and caused some citizens to fear and others to wonder, but then it faded, as quickly as it had blossomed.

The Warden witnessed this event from the planet's surface. Although not appreciated at the time, the flash signaled a shift in reality; it would not be long before the Warden's perception of reality, and that of the entire planet, would be brought into a slightly better alignment with the reality of the great unknowable.

The Guardian, the One, the Teacher of Reality had made his final contribution to those he loved and his fate, along with that of his friend, Yamaguchi, could not be known by those who still rode the peak of their own personal waves. What would Casey and Yamaguchi find when their waves settled into the sea of reality? The sea is vast. It has no shores. Who can say what lies beneath?

ABOUT THE AUTHOR

Gary Moreau grew up in a small town in Iowa called Estherville. He discovered science fiction in the fifth grade, beginning with a book by Alan E. Nourse entitled *Star Surgeon.*

He graduated from medical school at the University of Iowa and then completed a residency in emergency medicine at Los Angeles County/USC Medical Center. Following his training, he practiced emergency medicine at Long Beach Memorial Medical Center.

It is not likely that he became a physician because of Nourse's book, but it was the beginning of a lifelong love of science fiction. His plans for the future include a focus on his passion for storytelling. *The Pinnacle* bridges the timeline between *Judas Gene* (2016) and *Almost Human* (2001--both by Yard Dog Press).

He and his wife Gloria have two daughters, two sons-in-law, and five grandchildren. His greatest joys in life include family, friends, writing, art, and travel.

Gary Moreau's web address is www.garymoreau.com.

ABOUT THE COVER ARTIST

Artist **Mitchell Davidson Bentley** spent the last twenty years moving physically from place to place and artistically from traditional oils to cyber compositions. Trained in the traditional medium of oil by his mother, and inspired by his grandfather's love of science fiction, Bentley began his career as a full-time science fiction artist in 1989 from his home base in Tulsa.

While actively involved in the science fiction art world, Bentley also moved from Tulsa to Austin to Central Pennsylvania where his search for knowledge earned him bachelors and masters degrees from Penn State University. Over the same period of time, Bentley shifted from the more traditional oil painting to airbrushed acrylics, and since 2004 has been working exclusively in electronic media.

As the Creative Consultant of Atomic Fly Studios, Bentley produces cover art, marketing materials and Web sites while he continues to produce quality 2D artwork marketed through the AFS Web site and at science fiction conventions across the United States.

Bentley has lectured at universities, worked in film (also as a part-time actor), edited publications and served as Artist Guest of Honor at more than a dozen science fiction conventions. He has also earned over 35 awards, and is a lifetime member of the Association of Science Fiction and Fantasy Artists.

He currently resides in Harrisburg, PA with his partner Cathie McCormick and their spoiled cats, Mr. Spike, Zöe and Drucilla.

Bentley's Web address is: www.atomicflystudios.com.

A Bubba in Time Saves None, Edited by Selina Rosen
A Man, A Plan, (yet lacking) A Canal, Panama, Linda Donahue
Adventures of the Irish Ninja, Selina Rosen
The Alamo and Zombies, Jean Stuntz
All the Marbles, Dusty Rainbolt
Almost Human, Gary Moreau
Ancient Enemy, Lee Killouth
The Anthology From Hell: Humorous Tales From WAY Down Under, Edited by Julia S. Mandala
Ard Magister, Laura J. Underwood
Assassins Inc., Phillip Drayer Duncan
Bad City, Selina Rosen & Laura J. Underwood
Bad Lands, Selina Rosen & Laura J. Underwood
Black Rage, Selina Rosen
Blackrose Avenue, Mark Shepherd
The Boat Man, Selina Rosen
Bobby's Troll, John Lance
Bride of Tranquility, Tracy S. Morris
Bruce and Roxanne from Start to Finnish, Rie Sheridan Rose
The Bubba Chronicles, Selina Rosen
Bubba Fables, Sue P. Sinor
Bubbas Of the Apocalypse, Edited by Selina Rosen
The Burden of the Crown, Selina Rosen
Chains of Redemption, Selina Rosen
Checking On Culture, Lee Killough
Chronicles of the Last War, Laura J. Underwood
Dadgum Martians Invade the Lucky Nickel Saloon, Ken Rand
Dark and Stormy Nights, Bradley H. Sinor
Deja Doo, Edited by Selina Rosen
Dracula's Lawyer, Julia S. Mandala
Dragon's Tongue, Laura J. Underwood
The Essence of Stone, Beverly A. Hale
Fairy BrewHaHa at the Lucky Nickel Saloon, Ken Rand
The Fantastikon: Tales of Wonder, Robin Wayne Bailey
Fire & Ice, Selina Rosen
Flush Fiction, Volume I: Stories To Be Read In One Sitting, Edited by Selina Rosen
Flush Fiction, Volume II: Twenty Years of Letting it Go!, Edited by Selina Rosen
The Four Bubbas of the Apocalypse: Flatulence, Halitosis, Incest, and... Ned, Edited by Selina Rosen
The Four Redheads: Apocalypse Now!, Linda L. Donahue, Rhonda Eudaly, Julia S. Mandala, & Dusty Rainbolt
The Four Redheads of the Apocalypse, Linda L. Donahue, Rhonda Eudaly, Julia S. Mandala, & Dusty Rainbolt
The Four Redheads: The Wrath of Satan, Linda L. Donahue,

Rhonda Eudaly, Julia S. Mandala, & Dusty Rainbolt
The Garden In Bloom, Jeffrey Turner
The Geometries of Love: Poetry by Robin Wayne Bailey
The Golems Of Laramie County, Ken Rand
The Green Women, Laura J. Underwood
The Guardians, Lynn Abbey
Hammer Town, Selina Rosen
The Happiness Box, Beverly A. Hale
The Host Series: The Host, Fright Eater, Gang Approval, Selina
    Rosen
Houston, We've Got Bubbas!, Edited by Selina Rosen
How I Spent the Apocolypse, Selina Rosen
I Didn't Quite Make It To Oz, Edited by Selina Rosen
I Should Have Stayed In Oz, Edited by Selina Rosen
In the Shadows, Bradley H. Sinor
International House of Bubbas, Edited by Selina Rosen
It's the Great Bumpkin, Cletus Brown!, Katherine A. Turski
Judas Gene, Gary Moreau
The Killswitch Review, Steven-Elliot Altman & Diane DeKelb-
    Rittenhouse
The Leopard's Daughter, Lee Killough
The Lightning Horse, John Moore
The Logic of Departure, Mark W. Tiedemann
The Long, Cold Walk To Mars, Jeffrey Turner
Marking the Signs and Other Tales Of Mischief, Laura J.
    Underwood
Material Things, Selina Rosen
Medieval Misfits: Renaissance Rejects, Tracy S. Morris
Mirror Images, Susan Satterfield
Mirror, Mirror and Other Reflections, James K. Burk
More Stories That Won't Make Your Parents Hurl, Edited by
    Selina Rosen
Music for Four Hands, Louis Antonelli & Edward Morris
My Life with Geeks and Freaks, Claudia Christian
The Necronomicrap: A Guide To Your Horoooscope, Tim Frayser
Playing With Secrets, Bradley H & Sue P. Sinor
Redheads In Love, Linda L. Donahue, Rhonda Eudaly, Julia S.
    Mandala, & Dusty Rainbolt
Reruns, Selina Rosen
Rock 'n' Roll Universe, Ken Rand
Shadows In Green, Richard Dansky
Stories That Won't Make Your Parents Hurl, Edited by Selina
    Rosen
Tales from Keltora, Laura J. Underwood
*Tales Of the Lucky Nickel Saloon, Second Ave., Laramie,
    Wyoming, U S of A,* Ken Rand

Fantasy Writers Asylum
(A YDP Imprint):
Blood Songs
Julia Mandala
Gateway to Corimar
Julia Mandala & Linda L Donahue
Tale of the Black Heart
Linda L. Donahue

Non-YDP titles we distribute:
Chains of Freedom
Chains of Destruction
Jabone's Sword
Queen of Denial
Recycled
Strange Robby
Sword Masters
Selina Rosen

Three Ways to Order:

1. Write us a letter telling us what you want, then send it along with your check or money order (made payable to Yard Dog Press) to: Yard Dog Press, 710 W. Redbud Lane, Alma, AR 72921-7247

2. Use selinarosen@cox.net or lynnstran@cox.net to contact us and place your order. Then send your check or money order to the address above. *This has the advantage of allowing you to check on the availability of short-stock items such as T-shirts and back-issues of Yard Dog Comics.*

3. Contact us as in #1 or #2 above and pay with a credit card or by debit from your checking account. Either give us the credit card information in your letter/Email/phone call, or go to our website and use our shopping carts. If you send us your information, please include your name as it appears on the card, your credit card number, the expiration date, and the 3 or 4-digit security code after your signature on the back (CVV). Please remember that we will include media rate (minimum $3.00) S/H for mailing in the lower 48 states.

Watch our website at
www.yarddogpress.com
for news of upcoming projects
and new titles!!

A Note to Our Readers

We at Yard Dog Press understand that many people buy used books because they simply can't afford new ones. That said, and understanding that not everyone is made of money, we'd like you to know something that you may not have realized. Writers only make money on new books that sell. At the big houses a writer's entire future can hinge on the number of books they sell. While this isn't the case at Yard Dog Press, the honest truth is that when you sell or trade your book or let many people read it, the writer and the publishing house aren't making any money.

As much as we'd all like to believe that we can exist on love and sweet potato pie, the truth is we all need money to buy the things essential to our daily lives. Writers and publishers are no different.

We realize that these "freebies" and cheap books often turn people on to new writers and books that they wouldn't otherwise read. However we hope that you will reconsider selling your copy, and that if you trade it or let your friends borrow it, you also pass on the information that if they really like the author's work they should consider buying one of their books at full price sometime so that the writer can afford to continue to write work that entertains you.

We appreciate all our readers and *depend* upon their support.

Thanks,
The Editorial Staff
Yard Dog Press

PS – Please note that "used" books without covers have, in most cases, been stolen. Neither the author nor the publisher has made any money on these books because they were supposed to be pulped for lack of sales.

Please do not purchase books without covers.